William Justin Harsha

Ploughed Under

The story of an Indian Chief

William Justin Harsha

Ploughed Under
The story of an Indian Chief

ISBN/EAN: 9783337304058

Printed in Europe, USA, Canada, Australia, Japan

Cover: Foto ©Andreas Hilbeck / pixelio.de

More available books at **www.hansebooks.com**

PLOUGHED UNDER

The Story of an Indian Chief

TOLD BY HIMSELF

WITH AN INTRODUCTION

By INSHTA THEAMBA

(BRIGHT EYES)

NEW YORK:
FORDS, HOWARD, & HULBERT.
1881.

INTRODUCTION.

By Inshta Theamba.

("*Bright Eyes.*")

The white people have tried to solve the "Indian Question" by commencing with the proposition that the Indian is different from all other human beings.

With some he is a peculiar being, surrounded by a halo of romance, who has to be set apart on a reservation as something sacred, who has to be fed, clothed, and taken care of by a guardian or agent, by whom he is not to be allowed to come in contact with his conquerors lest it might degrade him; his conquerors being a people who hold their civilization above that of all others on the earth, because of their perfect freedom and liberty. "The contact of peoples is the best of all education." And this the ward is denied.

With others again he is a savage, a sort of monster without any heart or soul or mind, but whose whole being is full of hatred, ferocity, and blood-thirstiness. They suppose him to have no family affections, no love for his home, none of the sensitive feelings that all other human beings presumably have. This class demand his extermination.

Under the shelter of the conflicting laws imposed by these two extreme views, the clever operators of the Indian Ring—not caring what he is, but looking on him for what he has, and the opportunities he affords, as legitimate prey—pounce on him and use him as a means of obtaining contracts, removals, land speculations, and appropriations which are to be stolen. They tear him from his home, disregarding all the rights of his manhood.

Allow an Indian to suggest that the solution of the vexed "Indian Question" is *Citizenship*, with all its attending duties and·responsibilities, as well as the privileges of protection under the law, by which the Indian could appeal to the courts, when deprived of life, liberty, or property, as every citizen can, and would be allowed the opportunity to make something of himself, in common with every other citizen. If it were not for the lands which the Indian holds, he would have been a citizen long before the negro; and in this respect his lands have been a curse to him rather than a blessing. But for them, he would have been insignificant in the eyes of this powerful and wealthy nation, and allowed to live in peace and quietness, without attracting the birds of prey forever hovering over the helpless; then his citizenship would have protected him, as it does any other ordinary human being. As a "ward," or extraordinary being, if he is accused of committing a crime, this serves as a pretext of war for his extermination, and his father, mother, sister, brother, wife, or people are involved in one common ruin; while if he were simply a citizen, he would be individually arrested by the sheriff, and tried in court, and either protected in his innocence or convicted and punished in his guilt. The Indian, as a "ward," or extraordinary being, affords employment to about ten thousand employés in the Indian Bureau, with all the salaries attached, as well as innumerable contractors, freighters, and land speculators. He requires also, periodically, immense appropriations to move him from place to place. Imagine a company of Irish immigrants requiring from Congress an appropriation to move them from one part of the country to another! No wonder that the powers-that-be refuse to recognize the Indian as an ordinary human being, but insist that he be taken care of and "protected" by the decisions of the Indian Bureau. In this "land of freedom and liberty" an Indian has to get the permission of an agent before he can either step off his reservation or allow any civilization to enter it; and this, under heavy penalty for disobedience. In this land, where the boast is made that all men are "equal before the law," the Indian cannot sue in the courts for his life, liberty, or property, because, forsooth, the Indian is not a "person," as the learned attorney employed by a Secretary of the Interior argued for five hours, when an Indian appealed to the writ of *habeas corpus* for his liberty.

The key to this complicated problem is, simply, To recognize the Indian as a person and a citizen, give him a title to his lands, and place him within the jurisdiction of the courts, *as an individual.* It is absurd for a great government like this to say that it

CONTENTS.

Chap.		Page.
I.	The First Puzzle,	11
II.	On the Prairie,	18
III.	An Indian Battle,	27
IV.	The Buffalo Hunt,	35
V.	The Arrival of Gray Coat,	42
VI.	A Chapter of Love,	57
VII.	The Winning of a Name,	66
VIII.	Bitter Counsel,	76
IX.	Ma-shán! Home!	86
X.	A Vain Sacrifice,	97
XI.	An Empty Success,	105
XII.	Blindfolded Justice,	119
XIII.	Kind Face and Gray Coat,	130
XIV.	The Bridal Eve,	152
XV.	Blood-hounds and Lunacy,	170
XVI.	Little Swallow takes the Trail,	185
XVII.	The Peril of Prairie Flower,	202
XVIII.	Returning Reason,	216
XIX.	Chopping Logic,	227
XX.	Ploughed Under,	239
XXI.	The Two Voices,	259

CHAPTER I.

MY earliest memories are concerned with the shining of a great river, which, flowing by the spot where our simple village stood, gave sport to the boys, fear to the girls, toil to the men, and food to all. By the banks of this stream, with my feet in its current, I would sit for hours, and it was to me the suggestion and type of thoughts I could never hope in our simple language to express; I doubt if they could be defined even in the sweetest and most powerful words that other peoples know so well how to use. Sometimes I would pick a dandelion and fling it out into the swirl, and how strangely I felt as I saw it sweep dancing away! Or I would lose my arrowhead in its quicksands and would forget to search or even weep for it, because of the flood of strange meditations that would come over me. Or I would lay my cheek on the grassy bank, my eyes on a line with the river's surface; and usually at such times there was another cheek, a softer one than mine, on the grass beside mine—and I know not what made me think of rushing down great lengths of time with *her* by my side, of struggling with other men when I should be a man, of going into still places and then into stormy places, and at last coming to a wide, beautiful quiet.

Our village, at the time of my boyhood, was built under great trees whose whispers at night put us to sleep and whose laughter in the fresh morning breeze wakened us. The lands of my fathers stretched away for many miles to another great river, but it was the custom of my

people to live clustered together, in this one most beautiful spot of all, for mutual happiness and protection. Our
fathers had lived upon this spot for so many years that
our oldest traditions spake not of their coming—their
graves on the neighboring hill far outnumbered the
members of our tribe who now lived or could live for
many years. They had mostly fed upon buffalo-meat from
the prairies and fish from the river; but in addition to
these, which were now becoming scarce, we had potatoes
and grain from our own lands, cultivated by our toil. How
we came to plough the earth and raise corn upon it, mar-
ring beauty for utility's sake, was told to me when I was
of years to understand by Um-pan-nez-zhe, or " Standing
Elk" as the white man would call him, who was the "wise
man" of our tribe.

"Some years ago," he said, as we sat under the deep
shade of a tree and he made a new bow for me while I
whittled the arrow, "there came a white man to our
tepees,* and we received him as a brother. His hair was
white as yonder foam upon the Missouri. His form was
bent by the winds of many years. But his words were
soft and sweet as the rippling of Niobrara over the sand.
In his hand he brought The Book, the holy teachings of
which were like the gentle fall of rain, causing to spring
up from our hearts grains and flowers whose seeds had
long lain there. Our fathers had dim traditions of all
the good man taught, but the words of the holy Book
made these buried sproutings to rise and bud. He gathered the chiefs and head men of our tribe together and
told them of Wakanda, whom the white men call God.
The chiefs reverently told him that they and their fathers
had always known and worshiped Wakanda, who was

* Tents.

the kind Father of red men as well as white. Then the good man told them of the wrongfulness of anger, lying, and revenge, and the chiefs said they had known all this too. But when he told them of Wakanda's Son, who loved the simple-hearted and the poor and died for them, our fathers wept and said, 'We had hoped for such an E-Ká-gah, or "Friend," but we knew not he was ours.' For many days the good man staid with our people, and taught us how to build these houses of the logs felled from the brook-sides. He told us many of the strange ways of white men, who live in close and dirty cities, and many of whom have never felt the sweet breeze of the prairies on their cheeks, or watched the scarlet bursting of a blizzard-storm. He chided us for not plowing the ground and raising corn, and seemed to think his people were wiser than ours that they did so. But our chiefs said that their fathers had raised corn upon that continent before white man's foot had pressed it. That we had departed from their ways was a matter of proud choice. 'Our fathers,' they said, 'were like the prairie-dogs who burrow into the ground on one spot to gain their food. We are like the eagles who in unchained liberty snatch their prey from the foamy tops of river-waves. We might be squaws to dig, we choose to be free.' And there was like to be hatred between the chiefs and the good man; but his face was so calm and he showed so well how strong it is to forgive that instantly there was peace. Then he pointed out, in words as cooling as balsam-salve, how the game was disappearing from the divides and how the Hu-hú* were netted, and so slaughtered, in every stream, and how the Ma-chút† was seldom met in the everglades, and how the Um-pan‡ and Dta § no longer swarmed in

---

* Fish. † Bear. ‡ Elk. § Buffalo.

droves upon the wide prairies, and how the white men were pushing on to hem us in, so that a fierce necessity was on the red men to adopt the ways of the stronger race. At these words, Eagle Wing, thy father, who was a young man then, started up and said : 'Better to die than be as squaws.' But the oldest chief of all, Stern Face, who has since been laid with his fathers, answered, 'Thou art a young man, Eagle Wing. Upon thy skirts even now hang the trophies of the chase. Thou hast but one child : dost thou wish to see him die ? We might face death ourselves rather than be oppressed, but shall we bring worse than death upon our little ones who smile at us and reach up their soft hands to pat our cheeks ?' The young men could not answer when the chief had spoken, but for that day and for many days they preserved a sullen silence ; and for the first time there were anxious faces in our village. But the counsel of the old chiefs prevailed, and the good missionary set about teaching us to leave, as he called it, the state of savages."

When Standing Elk had reached this point in his story I dropped my arrow and, springing up, exclaimed :

"Savages ! How can they rightly call us savages ? Is it because we prefer the bounding air to their shut-up houses ? Is it because the narrow ways of their kind of life are hateful to us ? I have heard of it all. Is my mother a savage because she nursed me in a bed of wild mosses instead of a covered mattress, and gave me dandelions and wild roses instead of painted balls for playthings ? So long as we do not interfere with the happiness of others, who can call us savages without sinning against us and himself as well ?"

"Hush ! my passionate boy," the wise man said. " There are some having the dusky skin who have committed deeds of violence when maddened by the exactions of the white race, and they are taken as examples of us all. Nay, there are some tribes who are bitterly hostile to the whites and lose no chance of harming them; we friendly tribes are measured by those "hostiles"—although, it is true, the white man treats the hostiles with more consideration than those who befriend him."

"This is a greater evil still," I cried. "That there be wild-beets which poison and destroy should not be held against the healthful roots. And are there not some white hands which have robbed and murdered, and are all of their race held guilty?"

"My son," the wise man said, "the world can see but one character among all Indian races. It is for you to bear your destiny as Wakanda has ordered it. They are the stronger race. The weak rush must go down before the mighty wind. Meanwhile we have our lands secure. Our fathers have always dwelt upon them and called them theirs, and the great nation within whose bounds we live have in many treaties acknowledged our claim to them. Let us cultivate the soil as we have been taught by the good Wa-gá-za* to whose word you are so much opposed. He marked out the trail which will lead you to happiness; follow it like a brave and faithful son of a brave and noble chief."

For many days—oh for so many days! did I think of these words of the wise man, and they became vividly real to me when certain terrible events, which I must tell you of, had taken place. But at this boyhood-period of my life every day was a constant joy, increased rather than diminished by the sober thoughts awakened by such conversations as this with the wise man.

* Missionary.

Our village was built in the form of a circle, and the large, clear, open space left in the very heart of all was reserved for a common play-ground. Here the boys learned to shoot their arrows, with such accuracy that a little daisy from the plain could be cut in twain; and one part of it was to be kept by the archer himself, while the other must be laid in the lap of the little maiden whom he loved the best and whose bright black eyes had been watching timidly and anxiously the whole test. Here the older youths matched their athletic skill in many a leap, handspring, and race. Here they led their beautiful ponies and matched them against each other for speed and spirit. How their smooth flanks would shine, and how their intelligent eyes would twinkle, and how their strong muscles would fling them over the sod, and with what prodigious leaps would they clear the highest obstructions placed in their way! How the riders would bend them- selves on every side, now standing upright on the ponies' rumps, now lying prone on their backs, and now stooping to pick hats or moccasins or even arrows from the dust beneath their ponies' flying feet! And then after the sport, how those whom they loved would deck ponies and riders in their brightest ribbons and grasses, and timidly smile their admiration!

But by far the greater part of our happiness was in association with the beautiful world which Wakanda had made. Oh, how we loved the gentle voices of the grove, and the tender murmurs of the tall wild-grass, the sweet shining of moon-rays, and the rumble of the storm! What long excursions would we take—whole troops of us —to count the spears on the bunches of buffalo-grass, and chase the butterfly to the woods or the prairie-dog to his burrow, and watch the green eyes of the turtle sunning himself on the logs, and plait our hair with sweet scented grass, until, worn out with such activity, we would lie upon the banks overlooking a spring and watch the bubbles bursting on its surface. And when at evening we sat around the great camp-fire and told our mothers of the day's sport, they would tell us that Wakanda made all these beautiful things and we must love them for His sake and Him for theirs. And our fathers and brothers would point out to us on their fingers how much the corn had grown in a day, and some one would take The Book which the good missionary had left and read to us the sweet words of Wakanda's Son. Then when I laid myself down to sleep I would puzzle myself with the ever-recurring question: "Is this to be a savage?"

CHAPTER II.

ON THE PRAIRIE.

I HAVE spoken of the softer cheek than mine which often lay upon the bank beside me when I thought, and surely you who know anything of that love which must be the same in every race have already guessed that that cheek belonged to the sweet maiden I loved best. Her father was Standing Elk, the wise man, and truly he was never wiser than when he called her Wágh-ta, or "Prairie Flower." To my young eyes she was fairer than the morning, and her eyes outshone the stars of night. Her form was as slender and shapely as the spring-time growth of the mountain aspen, and her footfall gentler than the dew on the wild-rose. The young doves hatched together in one swinging nest upon the birch-bough are mated from that moment, and when the one is absent the other can but sit with breast to the wind and mourn ; thus it seemed to us we had loved forever, and neither could be happy alone.

There was one line of events in our lives involving us in a common peril, and bringing to us a common deliverance, which seemed to unite us with a bond of renewed life almost as strong as our spontaneous love. I must tell the story to you as I heard it, mentioning also my own vivid memories of such things as would strike a boy's fancy.

When I was about eight years of age, my father, Khé-tha-á-hi, or Eagle Wing, determined to take the branch of our tribe of which he was chief upon a grand buffalo-hunt. The plans were talked over for many nights around the camp-fires, and when at last the day came for the start everything had been carefully arranged. There were about one hundred warriors, all mounted on their fleetest ponies, drawn up upon the plain when the moment came to start, Other ponies were hitched to the tent-poles, across which were stretched skins, and the children and the camping outfit were then placed upon these drags. My father, when we were on the way, rode at the head of the little band on a magnificent horse, so white that the foam from his trembling lips could not be detected when it had fallen on his flanks. It was a grand and beautiful sight. The horses' heads were decked with ribbons and strings of wolves' ears tipped with paint. The warriors were dressed in their brightest garments, and the children vied with the birds in the beauty and variety of the feathers with which they were adorned. On one of the foremost of the sleds little Prairie Flower and I were placed; and although I was not fully conscious of it then, I am quite sure now that I needed no other ornament than her simple presence to make me the most attractive and envied of all. So with shouts and merry laughter; with jumping off our sleds to pluck a dandelion or snatch a spread plover's wing from the hand of a comrade and then hastily springing to our seat again; with many trials of speed between the best ponies on level spots; with cautious reconnoitering of wooded places to see if the Sioux were lurking there; with the gathering of sticks beside the cool spring at noon to roast the plover or the grouse to satisfy our hunger, while the ponies browsed upon the tender and savory grass; with the pitching of our camp in some secure spot at nightfall, to rest after the hard day's ride; with the starting up again and speeding away—when the first streaks of blood appeared in the East stabbed by the Sunbeam—with these and a thousand other delights, gayly we went upon our buffalo-hunt. Our course lay toward the north-west, where great herds of the noble game congregated. We crossed wide stretches of daisy-dotted plain and many little streams. I did not then love, as I have since learned to love, these gracefully rolling prairies, presenting, as they do, so many picturesque views. How often have I sat with Prairie Flower by my side, and watched for hours, that seemed but as moments, the ever-varying shades of green upon those magnificent contours, and felt emotions that I wish I could tell you of! I loved it best at evening-time, when the wondrous, untrained music of the valleys was fully abroad. Oh what sweet and varied harmonies the winds of the twilight can breathe into the swaying reeds and rushes which grow by the watercourses of the West! The heart of the red man loves that Wá-e * well! The patter of frost-drops upon the decaying fringes and cones in the neighboring pine-grove; the thunder of the stone dislodged by the badger's foot and sent bounding down the hillside into the river; the whisper of the night-wind in the nodding cups of the prairie lily and ane-mone; the crash of the tree at whose root the worm has been gnawing, and which now is overblown to fall into columnar decay; the "*honk*" of the wild geese sweeping in triangular bands toward the south, and the startled cry of the wild ducks rising out of the swamps; the splash of the beaver's tail as he builds his watery home; the whistle of the thrush, the drumming of the prairie-cock's wings, and the occasional whirr of the belated quail hastening back to her young; the snort of the elk, the barking of the wolf, and the voice of man,—all these, and a thousand other strains, grave and gay, shrill and melodious, enter

* Music.

into this song of nature, so sublime that no sound of forest or valley, or creeping thing or fowl of the air, can be out of time or tune to it or mar in the least its harmony. Wakanda smiled and the melodies began. All this I loved and Prairie Flower loved, for I loved her loves and she mine.

In the progress of our hunt toward the north-west, we soon reached a region where increasing caution was necessary, as we were approaching the hunting-grounds of the Sioux. This powerful tribe was at war with all others of my people. Deadly feuds had for many generations existed between them and all neighboring tribes, and many had been the romantic and bloody encounters betweeen members of the opposed parties. The cause of the difficulty was the great pride of the Sioux chiefs to unite all Indian races under their leadership and control, and hence the tribes which refused to recognize them as supreme were treated as rebels. The tribe of which my father was one chief had for generations been distinguished for its scorn of the Sioux's pretensions and its successful conflict with them. It was known to us that throughout the great Sioux nation runners were sent proclaiming that whoever would bring in the scalp of Eagle Wing should be rewarded with the chieftainship of one of the inferior bands. This of course increased the desire to encounter and kill him, but, such is the strange nature of my people, it also increased my father's importance in the tribe, and his own and his followers' willingness to be encountered. There was on both sides a thirst for conflict such as is felt when in the forest glades in the time of mating there is a sudden meeting of rival Um-pan-nu-gas.*

* This name is used by the Indians to distinguish the elk bucks in the spring time, when mating occurs. They are then supposed to possess souls, and on no account must one of them be killed.

On this trip, therefore, my father's warriors were magnificently mounted, and armed, as well as their means would permit, with rifles and our more primitive weapons, which are almost as effective in skillful hands—bows of great length and power, tomahawks as sharp as wild-grass-blades, and long hunting-knives. Runners were constantly kept in advance, every spot available for an ambush was carefully examined, and at night watches were posted to prevent a surprise.

There is one other circumstance I must tell you of before you can understand the animosity exhibited in the scenes I am about to describe. In all the wars with the Sioux our people had championed the cause of the whites, and many were the settlers who in those early days had taken refuge in our wigwams from bitter pursuit. Our tribe had never been at war with the whites. The chiefs had always been of the opinion that the only safe policy for us, as a weaker nation, was to preserve the utmost faith with the whites, and our hope was that this would recommend us to their mercy. The sickly or wounded wolf must not bark too noisily, else all the others of the pack will pounce upon it and tear it rib from rib. As we thus lifted our tomahawks in defense of the settlers, the Sioux regarded us as betrayers of the glory of the Indian race, and hence their hatred for us was bitter. When the prairie-dog seeks to defend the little bird who nestled with him in his home, the rattlesnake conceives of both as equally enemies, and drives them equally forth. It was so with the Sioux's hatred of us. On the side of my people the feeling was strong that it was not treacherous in us and our fathers towards the Sioux that we had never entered into treaty with them to destroy the whites. We thought we had the right of all free things to choose who should be our friends and who our enemies; and as we had chosen to be friends with the whites and to fight the Sioux, we stood ready to make our boast good with our blood. Thus the hatred was bitter on both sides—they calling us false as the sneaking badger, we calling them liars and base as the sand-hill lynx. Many bleeding wounds and ghastly corpses on both sides called for bitter revenge, and whenever their followers and ours met, whether singly or in companies, there was instant battle and no backs turned. But now to my story.

One lovely afternoon my father had taken me to ride before him on his pony's neck, from which station of high honor I was hailing my less fortunate companions. Suddenly my father's face, which had been smiling and gentle as the afternoon itself, was clouded with a look of awful hatred, with tracings still of a fierce delight. In the crushing of a dandelion he had seen the trail of the Sioux. With one majestic wave of his hand he stopped the advance of his band.

"Boy," he said sternly to me, "there is bloody work here to be done." With these words he lifted me from the pony's neck and dropped me to the earth.

His followers gathered breathlessly around the crushed flower, which seemed to contain tidings of some awful woe.

"Call in the runners," my father said, "and let watchers be hidden on every side."

When Great Bear, the most trusted of the runners, made his appearance, my father eyed him as if he were an inexcusable culprit, and sternly said :

" If Ma-chú-ta-ga* sees not such prints as these, whom can we trust ? Do you pass such sod-cuts with a dreamy eye ?"

"No one," Great Bear replied, with downcast look,

---

* Great Bear.

"could have seen so slight a trail as this save Khe-tha-á-hi himself."

"Thou art generally as faithful as my own right hand," my father replied ; "see that this happens not again. But who is this?"

The question was called out by the breathless coming of another runner, who at a hundred lariats' distance to the northward had skirted our little party's advance. When he caught his breath he exclaimed :

"Two hundred Sioux warriors are skulking down upon us from the north. I met their runner, and his scalp is mine."

"This shall be a token of our larger victory," my father said. "Meanwhile, be active. Get the women and children into yonder hollow place ; let them hide behind the bank. And let the warriors who have squaws-hearts crouch beside them. But you who are brave, think of what the Sioux have done, count in your quiver an arrow for every home they have left desolate in our tribe, and let each arrow shout the U-gthá-a* as it flies!"

The greatest confusion instantly began. It was as if the great shadow of a hovering crow had been seen by a nestful of thrushes. The wise and noble Standing Elk led us to the safe hiding-place my father had mentioned, and kissing Prairie Flower, left her by my side. The tears of the gentle girl ran wildly down her cheeks ; for, though she knew not the awful woes of war, her heart feared by instinct its tumult and pain, as the wild fawn starts unwittingly at the first hearing of the voice of man. My mother was beside us, and was a mother to both; for little Prairie Flower had none. She held our bursting pulses and bade us not to fear. So from our bank we

* War-cry.

looked out upon the hurrying warriors. Some were daubing their faces with high-colored earths. Some were testing bow-strings to see that they failed them not at the sore moment. Some were quieting restless ponies by a word of tenderness or one of command. My father had placed upon his head a peculiar tuft of long hair—the most sacred emblem in our whole tribe, handed down for generations that no one could count, and supposed by us to make victory sure. He had also upon his head his own war-bonnet, made of a crown of white eagle-plumes and two strings of the same noble feathers hanging down his back. Some of these feathers were painted red, for our custom was thus to color one for every wound the wearer had received in battle, and to place the colored plumes opposite the part of the body injured. Thus arrayed, and seated proudly upon his white pony, my father awaited with perfect coolness the coming of the Sioux; and, while the maiden by my side still wept for harrowed gentleness, I wept for admiration when I saw him. Everywhere the wise Standing Elk went attending to the details that were regarded as beneath the notice of the chief, and when he came near where Eagle Wing sat, he whispered in his ear a word which was both caution born of years, and encouragement born of pride. One by one the warriors, having completed their war-dress, arranged themselves in line on each side of my father, until of all the number only one was absent—the rebuked trail-finder, Great Bear. The chief cast his eye sternly down the line, and demanded :

"Has our Ma-chú-ta-ga gone into a winter sleep while yet summer shines and his enemy, the wolf, steals upon his young ?"

Either no one dared to speak or no one wished to defend the absent warrior; at least there was silence. A few moments passed, and then the missing man suddenly appeared from behind a clump of dense bushes. I was amazed to see that he was dressed precisely like my father, and this at first I supposed would be taken as a great insult by the chief. But I afterwards learned that it was the noblest and most faithful service any warrior could perform for his chief's safety. Great Bear without a word mounted a white pony of the shape and size of that my father rode, and took a place at the end of the line. At the distance of a few yards it was impossible to distinguish him from Eagle Wing, and indeed the very object in his heart was by his disguise to deceive the enemy and draw shafts meant for my father's breast into his own. He had determined, out of a real love for his chief and a sense of deep shame that he had been so blamed, to sacrifice himself, if need be, for the safety of his chief. When the chief saw him, he said softly to Standing Elk :

"My heart bleeds, wise man ; my heart bleeds! If it were not for the need to preserve the high honor of my chieftainship I would command Ma-chú-ta-ga to seek his own safety by mingling, in common dress, with the other warriors. Would that I could take him as a brother to my arms and forgive him, for he is a noble man and, save yourself, my best warrior !"

"It is better thus," the wise man answered, though tears were in his eyes, for Great Bear was his younger and well-beloved brother. And so they awaited the coming of the Sioux.

CHAPTER III.

AN INDIAN BATTLE.

I HAD but time to kiss one tear from the cheek of the trembling maiden, when the thrilling U-gthá-a of our people announced that the enemy was in sight. I held my breath to hear the answering shout of rage and defiance, but all was still. The Sioux were either squaw-hearted or reserved their breath for the close encounter. From our bank we could now see them riding forward in a line fully twice as long as that my father's warriors formed. They came in a gentle trot ; no weapons were visible about them, and for a moment my heart took great leaps of joy, supposing that after all the meeting would be as one of brothers. " Oh," I thought to myself, " how much better to join hands instead of arrow-tips ; or, if there must be some strife, let it be between the fleetest ponies down this lovely valley, or between the friendly wrestling power of the young men upon this green plain ?" Certainly it would have been a far nobler test of relative prowess ; for when past grievances can only be righted by the stretching of a row of ghastly corpses upon the grass, even that fails to satisfy both tribes, and there are new grievances to the number of these very corpses, which must be avenged in future encounters. War is sad and foolish enough.

However, the Sioux came quietly forward, and, though my father's followers taunted them with cowardice and treachery by turns, shouting "Coo! coo!"* until the

* " Coward! coward!"

very sand-ridges echoed, they revealed no weapons and made no reply. It being the custom of my people to tie a knot in a pony's mane every time we can shout "Coo!" to an enemy without a reply being made, the hands of our warriors were busy preparing these score-marks against the Sioux, and the very ponies tossed their knotted manes in pride and defiance as if they understood the sign. I noticed on the arm of each of our enemies a folded red blanket, and I innocently thought they were to be presents to our people. Still coming forward, they were soon but twenty paces from the nose of Eagle Wing's horse. Our warriors had now an arrow set in every bow, and such as had rifles sat with deliberate aim; yet, to my great wonder, my father did not order them to fire. Evidently he wished to scan to the full the intent of his enemies, thinking it beneath a chief to take any advantage of them. Now they were within ten paces of my father's line. Suddenly each of the Sioux, rising upon his horse's neck, whisked his blanket from his arm and shook it full-spread and in all its dazzling color before the eyes of our ponies. Oh then was seen the wonderful command that love exerts over the animal! Our ponies, trained to obey by long influence of kindness, did not wheel and dash away, as the Sioux hoped they would, to render our warriors' backs an easy mark for their weapons. Not a hoof moved from its print in the grassy sod. The poor creatures, unused to such warfare, trembled as the wild cottonwood leaves do before the storm; many of them crouched in mute fear until their bellies touched the grass; some snorted and whinnied wildly, as they do when a grizzly tramps upon their lariat; but all stood their ground. And before the Sioux could drop their blankets and seize their weapons, my father's voice was heard, shouting:

"Ké-da!" *

* "Fire."

And many Sioux fell headlong to the earth, while the survivors, having failed in their trusted device, were now put to personal skill and strength for safety. Then followed indescribable confusion. There was wild scrambling of horses, there were fierce struggles of hand-to-hand combatants, there was a mingling of hoarse battle-cries, shouts of defiance and victory, screams of pain, whirring of arrows, and cracking of rifles. Oh, the beautiful sod which Wakanda had made had bitter draught of blood that day! I hid my eyes to keep out the dreadful knowledge that brave men were uselessly killing each other, but my ears continued to tell the tidings, and when I closed my ears as well, my fancy took the story up. How long I continued thus I know not, but at last I felt a touch upon my arm, and, opening my eyes, saw Prairie Flower looking, too horrified to weep, into my face. She gently took my hands down from my ears and said :

"Oh listen to the dreadful shout of the Sioux! Thy father is dead!"

As she spoke a prolonged cry arose, a cry such as a hundred mountain lions might make in depth of hungry winter over the carcass of an ox:

"Khé-tha-á-hi is dead! Khé-tha-á-hi is dead!"

While the cry thus rang, a Sioux warrior dashed by, within six paces of where we were crouching, and holding aloft a bloody scalp, he cried :

"Khé-tha-á-hi is dead! My hand did the deed! I claim the prize! I shall be a chief!"

My heart sank within me as I heard these words, and my poor mother wrung her hands and moaned in pitiable despair. The cry "Eagle Wing is dead!" was caught up by the enemy in every part of the field, and it seemed for a moment as if our fate were sealed. Anxiously I cast my eye over the tumult to catch, if I might, any glimpse of my father to show the shout untrue. At last, in the very deadliest spot of all, I saw his plumed head-dress rising above the multitude of those who beset him; as I have seen the white feathers of the eagle's crown rising out of tumultuous waves after having dashed after his prey. And as also the eagle might shake himself free from the scattering drops that still clung to his wings, so my father threw off the Sioux who clutched at his arms and legs to drag him down, and running to a high spot in plain view of all, he waved his tomahawk above his head and cried: "Khé-tha-á-hi is *not* dead! He lives to avenge his slain, though Great Bear has died in his stead."

The lightning's flash, calling forth from the cloud the sudden storm of spring, swells the rivulet and makes it a mighty, resistless torrent. So my father's brave shout swept his remaining warriors into the sure course of victory. On the other hand the Sioux, disappointed and amazed that he, upon whom they had burst with so much fury and who had stood so long and bravely before he fell, was the noble Great Bear and not Eagle Wing, could strike now but feeble blows, gave way in every direction, and at last fled on their fleet ponies away.

When they had gone, we who had been so secure while others suffered for us came out of our retreat, anxious to do what we might to stay their loss of blood. Oh then there were sad scenes! Would the white man call us savages if he could see this mother holding upon her lap the head of her dying son, who poured his blood forth freely that her gray hairs might be undefiled? Would he call this wife a savage who, with her crowing babe clinging to her breast, kneels here beside the body of her young husband and whispers tender words in his dull ear? That love shines not in satins, is it love the less? Or is this a savage scene—this sister clasping her brother, safe and

well, in her arms; this little family clustered together in a
quiet spot, thanking Wakanda, with a mingling of aged and
infant voices, that He had saved the loved father from
death? Over the fallen Great Bear was bending the gray
head of the wise Standing Elk. Prairie Flower and I,
hearing his mourning, had hastened to his side, and while
she fondled one of his hands I reverently held the other.
She wept to see her father thus distressed; I wept because
the Great Bear had died to leave me mine. When we
had sat thus a moment, Standing Elk began the touching
Dta-wd-e, or lament for the dead, which springs naturally
from the heart of the red man as the alkali waters bubble
from the swamp-spring.

"Alas! my noble brother!" he cried. "Thou wert
swifter than the antelope, and as tender in thy love. Thou
wert wiser than the wild-bee! Thy sight was sharper
than the king-fisher's, and thy strength as lasting as the
hart's. From the day on which thou didst meet the
mighty bear on the foot-hills of the west and kill him
alone, and take his great name, where has been the glaring eye of animal or man that thou daredst not face?
And when until now wast thou ever overcome? But, my
brother, these crossed heaps of Sioux around thee show
thou didst not die the badger's death. Who now shall
find for us the light footprint of the deer, who shall lead
us on the covered track of the spoiler? Whose voice but
thine can bring one small pulse of joy to hearts left sad by
thy untimely death? And yet thou couldst have had no
nobler death—to die to save thy chief were worthy of
Great Bear! Alas! my noble brother! Alas! Ma-chú-
ta-ga! Ma-chú-ta-ga! thou hast fallen!"

When he had finished his lament, he sat silent for a few
moments and then rose, wrapped his blanket about him
and walked away. I lifted my eyes to follow him, and

they encountered the tall form of my father standing
with folded arms and gazing tenderly upon the prostrate
body of him who had died in his stead.

"'Tis a noble thing, my son," he said to me, "to die for
thy people's sake and for the life of thy chief. Thou wilt
be chief one day, and then thou wilt know how sad it is to
see thy children fall. My heart weeps for Ma-chú-ta-ga
to-day. But get thee to thy mother. They come who
will prepare the brave warrior for his long sleep."

The twilight had now come down. Over the spot of
prairie where lately such fury and hatred burned a
strange silence rested. The whispering of the wind
through the long prairie grass, the moaning of some
heart-broken one by the side of a body, the barking of the
wolves who from afar had smelt the flowing blood, and
the distant falling of worn-away banks into the eddying
river, were all the sounds we heard. I held sweet Prairie
Flower's hand tightly as we walked away, fearing that
some stray Sioux-shaft might still come to strike her
from my side.

Around the camp-fires that night there were many
breaking hearts. Only the young and innocent could
sleep. Upon a little hillock near by those who had been
killed were laid, and at their heads a row of pine torches
burned. Watches were stationed to do them every possible
honor, and at stated intervals to chant the Dta-wá-e—the
death-song of my people. Upon the highest point that
had been covered by the battle shadowy forms were seen
at work during the long hours, and the dull thud of their
implements striking against the earth told the sad story
of the digging of graves. Oh how many silent and lovely
spots have heard that weird and dreadful sound!

. With the first streaks of light on the following morning
the camp was astir. A mournful procession was formed

out of every member of our little party to convey the
bodies of the dead warriors to their last resting-place.
On wicker-work of wild aspens, covered with soft furs and
bright blankets, they were placed. These were borne on
the shoulders of the bravest warriors, my father still in
his war-dress, and Standing Elk, with his blanket folded
tightly round him, taking the lead. After the bodies
came the warriors who were able to walk; after these the
women, many of whom wrung their hands in deep despair;
and after these the children, who little knew the dread
solemnity of the spectacle of which they formed a part.
Upon this sad march the most perfect silence was demanded. When we reached the graves and had ranged
ourselves around them, the wise man, Standing Elk,
turned to us and said:

"Let us call to mind the words spoken to us by the
good Wa-gá-za* of the great love of Wakanda and the
great Love-Gift. I see before me my brother and my
friend. You see your husband and your son. We lay
them where the wild winds shall sweep and the dandelions blossom. Here the storm shall burst, but they shall
not fear it. Here the soft snows shall rest, but they shall
not feel them cold. But shall nothing else be here? Yes,
here shall be Wakanda's smile, and this they shall feel!"

As he spoke these words the bright sun rose above
the horizon, and while its rays touched hill and tree
with a gold richer than that the white man seeks,
our warriors were laid to their rest. Their ponies, fallen
in the fight, were buried beside them, and over all was
built a framework of poplar boughs. Oh, if you pass that
way, drop a tear for Great Bear's sake, who followed the
full extent of duty as he knew it, though it demanded his

* Missionary.

life—as dear to him as yours to you; and as you stand upon that lovely, lonely spot, think of my people as—ignorant, if you please, but—possessed of a love and sympathy which in any condition avail to make life worth the living; think of us with pity, not with scorn, because our usages seem strange to you.   We were made by the same Wakanda who fashioned you, and whom in our simple way we love.   Possibly we are peculiarly his own because we are weak and ignorant.

CHAPTER IV.

THE BUFFALO-HUNT.

THE weeping of the night-dew is soon dried from the short grass, and abides not many hours upon the long, save where the shade of shrub or willow wards off the sun-rays. So the tears of sadness remained but for a short space upon the eyelashes of those of us who were young, and even the older members of the tribe were soon so interested in the progress of our hunt that their hearts had no room for bitter thoughts. Only those who had peculiar reason for sorrow, in the loss of near relatives, continued long to mourn. It may be that this shortness of grief is the foundation of the charge that we are savages. One mark of the civilization we lack may be the lasting love that friend has for friend, and husband for wife—a love like that of bald eagles once mated in youth, which never cease to mourn when the object of it is dead, and never seeks to supply the vacant place. I know not how this is.

There was one circumstance connected with our conflict with the Sioux which struck even my childish fancy as peculiarly important. When we came to gather up the blankets with which they had hoped to gain an easy victory, and which had been left where they had fallen, we found them in every respect superior to any we had before seen. They were thick and warm and durable. The wise Standing Elk showed one of these blankets to me, and, child as I was, impressed me deeply as he said:

"In these blankets there is a bitter story folded. You must know, my son, that they were given to the Sioux by the Great Father who rules the whole land in which we dwell. To him we also owe the blankets which keep us warm and the implements with which we cultivate the soil. But you have already noticed that the Sioux's blankets are much better than any we have ever received, although we have always been faithful to the whites, while the Sioux have been their bitterest enemies."

"Do the white men treat their enemies better than their friends?" I asked in astonishment.

"They do. And so they encourage the red men to slaughter and revenge. Frequently in our councils it has taken all my eloquence and all thy father's authority to prevent the young men going to war, because, as they truly said, the red man can get his right only by making himself feared. If we were bad Indians as the Sioux are, we would have as beautiful blankets as they. It seems an unmerciful and unthinking policy adopted by the whites to treat the red men who have fought and suffered for them with indignities and cruelty, while those who threaten them with murder and robbery are conciliated with the brightest presents and the greatest favors."

Oh how often in after-years did I think of these weighty words! On how many cruel occasions, and in how many bloody scenes, did I learn that they were true!

When the wounded among our warriors were able to mount their ponies again, we pursued our journey toward the great north-west. Our way now led us over wide stretches of untrodden prairie, crossing here and there a little stream with wood-dotted banks. Oh how free we felt—able to hold our path against all disputers; dependent on the skill of our hunters alone; careful simply that no sunrise or sunset pass without receiving due admiration, and obliged only to Wakanda who kept us securely and well. At last we reached a lovely camping-spot in a grove of great trees which, because they stood in a defile of the prairie, had been spared for many years by the fires. Here never-failing springs burst forth, offering their cool and healthful refreshment. Is it one mark of the "savage" to love these quiet retreats better than the noise and anxiety of a great city ; and are we to be spit upon and shot at sight because Wakanda has made us with these simple tastes? Is it because liberty is more to us than life that the white men say sneeringly of all red men, whether good or bad, "The only good Indian is the dead Indian"? We love liberty because the world is full of it, and we are a part of Wakanda's world. From the moment of our birth, nature around us has rippled with freedom in every rill, and bubbled with it in every spring, and shone with it in every glistening sand-grain, and waved with it in every grass-spear and nodding dandelion. Why, then, should we be called "savages" because of all races we love the rills and springs and grass the most, and are most akin to their nature?

In this free and beautiful spot we pitched our permanent camp. Here we were to remain until our hunters had secured all the game we desired and the buffalo-meat was sufficiently dried to be taken home for winter use. Every morning our scouts went out in every direction to watch for the coming of a buffalo-herd, when they were to report to us at camp and the sport was to begin. And we had not long to wait. The second morning after our reaching this camping-spot, our scouts came in, wild with excitement and shouting, "Dta! dta!"* They announced that an immense herd of the noble game we sought blackened the whole horizon to the northward.

* " Buffalo ! buffalo !"

Instantly there was the greatest confusion. The warriors, who had been sleeping in the shade, or mending their bow-strings, or fashioning new arrows, sprang up and began to prepare for the hunt. The ponies were hastily loosed from their tethers, the long hunting-knives were thrust into the hunters' belts, outer garments were thrown away, and in a time so short that you would scarce believe it could be done the whole company was ready for the start. The ponies seemed to share in the common excitement, for they pawed the ground and whinnied ceaselessly, wild to be away. When all was ready my father gave the word, and the whole hunting-party, dividing into three bands so as to encompass the herd, rode gayly forth. Those of us who were not permitted to enter actively upon the sport took a station upon a high spot of ground near by, where we could share in the general excitement and watch the entire proceedings of the day. The very children danced about in uncontrollable delight, shouting, "Dta! dta!"

When the hunters gained the open prairie the bands separated, one going eastward, another in the opposite direction, while the central band continued to advance directly upon the game. We could see the flanking parties galloping away, taking advantage of every little hillock, riding along dry creek-beds, or pursuing lines of long prairie-grass, so as to come as near as possible to the grazing buffaloes without alarming them. At last we saw one of the leaders of the herd lift his head and gaze steadily toward the right flanking party. This the hunters knew would be instantly followed by the stampede of the whole herd; and therefore, with wild and joyous cries, the three bands dashed in full speed upon the noble game. For a few moments the buffaloes, confused by the loud and opposite shouts, stood irresolute,

and then, forming a column of shaggy might that shook
the very earth, they galloped away. The delay, however,
was sufficient to allow our hunters to get within gun-
range and even arrow-shot of the stragglers, and in the
dust which instantly arose, a great cloud, to heaven, we
could see the blaze of the rifle and the stumbling fall of
the victims. The custom was to ride up beside the
buffaloes and shoot them in the back, and one arrow or
ball was generally sufficient to stretch them upon the
earth, where they could afterwards be dispatched with the
long knives. For many hours that day the dust continued, rolling away toward the north; and though the
shouts and reports grew gradually less and less distinct,
and finally ceased entirely, we knew the sport continued
still.

It was late at night when the hunters returned to
camp, bringing such tender and savory parts of buffalo-
meat as were designed for the evening meal, but leaving
until the next day the great work of carrying in the hides
and joints for drying. We had bright fires blazing for
them when they came, and every preparation, except the
roasting of the meat they were to bring, made for their
evening meal. The hunters threw themselves down
before the fires, and after their more pressing hunger was
satisfied, each took a buffalo-rib and held it in the coals,
watching it as it roasted brown and savory. Then began
the recalling of the day's adventures and incidents. What
ringing laughter was heard as some amusing exploit was
related, and how they gloried in the swiftness of their
ponies and the strength of their own right arms! Little
Prairie Flower and I loved to sit beside our fathers and
hear these thrilling stories. The fire's glare lit up the
little hillsides around us, and peopled the pine-tops with
angels of light who evermore whispered joy and love to

our hearts. As I look back upon that happy, cheerful evening, it seems very strange that men like those, who dwell together without jealousy and without cheating, with no hard words and no cruel exactions, with none of the niggardliness of riches or the grumbling of poverty, should be hated of the white men and beloved of Wakanda: for the self-same reason that they fulfill their simple natures as Wakanda has taught them, and wish only to be left alone in bounding, joyous liberty !

That day was the type of many others as our hunt went gayly on. There occurred, however, an incident which more nearly concerns my story, and I must tell you of it. As the twilight came down upon us one evening, the warriors had not returned from the day's expedition, and the women were preparing their supper around the camp-fires. Suddenly from a thicket near by a dozen Sioux sprang upon us, screaming their terrible war-cry, and began to strike the defenseless women and children to the earth. I clasped little Prairie Flower in my arms, expecting that our turn to die would soon come, and wishing only that I might hold her thus when the blow came. Oh, how often in the weary and sad years that have since passed have I wished that we had then and thus died ! As we were thus crouching on the grass, clasped in each other's arms, my mother rushed to us, her frightened face streaming with tears, caught us by the arms and thrust us into a little pit which we, in our play, had dug in the earth. She then threw herself over us, with her face downward, and in this manner completely hid us from sight. The next moment one of the lynx-hearted murderers came by, and supposing her to be dead, as she feigned to be, gave her a cruel kick in the side and passed along. She uttered no groan, but whispered to us to remain perfectly still, and by the blessing of Wakanda

she would save our lives, though it took her own.
Another of the Sioux, discovering her, came and with
horrid oaths thrust his arrow again and again into her
quivering back and sides. Still she did not move a
muscle or moan in the slightest, though I could feel the
hot tears falling upon my cheek. Just as he had started
away, satisfied that my mother was dead, we heard the
shouts of a party of our warriors returning from the hunt.
They soon understood the cause of the screams and commotion in our camp, and, with cries of hate and rage,
dashed upon the Sioux so fiercely and swiftly that only
two or three escaped. When the mother-partridge sees
the shadow of the hawk, she utters her chirp of warning,
and instantly the little brood scatters into the grass, hiding behind shrubs and crouching under leaves; but when
danger is over the little chicks come forth again. So
when the Sioux had gone as many of the women and
children of our party as had been saved made a sudden
appearance from little clumps of bushes and other retreats
whither they had fled at the first notice of danger. With
scarce a moment's delay of weeping, they began the sad
task of arranging the remains of those who had been
killed. The cruel wounds my mother had received bled
freely and became very painful, but she clasped little
Prairie Flower and me to her breast and said cheerfully:

"My dear children! I would die a thousand times for
your sakes!"

Oh! was I not right when I thought, as I have thought
many times since, that civilization can claim absolute
superiority to our simple ways only when it presents the
spectacle of holier love than this, and inculcates principles of a nobler self-sacrifice?

CHAPTER V.

THE ARRIVAL OF GRAY COAT.

FOR about two years after our return from this hunt, nothing took place in our little village of sufficient importance to be mentioned here. At the end of something like that period, however, an event occurred which changed the whole future history of our tribe, and brought us, ultimately, from the high hills of hope and liberty to the dark caves of slavery and despair.

One day a troop of us, boys and girls together, were chasing yellow-winged butterflies upon the prairie a mile or more from our homes. The rich green grass of spring had just burst up from the sod, and while our fathers and older brothers were preparing the soil in our fields for the year's crop, we who were happily released from such slavish work allowed our energies to escape in noisy romp and wild chase. While thus engaged, we saw four horsemen riding over the prairie toward us, and instantly our sport was stopped, and we gathered into a bunch, to speculate as to who the visitors might be. They rode horses much larger than any we had ever seen before, and their faces and garments and manner pointed them out as belonging to some race with which we children had never come in contact. We watched them closely until they had come within twenty lariats' length of us, and then one of our number shouted:

"Run! run! Wá-gha! wá-gha*! The white men! The white men!" and we scampered back to our village wild

---

* "White man! white man!"

with affright, and yet bursting ever and anon into peals of venturesome laughter. Oh! would that we had run so fast and so far that we had never seen their faces again!

They proved indeed to be white men, and as they rode proudly into the little open space within our village, my father received them with the kindness of a brother. He waved his hand in welcome to them, and, through an interpreter who was in their company, invited them to dismount and enter our homes. The white man who seemed of the most authority said to my father:

"Most noble Eagle Wing, we thank you for your generous welcome. But we come from the Great Father on business of the greatest importance to you and your tribe, and therefore we desire a council with you and your head men as soon as you may be willing to grant it."

The speaker was a fat man of about fifty years of age. He sat very erect, and even haughtily, upon his large bay horse, from which high station his restless gray eyes seemed to be taking in the several advantages of our village. To my boyish fancy he appeared to be sweeping, by his quick glances, all our possessions into his arms for his own use. The whole expression of his face was one of cunning, masked under a pretense of sincerity. His words were very gracious, and apparently so fair that many of our tribe were completely deceived. He wore a great gray coat, and the custom of our people being to give a name to every prominent person who comes among them, and to take that name from some striking circumstance or object about him, I could hear the members of our tribe saying to each other, as they watched him:

"U-nosh-e-chú-day! U-nosh-e-chú-day!" This in the white man's language means Gray Coat! Gray Coat! and by this title he was ever afterward known among us.

To his request for a council my father replied:

"The Indian always receives the white man as a brother when he comes in peace. We will have a large wigwam built here in the center of this open space, and in it our council shall be held. There we will smoke the pipe of peace."

The chief then gave a few words of direction and command to his warriors, and they departed instantly for a swamp, which was at no great distance from our village. A great forest of tall, slender trees grew there, and in a short time the warriors returned, bearing upon their shoulders a number of poles cut therefrom. The butts of these poles were planted in the ground in the form of a circle, and their tops brought together and fastened with strong thongs. Over this framework our brightest blankets and richest furs were flung, and thus a wigwam was formed large enough to seat thirty persons. A fire of the fragrant pine boughs was built in the center of the wigwam; the smoke escaped at the top, where, wedded to the gentle breeze, it curled upward to the sky. Into this wigwam the white men were invited, and then my father, dressed in all the gorgeous signs of his high chieftainship, and the head men of our tribe, including, of course, the wise Standing Elk, followed them. All were seated in a circle, on robes spread upon the ground, and before any conversation could be entered upon the pipe of peace must be passed from lip to lip. It may not be known to some who read these simple pages that our peace-pipe is a tomahawk, the hollow handle of which forms the stem, and the round top above the blade, the bowl. The extreme end of the handle is whittled down to fit the mouth. In this pipe we smoke pounded dogwood bark, called *kinni-kinic*, mixed with the very least tobacco. When the pipe is lighted, it is passed from mouth to mouth, each person taking a few puffs, and always exhaling the smoke through the nose, and no greater insult can be offered to your entertainer than to refuse to place the peace-pipe in your mouth. In this manner the pipe was passed around the circle in the wigwam that day, beginning with my father, who passed it directly to the white men, and ending with the youngest Indian in the council. When this ceremony was completed, Gray Coat arose and said:

"The Great Father is pleased with the tribe of Eagle Wing. He has sent me to tell you this, and to urge upon you to continue to be wise and friendly, that you may still enjoy his favor. You have for years received your blankets and farming implements, and, when in hunger, food as well, from the kind hand of the Great Father. But all these and many other dealings between you and him have been conducted by persons appointed specially to bring each gift; and, as men are apt to be treacherous, and some of these messengers have proven so, the red men have suffered much from robbery and deceit. The Great Father has now determined that I shall remain among you as his agent, to receive and deliver all his gifts to you, and convey to him any suggestions or complaints you may have to make. This gentleman at my side has been appointed trader with you. To him you are required by our law to sell all your grain and furs, and from him you must buy all your supplies. This other gentleman, who with the interpreter makes up my party, is a farmer, sent to teach you how best to cultivate the soil. We will live among you and be your brothers, and all we ask in return is that you obey our commands and grant to us a reasonable support from the annuities which the Great Father will send you. We wish you also to cede to us all the land that you now hold, except a tract which we will hereafter specify, sufficient for your support. This tract will be set apart as a reservation, upon which it shall be my duty to defend you, and from which you will not be allowed to go except by my permission. The food and clothing of all the members of the tribe are to be placed under my control. All the letters passing between you and the outside world must be open to my eyes. The expending of your annuities shall be in my hands entirely, since, of course, it would not do to regard so many various wishes as the tribe might express if a public consultation were held. In short, you are no longer to be neglected, but will be taken care of and protected by me."

"In short," my father exclaimed, with instant impulse, "we are to be thy slaves! Go thou to the Great Father and tell him we will not accept his plans. Tell him we do not trust his words. Why may not we live as we have always lived and as our fathers have lived before us? Must the nestlings of the eagle turn into prairie-dogs? Must the free-born become slaves? Must the wild colt, shaking the dews from his mane and snorting defiance at the elk-buck's horns, subject his flanks tamely to the spur? Go and tell him that we will not sell our land and let any of his servants, like thyself, live upon the money; go and tell him we will be free!"

"Most noble Eagle Wing," the white man replied, in a voice that was soft and insinuating, "the Great Father has already arranged that I should stay with your tribe. If you do not submit quietly to this regulation, which in time you will discover to be wise and fatherly, it will be the Great Father's unpleasant duty to send the soldiers to enforce his commands."

"His commands!" my father said, springing up and flinging the peace-pipe away from him. "Are we already slaves? When did we invite his patronage? When did we ask thy nation to be a father to us? Shall the brown bear lie down in the antelope's simple hiding-place, and,

just because his limbs are stronger, force the timid creatures to part with the larger share of their scanty room
and present their tender breasts and hams to his cruel
jaws? The white man dare not do so unjust a deed,
which in the end would make such savage work between
his race and my own, if he fear Wakanda!"

"Oh! Wakanda?" Gray Coat smoothly answered.
"Wakanda is all well enough in his way and in his place,
but we are dealing now with plain facts. I am sent to be
the Great Father's agent for this tribe, and if the best
and bravest of all your warriors should dare to disobey
my commands, your Wakanda should not-save him from
the piercing bayonet."

Oh! to what quarter of all this bright universe above us,
or of all this radiant earth around us, can the poor red
men turn their eyes for succor and sympathy when the
power of Wakanda, our only friend, the only one who has
fulfilled his promises to us or failed to enrich himself at
our expense, is denied and spit upon? Will the white
man not grant us even the slight hold upon their mercy
that a mute and tearful appeal to the Friend of all would
convey, as it would seem, to the most wretched suppliant
of the favor of the strong? Have tears lost their eloquence, and do bleeding wounds gape in vain? It is the
simple belief of my people that even the she-wolf, which,
springing suddenly from cover upon the antelope, stands
with dripping jaws and fierce eyes over the fallen victim,
will have pity and refuse to slay the poor creature if it but
turn its soft and pathetic eyes upward, as if seeking Wakanda's face. Will the white man show less mercy than
the she-wolf?

When Gray Coat had spoken his cruel and wicked
words, he arose haughtily, and with his three friends left
the council. For a long space my father and his people

sat silent and despairing around the ruins of the council-fire. At last the noble Um-pan-nez-zhe arose and said :

"You have often, since I came among you, taken my words as those of wisdom, my children. Will you regard them now ?"

"We will !" said my father.

"We will ! we will !" sorrowfully answered one after another of the head men, knowing perfectly what would be the old man's advice.

"My children," Um-pan-nez-zhe said, with great solemnity, "at least our lives are secure. For the present, and as long as we quietly obey, they are secure. And when the red man has even life remaining, and while his wife and babes are safe, though he has been stripped of every other comfort, he has all—nay! far more than all—he can expect from the stronger race. Still, if we send to the Great Father a petition, signed by all the head men of our tribe, he may regard our wishes and suffer us to be free."

This last hint, being the only hope that could be offered, was eagerly accepted by all, and a messenger was dispatched to the white men, begging them to return and hold another conference.

Gray Coat and his companions soon made their appearance, wearing upon their faces the injured look of those who have for a long time borne patiently with the whims and fancies of a childish people.

"Are you willing now to talk words of wisdom ?" Gray Coat asked, with as much severity as his soft voice could assume, and also with a trace of triumph in its tone.

All the warriors turned their eyes to Um-pan-nez-zhe as having proposed the petition, and as therefore being the proper person to explain and favor it. But the wise man had still another plan in his mind, and so when my father waved his hand to him to speak, he arose, with a dignity which I saw really affected the white men, and said:

"Is it our land that the Great Father desires? Has he not enough for his people in all the great prairies that sweep so grandly between the watering rivers? If so, let him send a few of his families to us and we will give them land. And if he desires all our land, but will still grant us life and liberty, we will move on toward the setting sun, the course our fathers all have taken, and there we will live and be out of the white man's way."

"Nay! my noble old man," Gray Coat replied, "I have come for the very purpose of defending you from the powerful tribes of Sioux who roam upon the prairies to the west."

"Is there such strength in thine arm, then?" the wise man replied sneeringly. "Surely I did not think it. And besides, for many generations we have been fully able to defend ourselves against the Sioux, and if this be the object of thy journey to us, we thank thee for thy kindness but we decline thine aid."

Stung by these words, Gray Coat angrily exclaimed:

"Cease such foolish talking! The Great Father commands you to remain where you now are, and to obey my directions."

"But if we should send a petition to him, stating that we prefer to remain as we have been and that we love not even our beautiful homes so much as we do liberty, would he not respect our wishes?"

"Most certainly!" was the reply of the white man, whose expression of face instantly changed from anger to quiet triumph. "And as I anticipated that you would desire to make such a petition, I have ordered my secretary, the interpreter, to bring writing materials to take your words down."

When Gray Coat had thus spoken he held a short conference with the interpreter. A look of understanding
between them and a smile of cunning and triumph played
for a moment upon the faces of all the white men. Ah!
it was only after many years of bitter suffering and cruel
robbery that I learned what that look and smile por-
tended to the unhappy Indian race! The paper which
was on that day prepared opened the way for one of the
most unjust of all the dealings that even the white man
has had with us, and is the cause and groundwork of the
sorrowful story that I have to tell; a story sad because
of the pathetic tears we were made to shed, and sweet
because of the graces which, by our suffering itself, were
nourished and developed in certain hearts very dear to
me.

When Standing Elk had heard the words of the white
man he took his seat, as it was our custom to delegate
the task of dictating treaties or petitions to the chief. My
father, therefore, arose when the secretary was ready to
take down his words, gathered his robes of command
about him, and spoke the earnest wishes of our hearts. It
was a grand picture. My father was so tall that he stood
very near the center of the council-wigwam, in order to
be able to lift himself erect, and even then the eagle-
plumes upon his head touched the robes that were flung
upon the roof. He made many gestures of majesty and
grace; and to the dignity of the orator added the earnestness of one who is conscious of pleading the most
sacred rights of the humble against the cruelty of the
strong. His words were as follows:

" Most noble Great Father! was it by your command
that Gray Coat came to deprive us of our liberty, and did
you tell him to threaten us with death if we did not submit to his authority? What crime have we committed

that we may not be free? When have we failed to stand between the white settlers and the Sioux, and when have we hesitated to die that those who have taken refuge in our wigwams might live? Does it not seem that we who have always been the white man's friends ought surely to enjoy our little possessions in security and peace? Our hearts are heavy and our eyes are dull with weeping. Our wives and children will moan and cry, 'Ma-shán! Ma-shán!' * through all the night if we may not live in liberty. For what is home if we be not free? If the Great Father wants our land we will move away, following the sun, which smiles with constant brightness upon us. The red man loves liberty. Will the Great Father grant it to him?"

These words were taken down, as we supposed, by the interpreter, and under them my father and all the head men present made their marks. There was a peculiar blotch upon the paper near where my father placed his cross, and this being fixed in my memory, I was able to recognize the petition when for a very cruel purpose it was presented to us many years thereafter.

"It will be some time," Gray Coat said, "before the Great Father will reply to these words. Meanwhile it is my *duty* to assume authority over you. I shall take up my residence in the little grove which crowns the hill to the east of us, and let no one of your tribe without my permission leave the reservation, as we shall now call the part of your land which I shall hereafter mark out."

Thus the "Indian Agent" came among us, and thus our slavery began. The results of his presence were not appreciated by me at that time; indeed it was some years before the very wisest of all our people knew what power

---

* "Home! home!"

for oppression and cruelty he had in his hands. There were even some in our tribe who regarded his coming as a favorable sign to us, since, as they argued, we thus had a representative of the Great Father at our very door, and could present our grievances to him in person. Moreover, they said, we can learn from him many wise ways and judicious customs, so that our lives will be happier and our children better educated. And it is only just to say that they were right in this last particular. The agent did indeed establish a school in which more than one hundred of our young people learned to read and speak the English language. To him I owe the power, which I now so poorly use, of writing my simple history, with the hope of securing sympathy and justice for my unhappy people.

It was not long before we began to discover how real and absolute was the power Gray Coat exerted over us. In a thousand ways he made us feel our subjection. The faces of my people gradually assumed more and more of a despairing look, until it seemed to me that one who had visited us when I was a child would scarce recognize us as the same race had he come again when I had become a youth.

I must anticipate my story a little while I tell you of the singular and original manner in which Gray Coat secured, without expense to himself, a large and comfortable home among the trees of which he spoke at the council.

When our first annuities, amounting to about six thousand dollars, were sent to our agent, he prepared to expend them without consulting our wishes in the slightest. He ordered a large number of our young men to leave their field-work, take their teams, and haul an immense number of bricks from a distant station on the white man's railroad. Workmen were also brought over, who began to build the walls of a large structure, many of the Indians being required to assist on the more simple and burdensome parts of the work. We wondered much what the building could be designed for; but as the walls rose higher and higher in such disproportionate grandeur to the simple homes in which we dwelt, the wiser among us began to suspect that it was to be the agent's dwelling-place. The weeds were growing rank between our rows of corn, and we were stared in the face by cruel hunger, which too really beset us in the following winter, but Gray Coat cared not. After many months of hard work the building was completed, and then the agent said to us:

" I have spent your six thousand dollars in this edifice, which I design for a hospital for the tribe. If any one among you should be sick, he will be cared for here. See how kind and thoughtful I have been of the interests of those under my charge. Do you not repent that you ever refused for a moment to regard my authority?"

But our chief answered him:

" We do not wish to be treated in a hospital. We have our homes, in which our wives and daughters may nurse us when we are sick. You have deceived us in this matter, and spent money which was not rightfully your own in a way that will not benefit us in the least."

" Do you refuse to accept the hospital that the Great Father has in kindness and love provided for you?"

" We do."

" Very well, then," the agent smilingly replied; " it would certainly be wrong to allow so noble a building to go to waste, and therefore I will move into it with my family."

Which he accordingly and cheerfully did.

The family of Gray Coat consisted of his wife and two sons, the eldest of whom seldom made his appearance

upon the reservation, as he had some lucrative office under the Great Father at Washington. The younger son
was a vile and unprincipled man, who brought more
agony upon my heart than it has felt from all other sources
and causes combined. I hated him from the moment my
eyes first saw him, and I instinctively feared that some
great calamity would be brought by him upon myself and
Prairie Flower. I dreaded him as I should dread the rattlesnake even before I had felt its fangs. He had a peculiar scar upon his cheek, and thus was always known to
my people by the name of Scar Face.

The wife of Gray Coat was a most gentle and lovable
woman. Many were the kindnesses that she showed to
my people, and if our gratitude could be known to her in
the grave, whither she was sent by the unnatural and infamous blow of her own son's hand, she might be repaid
for her mercy to the helpless. Oh, daily from hundreds
of hearts a prayer goes up to Wakanda that He will bless
her and lead her through all the beautiful places of His
Ma-shán, because she remembered in love those who were
far below her, just as she is below Him! It was singular
to see what a respect and even love Scar Face had for this
noble mother during her whole lifetime, and in all his
lustful and reckless deeds he took care that not a word of
it should reach her ears. He feared neither the laws of
Wakanda nor those of man, yet he would give up the
most fascinating scheme or prospect if he might thereby
give pleasure to his mother. I have often thought how
wonderful and how wise this provision of our nature is,
that a man, no matter what may be the color of his skin,
will reverence and adore the gray-haired mother who, in
great pain and sorrow, bore him; and if he be wise and
diligent, will hasten to lay at her feet all the honors or possessions he has wrested from the world; or if he be fool-

ish and sinful, will be kept back from many an evil deed
and many a cruel wrong by the sweet remembrance of her
love. In the case of Scar Face this peculiarity of his nature saved to me what little happiness my life still retains,
and therefore wherever I shall see the love of a son for his
mother, whether on the free prairies, where my people
dwell, or among the grand palaces of the stronger race,
who have so little in all their finery and elegance to attract my heart, I shall fall down and worship the spectacle.

It was not long before I could notice the most marked
change in the interest my people took in the cultivation
of the soil. Hitherto they had been proud of their progress in the ways and customs of the white men, but now
they seemed to regard them as tyrants, and all desire to
become like them was destroyed. The farmer who had
been sent to teach us agriculture made a great show of
his superior knowledge; and as he laughed much at our
simple methods without showing us any better way, there
were many of our people who refused to work at all. The
agent had no sympathy with our worship of Wakanda,
though his wife secretly encouraged us in it, and whenever he could interfere with it he seemed to take a particular delight in doing so. On many occasions he forced
us to work upon the Sabbath day, which in obedience to
the teachings of the missionary we had always observed
as sacred. He openly encouraged the thoughtless ones
among our people to disregard our worship, and spread
arguments against Wakanda wherever he could find ears
to hear. In short, in more ways than I have words to express he ground us down in hated slavery, and bound
upon us exactions and cruelties which galled the soul as
no spiked collar could possibly gall the neck.

Can the white men hope that such treatment will help

us up to a level with themselves? Do they not know that a slave is, by very hatred, kept from wishing to become like his master? Is it not the testimony of their histories that in all subjugated nations the inhabitants are spurred to continual revolt, dash themselves against the most fearful odds, take hope by brooding upon despair, grow desperate by defeat, and plan revenge in tears?

There is a beautiful bird, radiant with plumage of gold and green, which flies through the groves of the West, and, so long as he is left in glorious liberty, he takes pride in his own beauty of wing and feather. But when the bird has been caged by the Indian boy behind cruel bars of wild cherry, he plucks out with his own beak all the beautiful feathers he can reach, as if determined that the captor shall not be delighted with the glory of his plumage, since he cannot spread his wings upon free boughs. Thus the simple hearts of the red men disdain to exhibit forced virtues to their tyrants, and if they cannot be instructed and admired as brothers, they will not be instructed and admired at all. This, we admit, is the feeling of our hearts; are we to be shot at sight because it is so?

Meanwhile little Prairie Flower and I, but half conscious of the web of slavery that was being woven around us, were happy in each other's love, and, like twin wild-roses, lifted up smiling faces amid thorns which pierced the hearts of those who, being older and more experienced, could appreciate their sharpness.

CHAPTER VI.

A CHAPTER OF LOVE.

I HAVE described the adventures of our buffalo-hunt with some particularity, for the purpose of showing you how deep and sacred was the love between Prairie Flower and myself. Thrown thus into a common danger and saved thus by the self-sacrificing love of the most dear to both our hearts, we came to regard it as the will of Wakanda, as it certainly was our dearest wish, that we should live for each other's happiness. It was not, however, until some years after the events described in that chapter that I grew to know what this love really was, that was rooted in my soul, and found courage to express my love plainly to her and ask that her heart might always be mine. It was in the following manner. And I may venture to hope that the simple story of our love will not be uninteresting to you, since the entire bitterness of the events I must by and by describe is owing to the complete and sacred surrender of our hearts each to the other.

It was at our little village beside the shining river. For some time I had not seen as much of Prairie Flower as during the period of our childhood. I feared that her face was shadowed from me. Our quiet strolls together upon the divides and through the valleys had entirely ceased, and for a long time the softer cheek than mine had not rested on the grass beside me. All this I knew was right, as I was now become a young man and Prairie Flower was blooming into womanhood. The Indians are exceedingly careful respecting the regulations to be ob-

served in the association between the youths of different
sex.   Not even a brother and sister, after they have come
up out of childhood, are allowed to be alone together.   So
that I perfectly understood Prairie Flower's feeling in the
matter.   Still, that anxiety which is, perhaps, always present to real love, in whatever race, was in my heart also, and
I fancied that even in the company of our people the little
maiden avoided me.   So beautiful a girl was not without
other admirers among our people, and though I had at one
time received from her the very best evidences of her pref-
erence, there were times when my anxiety that she should
not forget me or prefer another overbalanced by far my
assurance of her affection.   For days together I revolved
the matter in my mind as I sat upon the river-banks or
strolled along the shady paths in the woods.   What if she
has changed in these changing years, I thought, and looks
back with laughing wonder at her childish love for me?
What if the face of some other youth seems to her hand-
somer than mine and his limbs more shapely?   But no!
true love can never change, and the touch of our childish
cheeks was not more real and tender than the touching of
our hearts.   She loved me once; has she changed, or have
I become less lovable?   If she did not love me, I was disposed to assign this last reason for it rather than think
that she could change.   But in the eyes of love the object
could never be other than lovely, though wrinkles may
have come upon the face and gray hairs upon the head.
Oh! if she loves me, how fair the days will be, and how
bright life will seem! but if she loves me not—I could not
bring myself to think of such utter gloom as my life then
would be.   Rendered miserable by these alternate emotions, I determined that I would formally present my love
to her, in the presence of her father, as is the custom of
my people.

Early one radiant evening when such stars as had come out were shining above, and the river was murmuring as it seemed to me it had never done before, I made up my mind to carry my purpose into effect. The air was throbbing with all the busy hum of night-life, and the varied music of the wind sighing through different lengths of grass soothed and encouraged my beating heart. It was in the early summer, and the perfume of the wild-rose and balsam delighted the sense and imparted the stimulus of health to the frame. It was a twilight such as only lovers can rightly appreciate.

I dressed myself in my gayest garments, and over my shoulder I flung a bright blanket, neatly folded. My hunting-jacket, leggings, and moccasins were richly ornamented with beads, and by my side hung a small looking-glass, supposed by the youth of my people to add a particular charm to the appearance of the wearer, and to render much assistance in the matter of love-making. Around my neck I tied a necklace of bears' claws, belonging to my father. This necklace was of particular value from the fact that the claws where white, as if carved out of pure pearl, whereas usually the claws of the bear have a brownish tinge. From the necklace hung a strip, to fall down the back, of the finest otter-skin, ornamented with rabbits' ears, tied in pairs, and dotted with brilliant colors. Upon this pendant also were two or three medicine-charms, supposed to be of great efficacy in the healing of diseases. Thus gallantly arrayed, I started for the home wherein my Prairie Flower bloomed.

I supposed it would be the easiest matter in the world to open my heart to her on this subject as it had been opened on so many others. Had I not played with her from the moment of my earliest recollection? Was not her sweet smile entwined with all that I knew of life?

Had we not passed days together by the river-side, or wandering in search of plover's eggs upon the plains? And, more than all, had we not had shelter under one bosom from the sharp thrusts of the Sioux's arrow-points? Why should I hesitate to tell her of my affection when I had shown it to her so often? But when I had crossed the open place in our village that I have spoken of, and came near the spot where Um-pan-nez-zhe's home stood, my courage suddenly deserted me, and I made up my mind that a short stroll upon the open prairie would prepare me to face my love. Turning from my course, therefore, I bent my steps to the grassy valley-sides where I had so often raced with her in our sport, and, throwing myself down upon my back, I gazed up into the early stars, and wondered why I was so timid. The stars seemed to whisper the answer: "It is because," they said, "there is a vast difference between childish love and that expression of sober and tried affection that manhood can make. It is one thing to ramble with a child-lover over flower-spangled prairies, and quite another to woo a wife, to be to thee another self. Look at us. See how we shine in glory, remaining in our glowing places not for ourselves alone, but for the lighting of the world. Let thy affection be as bright, as abiding, and as unselfish. Be thou not like yonder falling meteors, who, disregarding duty, dash away on selfish courses; for behold in their speedy extinction the sure type of every selfish career. Remember this in thy love for the sweet, blooming Prairie Flower and thou shalt be happy."

While I thus lay thinking and listening, I saw a white, fluttering object, far up in the sky, falling down toward me through the gathering gloom. It flitted and circled downwards, and reflected from its bright surface the rays of the rising moon. Quietly the object descended to the earth, and falling lightly at my feet, proved to be an eagle's plume, radiant with blended gray and russet and heavy brown. I looked to discover the bird, but in the uncertain light he was not to be seen. I watched to see him pass, but in that I failed as well. In some far region of infinite space the grand old bird was sweeping away, but had not disdained to send down this feathery messenger of his good-will to the cold earth. Oh, what lessons that one little plume taught me on that night of my anxiety. It taught me of a great region of purity and excellence far above the world in which I lived. It taught me that *she* was the brightest inhabitant of that celestial domain in all that concerned moral elevation and dignity. But it also taught me that perhaps she would send down to me some little token of affection which I might treasure side by side with my eagle's plume. As I thought of this I sprang up, snatched the feather from the grass, and determined to hasten away, lay it at her feet, tell the simple story of how it had fallen at mine, and beg a return of my great love for her.

Simple as this purpose seemed, it was hard to carry it into effect. Twenty times on my way to her father's home I stopped, threw myself on the grass, and half resolved to postpone the eventful declaration. Had the prize been less in value, I should have turned to my own home; but when I thought of her sweet face and simple ways and thrilling voice, I could not but go forward. And as I found that thinking of these gave me courage to advance, I bound myself to think of nothing but these, and so I reached her father's door.

I found him, the wise Standing Elk, sitting just at his door-step, twisting a sinew for a bow-string.

"Good-evening, my son," he said; "have you been on one of your thinking-journeys over the prairies?"

"I have only been listening to the night-music," I said.

"But what have you in your hand?" he asked.

"An eagle's plume," I answered.

"And did you find it out on the prairie?"

"Yes," I said shortly, not wishing to tell the story of the feather until the one for whom it was designed could hear.

Of course the wise man knew whom I had come to see, and I supposed he would call her without my being obliged to ask directly for her. But for some moments this seemed the very farthest thing in all the world from his thoughts. During this time I was painfully embarrassed and conscious that he was enjoying my perplexity. At last he called:

"Prairie Flower, my child, there is a looking-glass and a young man here, and they both wish to see you."

At this jocose reference to my attire and the particular significance in love-making of the ornament mentioned, I am sure my cheeks colored deeply. Nor was my embarrassment relieved in the least when I heard Prairie Flower's voice saying sweetly:

"It seems to me I hear a voice here, beside that of my father, that I ought to know."

Instantly she stepped forth. How I blessed the dear girl for not partaking of her father's merriment! And what a sly little maiden she was that she did not even look at the looking-glass hanging at my side, which betrayed my purpose. Nevertheless, I was exceedingly confused in her presence, and although I had seen her almost every day of my life, it seemed to me at this moment that I had not seen her for years. And before her bright smile how soon all the fascination faded from the story of the eagle-plume! It seemed the most simple and silly thing I had ever imagined, and I instantly determined not to make any use of it—at least on that occasion. How many of

our twilight visions seem trivial and absurd in the light of
day! Her smile was the sunshine in which my carefully
prepared story paled to insignificance.

While I was thinking these things, an awkward silence
reigned; but Standing Elk, who was as good as he was
wise, noticing the rabbits' ears on the pendant to my necklace, asked:

" Do you know, my children, why the chief of our people always has these rabbit-ears upon the necklace that
marks his chieftainship?"

"I do not," I said, eager to have the silence broken,
partly because it was exceedingly painful to me, and partly
because I really delighted in the wise man's stories.

Prairie Flower likewise protested her ignorance in the
matter, and her father, with the greatest consideration,
turning away from us, thus affording me an opportunity
to sit at my dear one's feet, began his story:

"One of the greatest of our chiefs, who lived many years
ago, became a very old man before he was blessed by
Wakanda with the gift of a boy. For long years he had
wished, and the whole tribe had wished, that the sound
of a son's voice might be heard within his wigwam, that
he might have a successor in the chieftainship. This was
before the good Wa-gá-za had come to our tribe, and
our fathers knew no better way than to practice their simple rites of superstition, hoping thus that their great desire might be granted. At last Wakanda heard their unconscious prayers, and a son was born to the chief. Oh,
how they tended and watched him during his infancy and
early childhood! It seemed as if the entire hope of a
proud and powerful race were wrapped up in one little
bosom. The wisest men were chosen for his instructors,
and the most careful matrons were appointed for his
nurses, and if the child received so much as a scratch the

one through whose inattention it occurred was instantly put to death. You are a chief's son yourself, but you can scarcely appreciate the extreme care taken by the entire tribe of that tender child's life.

"One day the father of the boy was out hunting, to secure for his son a savory rabbit or a tender quail. Behind a little sage-bush he discovered what he supposed to be a rabbit. He was sure that he saw a pair of rabbit's ears bending and rising, as if the animal were picking the sage berries and leaves. Instantly he let fly an arrow, and what was his amazement to see his own son rise from behind the sage-bush, to see who was thus interfering with his innocent sport. The boy had escaped from his sleeping nurse, and had there thrown himself down to enjoy the beauty of all things around him. Clasped to his bosom he held a pet rabbit, which his father had seen, and the ears of which the father's arrow had smoothly cut away. The chief caught his boy in his arms, frantic with delight that he had not slain his own child, and rushed wildly back to camp. The nurses, who had for this time been forgiven on account of the wild joy of the chief that his son was safe, went out, found the rabbit's ears, which spake so plainly of their own carelessness and the nurseling's narrow escape, tied them together with bright-colored thongs of deer-skin, and the boy ever afterward wore them about his neck, to recall this crisis of his life.

"Thus," said Standing Elk, completing his story, "the chiefs of our tribe, descended from this saved boy, have worn upon the pendant of their necklaces a succession of rabbits' ears, tied in pairs, and bringing to their memory the simple story of how their ancestor, Má-shti-ga Né-ta,* was saved from the arrow of his father."

When the wise man had completed his story he relaxed into deep meditation. I was naturally very deeply im-

* Rabbit's Ears.

pressed by what he had said, as it concerned the history of one of my own ancestors, and explained the wearing of an emblem which I would be required to wear on many important occasions if I should live to become a chief. But I was even more concerned to effect the real object of my visit, and as the deep meditation of the wise man rendered us practically alone, I turned to Prairie Flower and said :

" And what do you think of this pretty story ?"

She waited a moment before replying, and then, looking up shyly and sweetly into my face, she said :

" I love to hear these simple stories of our people. I do not know much about them. But of rabbit ears," she whispered after a moment, " I know only this, there are always two of them found together."

This was said with such a pretty meaning, and she looked so pretty too, that without further consideration I clasped her in my arms and exclaimed :

" We shall be like rabbit-ears—we two found always side by side !"

Then I poured into her ear all the love of my heart.

" Think, my sweet Prairie Flower," I exclaimed, " how often we have roamed the prairies together ; shall life not be one great, beautiful, and flower-dotted plain to us ? Think how many times as children we have whispered our mutual love ; shall it change now, that we are simply older ? Think how the self-sacrificing pain of my mother by right, and thine, wedded us in the most sacred way at the arrow-points of the Sioux. Shall we not reaffirm that right to each other's love ? Speak to me, and speak happiness or woe !"

To my passionate entreaty the little maiden simply looked up into my face with tears, and said :

" Khta-wé-tha ! * Khta-wé-tha !"

* " I love thee."

CHAPTER VII.

THE WINNING OF A NAME.

THE wise man seemed to be by no means startled or displeased by the turn affairs had taken when he returned from his absorbing trip of meditation. .Calling us to his side, he caused us to kneel there and, placing a hand on each of our heads, said :

" My children, dear to me by every thought and memory that can make us treasure an object, I have noticed with joy the growth of your affection, and now see with the greatest happiness its consummation. The prairie-cock could never watch with more tenderness the feathering of his brood of two nestlings, the others having been snatched away by the cold rains of spring, than I have watched your growth, my dears—the one the last of a great line of chiefs, the other the orphaned last of as great a line of wise men."

" I boast, my son," he said to me, " but I boast humbly, for I am the least of all my ancestors, the wise men that our tribe has had. Yet I am glad that in little Prairie Flower thou wilt have a wife worthy by birth, as she certainly is by character, to sleep by the side of a chief's son."

" Worthy ! " I cried; " noble father, she dwells far above the blue region which my lightest arrow could find. See ! You asked me whence I got my eagle-plume. It fell at my feet out of the twilight as gray as it, and I picked it up to lay at the feet of my Prairie Flower, to ask that she would, like the eagle, send down from her far height one little token of love to my heart."

"You can talk more beautiful words than I," Prairie Flower whispered to me, "but I love you more! The male thrush has the brightest plumage and a breast streaked with the deepest brown, but his mate has the tenderest heart.'

"My daughter," the wise man said to her, "my hair is white—whiter than the down of the ripened dandelion. But as the flower then is ready to fly away over many valleys and live again, by the dropping of its seed, in a score of young and fragrant blossoms—so I shall soon be gathered to my fathers; but let the principles of my wisdom live again and again in those who, if Wakanda please, shall spring from thee. I saw not thy mother die; of her cruel and unrighteous murder by the white man I will tell you, again; but while she lived she had but one wish for thee, that thou mightst be as happy and true—happy because true—in thy wedded life as she was in hers. So I charge thee to do thy part to fulfill her wish."

The gentle Prairie Flower could only answer with her tears.

"Give me thy hand, my son, and thine, my daughter, and as I unite you this night under the full moon, in token of your love, let me tell you the first principle of the red man's glory. It is to remember your fathers, to honor their memories, to practice their virtues and defend their graves. In you the lines of power and wisdom meet; in you also, and in all your actions, let power and wisdom blend. Power may seem to have a dignity and value wanting to mere wisdom, and power is rightly represented in thee, my son. But wisdom exerts a milder influence and a mighty because gentle restraint upon power, so that the one is never truly itself without the other, and thus wisdom is rightly represented in thee, my daughter. If you thus live in mutual assistance, you will be able to call down the blessings of Wakanda upon the members of your tribe, as the tall twin-trees draw the showers out of the sky to revive the shivering aspens that grow between them. Thus also I call down the favor of Wakanda to rest upon thee now."

"We thank thee," we said together.

"And now one word of caution," the wise man said. "Have you ever seen the young red foxes mating? They stare upon each other with wide-open eyes for some minutes, and then lie down side by side in the shade of the rock with eyes half closed as if perfectly content. Keep your eyes well open upon each other's faults while you are in this period of courtship, but when you are married let your eyes be partly closed, in charity forbearing with, and in love helping to remove, your mutual failings."

After taking a tender leave of Prairie Flower, I started toward my home. What emotions and joys were entangled together in my heart! I seemed to tread upon the air. The dull earth could not rise to touch my feet. How brightly the moon shone upon the tips of the river-waves, and how the distant barking of a pack of coyotes seemed but to hail me to honor and happiness! The evening breeze had never had such delightful freshness for my cheeks, and I had never seen our village so peaceful and beautiful as it now appeared, slumbering in the moonlight. I knew that I was far too happy to sleep, and so I turned my steps again toward the prairie to think it all calmly over and charge the pale stars to keep watch over my love.

· Such is the strange paradox of our natures, however, that even in this moment of my greatest happiness I was haunted with a feeling of unworthiness and misery. In my heart the counter-currents of emotions met and swirls of anxiety were formed, wilder and fiercer than the eddies my boat had often passed upon the shifting Missouri. My thoughts were much engaged, as I walked along, with one of the most rigid of our customs which I had never fulfilled. My people had always held that a man was not worthy a fair maiden until he had performed some feat of bravery or skill of sufficient prominence to distinguish him ever after. It is perhaps known to you that we get our names from some remarkable circumstance attending our early lives or some exploit accomplished by us in youthful years. My Prairie Flower herself received her name from the fact that when her mother took her forth for the first time to see the broad valleys among the mountains where she was born, she bent forward, babe that she was, and clapped her little hands in the highest joy when she saw the wild flowers springing around her. I thought of this and of all the stories I had heard around the camp-fires, of how each member of our tribe had obtained a title of honor. But I was still known as Eagle Wing's son—a title proud indeed, yet not sufficient to commend me to the consideration of my people. While I had not been unsuccessful in fishing, and had always been among the first in the chase, I had not performed any individual act of prowess sufficient to give me a distinguishing title. So much of my time had been given to musing under the trees that I had employed little in pursuits which would throw me into places of danger. Thus I had acquired the reputation of an idler among our people, much to the uneasiness of my father, who frequently placed before me the glory of my ancestors and warned me not to tarnish their name. There was an additional circumstance that rendered my condition a perplexing one. The longer the exploit was postponed the more my people expected that it would be a great one, and while the crushing of a wild bee might have sufficed in my childhood, the slaying of a bear at least was demanded now.   It is perhaps difficult for the white man to realize how firmly this custom would become rooted, in the course of many years, in the hearts of a simple race. We clung to it as sincerely and regarded it with as much veneration as a far graver principle might be held among a more cultured race.

Thinking upon these things materially marred the happiness with which I had started out upon my walk. My step had gradually quickened, as I was distressed and stimulated by these musings, and, without taking note of distance, I sped rapidly over the prairies, crushing the flowers recklessly and caring little that I aroused many a bird from her night-perch. At last I came to a little grove of pines nestling around a sunken basin of a few yards' width, and, casting myself under one of these trees, I cried passionately:

" I will do something great.   I will, for her sake, distinguish myself. Oh! why have I watched the shadows on the hillsides when I should have been following the trail of the bear or crouching under sage-cover for the lion of the mountains?   What fatal spell has made a sluggard of me when I love so truly and wish so much that my little Prairie Flower should not blush for me? Oh that the glory of my ancestors should thus cease! Has their blood run into water in the long course before it reached my veins?"

Bitterly I wept that night as the moon-rays trickled down to me through the pine-fringes. It was the storm which at the evening relieves the passionate heat of the summer day.

" Show me some enemy worthy of a chief's son!" I cried, springing up and looking wildly around.

That look was the first notice I had that the event I had

so often wished was close at hand. Peering at me from beneath the underbrush, I saw four points of fire. As I looked at them, they seemed to expand and to assume the shape of interwoven rings of many hues, always coming back to the points of fire when I had looked away or closed my eyes for a moment. Well did I know that a pair of animals were glaring at me from their lair; but of what description they were I could not tell. Thought at such a time travels fast, and a hundred possibilities instantly sprang into my mind. Were they simply badgers, eying me from the rim of their burrow and wishing but to find a moment in which to make a sure retreat into the ground? Or were they the dreadful wild-cats, lashing their sides in the shade of the underbrush and licking their lips, while they purred softly to each other in anticipation of a lapping feast of blood? Were they the tassel-eared lynxes to creep slyly after me when I should turn homeward, to see if some stronger animal should fell me to the earth that they might then come in and share the spoil? Or were they a brace of lions who had bounded down from the foot-hills in search of prey, which they would convey thither again before the morning appeared? These thoughts flashed through my mind, and it was a matter of deep concern with me which conjecture was the true one. I had no weapon save a small hunting-knife, which by mere accident lay in the pocket of my jacket. Still, in my present mood, I sincerely hoped that a fierce encounter might be awaiting me, that in one night I might gain a bride and a name. I distinctly remember also that in that hour of my first consciousness of real peril I was perfectly cool, more so than I had ever imagined would be the case, and, as I held my hunting-knife in my hand and ran my finger along its keen edge, not a muscle quivered. All this took but a moment, though it requires some time to tell it. The echo of my wild cry had scarce died on the farther margin of the little pool when I determined upon a course of action.

I knew that the best way to discover the intent of a wild animal is to appear to retreat from him. If he is peaceably disposed, he will also retreat; but if thirsting for blood, he will think his moment of opportunity has come and will dash upon you. The fiercest wild animal is naturally a coward in the presence of man, and, unless wounded, waits for some advantage before making an attack. Knowing all this, I took a few cautious steps backward, keeping my eyes, however, fixed upon the spots of fire. Instantly a fierce noise, between a growl and a bark, issued from among the fire-points, and I could have no further doubt as to the nature of the animals before me. They were the savage timber-wolves, the most dreaded because the most active, knowing, and treacherous foes that man has among the animals of the plains. Well did I know that a conflict was before me in which the utmost bravery and skill would be required, and that the conflict could end only in utter death of one party or the other. Little howls of a whole pack of young wolves now I heard, and I knew that alone, and unarmed save with one small knife, I had burst into a den whence the she-wolf allows no one to pass out except over her dead body. As I retreated, therefore, I was not surprised to see the points of fire follow me, and when I stopped, knowing no flight could give me safety, the blazing eyes crouched among the aspen leaves as before, except that they were much nearer now.

I knew they were crouching for the spring. In the dread moment that ensued, a picture of my whole life passed before my mind. The scenes and dangers of my childhood, the shining of the great river, the blossoming of the wild-flowers I had loved so much, the wide stretches of grassy prairies I had crossed, every minute fault I had had, the sounding of every passionate word, the thudding of every revengeful blow, the sweet presence of my mother and the smiles of my Prairie Flower, whom possibly I was about to lose forever,—all this, and many other things that I had hoped to forget, flashed before me, and I saw it all plainly. Sometimes in the darkness of the storm a sudden flash of lightning lights up the whole village in which I had lived all these years, and I can see the outline of every familiar house and play-spot, and then all dies into darkness again. So some strange quick gleam lit up old scenes for me, and forgotten memories and buried hopes, in that moment when I waited for the she-wolf's spring.

I waited not long. Two shaggy and mighty brutes dashed upon me and I fell to the earth. Fortunately in the fall I happened to catch the fore-paw of one of the wolves in my left hand, and knowing it to be exceedingly sensitive I clutched it with the might of despair, crushing its joints together and causing the animal such intense pain that it could inflict very little injury upon me. Against the other wolf I plied my knife vigorously. This proved to be the she-wolf, and against her I knew I must carefully defend my throat. So I kept my knife flying before this part of my body, and at every dash she made, as she stood growling horribly above me, I would thrust it into her breast or neck. The wolf whose paw I held at last fastened himself upon my left arm; the she-wolf tore the flesh from my right side with her claws, and from my right shoulder with her venom-dripping teeth. I know not how long the struggle continued, but at last with a fortunate thrust of my knife I pierced her heart and the foul brute fell over upon the decayed pine-fringes, dead. Still holding on to the paw of the other wolf, I rose to a sitting posture and soon succeeded in giving him a death-blow, and with one howl of mingled pain and rage. he rolled heavily to the earth.   Then with a sigh of relief I fell back and, faint from loss of blood, became unconscious.

When I opened my eyes again I was surrounded by a party of my people whom my father had sent upon my trail to find me. It was midday, and as I became conscious after the long period since my severe contest I felt exceedingly faint and weak. On one side of me lay the she-wolf and on the other her mate, in whose bloody flank my hunting-knife still was sticking.

" Thou hast done bravely!" the leader of the party exclaimed. " Thou shalt worthily succeed thy father."

The other members of the party were full of admiration, and I found that they had already bound up my wounds with such natural balsams as the red man knows where to find and how to prepare, and had tied together a framework of wild aspens upon which to carry me back to our village.

We soon set out upon the return, and although my wounds were beyond expression painful, I forgot their heat and agony when those who conducted me so loudly and generously praised my exploit. A runner was sent forward to tell the people of our approach, and to rehearse the story of how I had conquered the two fierce wolves, so that the whole village turned out to meet us, with my father at their head.

" Bravely hast thou upheld the glory of thy ancestors, my son," my father said.

"Shá-ta-ga-dtá-tha" * shall be thy name," said the wise Um-pan-nez-zhe.

Sweet Prairie Flower was in the throng, and though she

* Wolf Killer.

said nothing to me, her hands were full of salves for my hurts, and her eyes were full of proud tears. And as we advanced into the village, past the familiar play-ground and before the well known houses, the people made the hills to echo with their shout : "Shá-ta-ga-dtá-tha! Shá-ta-ga-dtá-tha!"

CHAPTER VIII.

THUS I acquired the name by which I have ever since been known. I was required again and again to repeat the story of the contest with the wolves to the people of our village, and I am quite sure that their admiration of my bravery could not have been so hearty if it had not been sincere. This generous praise helped me to bear the pain of my wounds without complaint, and indeed I gloried in them as removing the stain that had previously rested upon my nameless youth. Even the young men of the tribe who had been my rivals in hoping to secure the affections of Prairie Flower were very noble in their praise, professing that not one of them could have done the deed. When one of the young eaglets has stolen a lamb and flown with it to his rocky nest the others of the brood gather fluttering round and scream with defiant delight, while the old bird blesses all with hovering wing. Thus was I the praised of our village. In the attentions of my little bride, however, I had the most delight. It was now known to all the tribe that we were to be married, and thus she was permitted, by our social customs. to wait upon me during my recovery, always, however, in the presence of my mother. The heart of her who had sustained such pain without a murmur to save my little friend and me from the Sioux was gladdened now and doubly repaid by seeing the happiness we had in love, and so our mother's presence was no restraint upon us.

On one of the days when Prairie Flower was beside me she asked:

"What made thee so brave, my Wolf Killer? How

bold, to stand alone against the terrible beasts, and in the night too, when there were no eyes to see thee and inspire thee with courage!"

"I fought for love of thee!" I answered. "The brightness of thy presence in thought gave me light, and the hope to win thy smile gave me strength."

"I prayed to Wakanda for thee," she answered, "for I felt a strange fear for thy safety."

"No obstacle is now between our union," I said joyfully, "and no longer will you blush for being loved by a nameless youth. O my blooming Flower, what happiness we shall know!"

"I knew that thou wouldst prove thyself brave," she said. "Even the little wren needs but a moment of danger to show the strength there is in her tiny wing and the courage in her russet breast. I knew that if Wakanda granted thee but the opportunity thou wouldst reveal thy might and bravery. There is truly no obstacle between us now, save one. Thou must recover. And that it may be speedily and happily accomplished talk no more, but sleep thus upon my arm, while I watch and sing beside thee."

Then in a sweet low voice, such as could only be caught from a constant dwelling amid prairie music, she sang a little strain of her own composing. It may not be known to you that the better tribes among the red men love to sing many little melodies, and our music is dear to us, although it might seem simple or even monotonous to those who admire the strained modulations that are heard in cultured nations. A most imperfect translation of my Prairie Flower's song might run as follows:

> The wild thrush lines her nest with moss,
>   And builds a shade above, dear;
> So would I screen thy rest from harm,
>   So soften it with love, dear.

For me, as bravely thou hast fought,
　　So tenderly I'll watch thee,
Most happy that thou'rt safe, my love
　　Nay! that thou still dost love me.

The wild bee will not sleep in shade,
　　But perches in the morn-ray;
So in thy love's light would I bask,
　　Which e'er shall be my noonday.

The sweet winds whisper of thy skill,
　　But sweeter I shall sing it;
The Shón-ga's * mane thy fame shall toss
　　From every knotted ringlet.

Sleep on, my love, renew thy strength,
　　Confess thee conquered never;
The wild buds blossom once and die,
　　But thou shalt bloom forever.

When other conflicts thou dost meet,
　　Wakanda still shall guide thee;
Through life, in death, oh let me pray
　　Thou'lt only rest beside me.

By the soft tones of her voice I was soothed into a refreshing repose, which did far more to restore me than many unguents could have done.

One beautiful evening, when I had gained sufficient strength to sit up, my father helped me out to a little camp-fire, before which Standing Elk and Prairie Flower, with my mother, were already seated. They gave me a comfortable seat at my father's right hand, the place of honor. I motioned my little bride to come and sit beside me, which she gladly consented to do, and during the evening she held my hand in both her own.

The conversation naturally turned upon my conflict

---

* Pony's. Reference is here made to the Indians' custom of tying knots in the manes of their ponies in token of bravery.

with the wolves, and my father seemed to find peculiar pleasure in rehearsing the difficulties of it. He was usually very silent, as became a chief. His noble face had always been stern to me, although his own and only living child. When in camp he was accustomed to pass backward and forward, demanding the greatest homage from his followers, and striking all with admiration of his immense figure, straight as an arrow and sinewy as a bow. How often had I seen his majestic form pass around the camp in the dim starlight when any danger might be near, and how I thought, as he came and went, of another Father who never sleeps at all! His character being thus august and almost forbidding, it was with particular delight that I heard him converse so freely and proudly of what I had done.

After a few moments of conversation upon this theme a short space of silence fell upon the little group. The pine-knots blazed up weirdly, and their light seemed to watch the covert creeping of the shadows until they came too near, and then it would spring brightly forth and drive the darkness to the woods again. We all gazed into the fire, and upon the faces of all came a look of solemnity. Possibly there was something in the dying embers to inspire that look, or perhaps we were all unconsciously thinking of the same deep meaning that life has to the simple-hearted. Upon the face of the wise man particularly there was a look of the most intense awe. Prairie Flower touched my arm gently and pointed to it. At last he broke the silence and began one of the most important conversations it has been my lot to hear.

"There is a fiercer foe to the red man than even the she-wolf robbed of her young," he said.

There was a moment of deep silence around the camp-fire.

"Thou hast spoken truly," my father answered with the greatest solemnity.

"Tell us, Eagle Wing," the wise man then said to him, "tell this son and daughter of thine and mine who is the worst foe of the Indian race."

I shall never forget the slow and august tone my father used, as, straightening himself up to his full height and looking sadly out upon our fields, he answered :

"Wá-gha!" *

"The white man!" I demanded, incredulous.

"Yes, my son," Eagle Wing replied, "the white man. This glorious land, running so wild with rivers and blooming back Wakanda's smile in such wealth of flowers, once belonged to the red man, and of most of it he has been shamelessly robbed. If those of our race who have been slain by the white man should spring up from the sod as trees, there would be one broad moaning forest from the great river to the sea. Those of us whose lives have been spared are sneered at, despised, enslaved, and spit upon as dogs."

"But," I asked, "are not the white men boasters of their love of liberty? Do they not profess to offer all men an asylum from oppression and outrage? Do they not claim to be the helpers of the weak and the upholders of those who fall?"

"My son," he answered, with a look such as I have seen his face wear only in battle, "the foulest scum of every nation under the stars can come to the Great Father's land and be protected and blessed by equal laws, but the red men, the original owners of the land, are trodden in the mire and esteemed worse than brutes. The bald eagle is their chosen emblem, but as you have seen this

* "The white man!"

noble bird upon the banks of yonder river snatch the putrid carrion from the very lips of the wolf, so will the white man debase himself to rob and outrage the poorest member of our unhappy race. Of all the many treaties we have made with the Great Father scarce a score have they honored with even the pretense of keeping."

"Why not rise, and join with other bands of our people," I exclaimed, "and sweep the white man from the land!"

"My son, your words accord with the message I received not many days since from certain of the great chiefs far to the west of us. While thou wert lying too severely hurt to be informed of any startling thing, a messenger came from these chiefs to me. He had in his hand the tomahawk of the greatest chief of all, and thus, as is the custom of our people, I knew that he was a trustworthy runner and that his words would be true. If he said one word that is false, our customs demand that he shall die as soon as he returns to his band. This young man rehearsed the names of the chiefs who had sent him, and added this message: 'Come to us with your warriors and people. Let us meet among the sand-hills. There let us await the coming of the white men, and die in one last battle. As it now is, we die like dogs. Let us be men. There is a universal tradition among our race that a noble chief, Tecumseh by name, dreamed of a time when his people would unite themselves together in one last stand against the white men. That time has come!' For many hours we solemnly thought of the message in our wigwams and when a council was held—"

"Of course you said you would go. Da-dé-ha! Da-dé-ha!* tell me you will go!"

---

* "My father."

"We said to the messenger, 'We will wait. The eyes of some of the white men are turned toward us in sympathy. We will see if they will grant us their law. If not, we can but die. If we act with treachery, we shall be despised by the white men and by ourselves as well. If we suffer patiently, we shall at least not despise ourselves, and that is something.' Then we sent the messenger away."

"You sent him away! You feared to fight!"

"My son, thou little understandest the power of our oppressors. They have mighty revenues and well-trained armies. The minnow is not more within the power of the fish-hawk when clutched in its talons than we are within the absolute control of the whites. It is for us to submit patiently, to be oppressed without answering, to be spit upon without shrinking, and to die without a murmur."

With these words the grand chief, my noble father, wrapped his blanket about him and with a strange look of craven submission upon his majestic features took his seat beside us.

"But, my father," I exclaimed, "even if we might not sweep the white man from the earth, we may at least slay those of his race who come within our reach. We may avenge many a drop of blood by many an individual sacrifice. The Missouri cannot bear yonder mountain bodily away to the sea, but it can tear many a particle of earth or rock from its side."

To this my father made no answer. He was wrapped in deep meditation. Seeing which, the wise man turned to me and impressively said:

"Never slay a white man. Bear to be robbed, bear to be tortured, bear to be murdered, bear to see thy wife torn from thee and outraged in thy sight—"

" What !" I exclaimed, interrupting him, " bear to have this blooming Flower polluted by the breath of foul evil? Can you, her father, counsel it?"

" Yes, I, her loving father, insist upon it, and further say, bear to have thy children scattered limb from limb before the whirlwind of their wrath, but never slay a white man, never answer him with sneers."

"Thou art teaching me to be a coward," I cried.

" I am teaching thee to be truly brave," he answered. " It is the part of a brave man to bear any personal harm and agony rather than bring death upon those to whom he has no right to cause distress."

" What is thy dark meaning?" I implored.

" My meaning is this. The white men hold the entire tribe responsible for the fault of one of its members. If you should kill a white man, however just might be your grievance, the papers which daily appear in all their cities would represent you as bloodthirsty and revengeful. The most false and unjust account would be given of the affair, making you wholly to blame and the white man a martyr. We have no means to deny the slander before the people of the Great Father, and so even the gentle and true-hearted of the whites come to believe us inhuman. Then the Great Father sends an army, and although your father and mother and your beautiful bride might be utterly innocent of any desire to do harm, they would all be put to death for your fault." .

" Horrible !" I exclaimed. " Is this justice?"

" It is justice as the white man knows and practices it toward our helpless race."

At this stage in the conversation my father started up again, not excitedly as before, but with the greatest dignity. The flickering light brought out his majestic form against the darkness around, and speaking as the apolo-

gist of his people, and in a tone of blended sadness and entreaty, said :

"This strange dealing of the white man is the cause of
every Indian war.   In all our tribes there are reckless men,
or there are headstrong young men, who, stung to madness by the exactions of the whites, forget the teachings of
their fathers and commit some deed of violence out of a
natural love of revenge.   Then the entire tribe, being held
responsible by the Great Father, is forced to take part in
the strife in mere self-defense.   If only the guilty could
be punished, as is the case with our brethren in Canada,
there would never be any difficulty in this country, as there
has not been in that, between the red men and the white.
But as it is, my son, the wise Um-pan-nez-zhe has taught
thee rightly.   Our only safety is in drilling every member
of our tribe to uncomplaining submission, no matter what
may be the provocation, and thou as the future chief of
this people must learn this lesson well.   But who is this?"

The question was occasioned by the approach of a
young man, a member of our tribe, who had been sent two
days before to trade at a neighboring outpost of the whites.
He came now to make his report to the chief.   But what
was our astonishment to see his garments covered with
blood! A fearful gash laid open his cheek to the bone,
one arm was terribly cut, and his right side was literally
torn to pieces.

"Strong Arm!" my father cried in amazement, "can
this be thou? What fearful calamity has befallen thee?
Have you too invaded the den of the she-wolf?"

"Nay! my father," the wounded man replied, "I have
been attacked by a white boy!"

"A white boy!" I exclaimed.   "Was he of thy size and
strength? Where was Strong Arm's boasted prowess?"

"I suffered myself to be thus stabbed," he said.   "I remembered the teachings of my fathers. I returned no blow, I answered not a word." *

"Oh! woe is to our race!" I cried. "Better that all our people die nobly defending their rights than that one be thus injured."

"Strong Arm!" my father said, without noticing my words, "thou hast vindicated thy name and shown that thou hast a strong heart as well. Go to thy home, and I will send salves for thy wounds. Always thus remember the safety of thy people and thou shalt always deserve their praise."

After he had departed, my father turned to me and said:

"My son, that we are utterly within the power of the white man is a bitter lesson to learn. It cost me many tears. But we must burn it into the heart of every Indian youth, and thou as my successor must take this task up at my death. The safety of thy people depends on teaching this lesson well!"

* An actual occurrence among the Omaha Indians in Nebraska, during the summer of 1880.

CHAPTER IX.

MA-SHÁN! HOME!

LONG and sadly I pondered these weighty suggestions of my father. I began to see that the Indians, although loving freedom so dearly and taught it by every breath of prairie air they breathe, and inspired by it in every flower they see, are really the slaves of the white race. True, no chains are riveted about our wrists and ankles, no yokes are placed upon our shoulders, no spiked collars gall our necks, and no lashes are laid upon our backs; but better have these merely physical sufferings than the agonies which I now became conscious we had to bear. When a man is so helplessly in the grasp of another that he cannot resent the deliberate taking of his property—is not that slavery? When the very love we have for wife and child and brother is made the excuse for murders which, because of this very love, we dare not avenge and cannot resent without involving these dear and innocent persons in a common ruin—is not that slavery? When those who have authority in the white man's government can withhold the money that is rightfully ours, can sell to others the provisions designed for us, can cause the wail of women and little ones to ascend from a thousand campfires on the prairies, and when there is no recourse left us but silent submission—is not that slavery? When a man must know that his dear wife is shamefully outraged by a white man, that there is no law by which the transgressor can be punished, that the Indian if he oversteps the limits of a martyr's self-control and shoots the white man down is bringing death upon hundreds of innocent ones in his race—is not that slavery? And does not the fact that the holiest emotions of our nature are made the shackles by which we are bound give a peculiar agony to our slavery that no mere physical smarts or salty tears can express?

All these things I thought of constantly and seriously. For a time it seemed that a great darkness had come upon my life. Eagerly I sought an opportunity when the wise Standing Elk might instruct me further in these terrible truths, hoping that he might be able to show me a wav out of the night.

One afternoon I was resting on a couch of wolves' skins in a cool arbor of aspens built for me under a great tree. My mother and my little bride were working upon a pair of moccasins, shaping and beading them for my feet. They worked secretly, hoping to hide the moccasins from me, since they were intended as my wedding-present. But at moments when they were intent upon their toil I caught sly glimpses of what they were doing, and although I said nothing it seemed to me a beautiful and a touching thing for these two persons, who loved me most and whom I most loved, to join in shoeing me for many a trip across the divides in search of game, and for long marches against the Sioux. Ah, it is well they little knew upon what journey I should wear them! I thought of that simple legend of my people which relates that the she-bears rub their cheeks so steadily and lovingly along the claw-points of their mates that they sharpen them for the bloody encounter with the mountain lion among the rocks, or with the elk-buck along the water-courses. So love prepared me for providing for my loves.

While they were thus engaged in toil, and I in thought, our company was increased by the coming of the wise Standing Elk. I never until that moment noticed how

old and sorrow-worn he seemed. His long hair was turning white in many places, and though his form was perfectly elastic and erect, and his eyes were bright, there was
a deep look of sadness upon his face which showed plainly
that his soul was bent and its lights were dim. He seated
himself with the air of one who lives in other days, and
the rapid and steady winking of his eyelids showed that
he was buried in thought.

"My father," I said to him, "the eaglet was never half
so clamorously glad to see the return of its sire with a fish
in his claws as I am to see thee to-day. My soul hungers.
Tell us more of this sad and terrible law by which the
white man, grinding us down in slavery, compels us to
submission by threatening the lives of our wives and
children. Is there no counter-law of theirs to give us
escape? Is there no ray of light in this horrible midnight?"

"Nay, my father!" Prairie Flower exclaimed. "Wolf
Killer has already distressed his mind too much with
these terrible thoughts. His very wounds will soon begin
to bleed with them. Tell us rather some sweet story of
thy youth, some pleasing tale of thy love for my mother
when she was fair. Or if thy soul is too sad for that, tell
us, as thou hast promised to do, how my poor mother met
her death."

The bright bass springs from the waters of the lake,
gleams in the warm sunshine for an instant, every scale
and fin radiant with rounded rainbows, and then falls back
into the darkness again. Thus the wise man emerged for
a moment from his thoughts when his daughter spoke,
the light of a smile played upon his shriveled face, but
then he returned with a sigh to his meditation.

"Thy voice, my Flower!" he said, "would recall me
from the very gloom of death and thrill me with life's

delight. But I am sad to-day. I feel that my trail is almost completed. Before I die I must prepare you both for living. And, strangely, I can answer both your requests with one story. Listen, my daughter, while I tell thee how thy mother was slain. Listen, my son, for in these same words thou shalt find one sad illustration of the dreadful hold the whites have upon us, and how they punish the innocent for the crimes of the guilty."

Seating himself more comfortably upon a pile of furs, he gave himself a moment's thought as a preparation for the story. The sun, just setting, scattered with most prodigal hands its wealth of rays upon the spears of wild grass and the fluttering leaves of the shrubs. The sky was lit up with scarlet and amber and gold, and such clouds as there were sought to hide themselves in light for very shame to mar such loveliness. The prairies which stretched away to the south and the hills which broke away to the north answered each other in all the varied voices of the twilight music; while, nearer, the whistle of the quail was heard calling to his mate. Not one sound was heard suggestive of human strife and passion; but oh, what a story we were to hear of how all that is worst and most devilish in man seems directed against our helpless race!

" I was not born a member of this portion of our tribe which Eagle Wing commands," the wise man began. "Our band was part of one great family with yours, spoke the same language, and practiced the same customs. There were about five hundred of us, all told, and we lived far to the west of this village. The rugged mountains rose above our wigwams in great uneven peaks, their sides were storm-worn and their summits crowned with snow. As you love the bending trees, we loved the unyielding rocks. We were a hardier, though certainly not a nobler, people than you. Our sport was to track the great bear over slippery paths and up lofty mountains, or to fish in the raging torrents which thunder through the cañons and throw out a thousand little white spray-arms to push away the stone which obstructs their course. Our joy was to watch the creeping of heavy sun-shadows down the mountain-sides as the sun rose or set, and to see the radiance that the highest peaks caught first at morning and held longest at evening. And oh, what lessons we thus learned of holy souls who catch and forever retain the brightness of Wakanda's smile, shining out of eternity! Our music was the scratching of the bears' claws upon the pine bark, the roar of mountain streams, the thundering fall of stones, and the moan of winds over trackless snow.

"I must pause in my story to call up, from the dark shadows of memory, a picture of that sweetest of all places, Mashán—home. Images of it come brightly back to all men alike in the most solemn, happy, and saddened moments. Listen, while the image flashes before my old eyes to-night and becomes radiant in my tears.

"Our village stood in a little valley which had been beautifully hollowed out in the heart of a great rocky range. There were but two entrances to our retreat, one at each extremity of the valley. These gateways were formed in the rocks by the cutting of a mountain stream which flowed through the length of the valley. The sides of these granite gateways were as precipitous as even those stupendous rocks could be, so that we were compelled to build, above the level of the stream, trails just wide enough for two ponies to walk abreast. Over what narrow footways will the most dreadful disasters come!

"The mountains ranged themselves in uneven ranks parallel to the stream, and seemed to our simple imagination to have assumed that position that they might the

more easily guard us from the intrusion of man. And
that they widened out above, so as to show a great belt of
blue sky, we interpreted as meaning that they wished to
afford free access to the benefactions of Wakanda. With
the blending of these ideas in mind, we called the mountains after the most renowned warriors that had ever lived
in our race. There was one great peak to the extreme
west, by whose foot the stream flowed in, and whose rough
head, reaching up far beyond the timber-growth, was
streaked and seamed with flowing snow. This mountain
we called the 'Old Chief.' Next to him were smaller
mountains, clothed to their tops with a green growth of
aspens, and these we adorned with the names of the noble
men who, by their gentleness and strength of nature, had
been as dear to our hearts as they were terrible to our
enemies. Then, on the farther side of the stream, came
a great mountain, bald but not rocky, which seemed to
extend two wide arms of mercy to hold our village in, and
this was named 'Gentle Face,' after the father of my
father, who was chief of the wise men. Then came other
peaks in one sublime succession of snowy might, extending around our village to the 'Old Chief' again. Some
were crowned with rocky heads, some shook the cloud-
mists from beards of pine, and some laughed forever in
the sunshine. These were named for other lesser persons
who in the past had given their lives to protect our race.
Within this circle of strength there were smaller, gentler
hills, covered with picturesque patches of aspens or
dressed in flowing garments of rustling spruce; and these,
leaning against the breasts of the higher mountains, we
called the wives and children of the warriors who lifted
their pleased faces above.

"My father was the wise man of that band as I am of
this, and his sole aim was, as mine has been, to teach his

children how to observe their own natures and thus be led to happiness. My wife, thy mother, was a noble treasure, faithful and devoted to a degree that only genuine love can produce. I had three noble sons and two daughters beside thyself, my Prairie Flower. Thy years then numbered but two, and we held thee close to our breasts as the child of our old age.

"The white men had a settlement about twenty miles from our village, and we had frequent intercourse with them. Until the dreadful day of which I now must speak, not the slightest difficulty had ever arisen between the settlers and our people. There was, however, a young man among us of most passionate disposition, and who frequently declared that the white man who failed to regard his wishes should die. Long and frequently my father urged him to be considerate and forgiving; but Long Knife, such was his name, would not be wise. There were some among our people, as there are reckless men in every tribe, who encouraged Long Knife in his boastful threats, and promised him their assistance in case he found himself in difficulty. The number of these foolish and wicked men was, however, very small in proportion to the vast majority of us who wished to preserve all good faith with the whites.

"One day Long Knife was drinking heavily with a dissipated white man in their settlement. The Indian proposed that they should together take a day's sport upon the mountains; but the white man would not consent to the project. He pleaded the press of business duties; he said he was no great hunter; in short, he would not go. A long and heated dispute followed—a drunken brawl—in the height of which Long Knife sprang upon the white man, bore him to the earth, and stabbed him to the heart. The murderer, instantly realizing the terrible consequences upon himself and upon his tribe of what he had done, took refuge among the high rocks of mountains above our village.

"An account of the transaction, distorted into the most frightful falsehoods, was published in all the white man's papers. Wicked men, who lived near us and thirsted for our land, represented our whole band as utterly evil, and the wildest reports were spread abroad that we had gone to war. It was said that we had fallen on many settlers, had burned their houses, slaughtered their wives and children, and stolen their property. We had no means to deny these reports, and many of the white people may believe them true to this day.

"The day after the murder of the white man, an officer with a few soldiers rode into our village, and from a paper in his hand he read these words: 'The Great Father is much displeased because a member of this tribe has done so cruel a deed. He requires you to find Long Knife before fifteen suns have set. If you do not, war shall be made upon this village.' The officer and soldiers then rode haughtily away.

"Our village was instantly the scene of the wildest confusion, such as you see among the white ants when a pony stamps his foot into the center of their mound-home. The women moaned and wrung their hands, and the children wept, not knowing why, save that they saw their mothers distressed.

"A sorrowful procession was formed which wound round and round the beloved homes, and under the familiar trees, and past the sacred places where our fathers slept, and the people smote their breasts and cried:

" Ma-shán! Ma-shán!* We love our homes; they are

* "Home! home!"

to be taken away from us. We love our lives; we are
to lose them. Oh, Ma-shán! Ma-shán! Ma-shán!'

"A council of all the male members of the party was immediately held, a heap of pine-knots was started into a
flame, and oh, I trust Wakanda has forgiven us for the many
bitter words we spoke around that fire. The chief was
the first, of course, to express his opinion.

"'My children,' he said, 'this is a bitter hour. Never
has my heart been wrung with such unspeakable agony.
There could be nothing more unjust—nothing that more
directly smites Wakanda in the face—than this law of the
whites by which we are made chargeable for the crime of
Long Knife. I did not command it; you did not know
of it; we all lament it. But if the punishment rested
with the destruction of the men of our band, I could die
content. Behold, the white men demand the lives of our
wives and little ones—those who never handled a bow,
and those who know not their right hand from the left!
This is hard. This makes even a chief weep! Were we
not helpless in their grasp, we might laugh such unjust
pretensions to scorn. But they have the right to make
what laws they please to bind us—the right that the tyrant
may ever exercise over the slave. We must submit, my
children, we must submit. Let it only be bravely and
proudly done.'

"When he had ceased speaking, one of the young men
started up and said angrily:

"'Must the elk-buck kneel to the hounds because his
mate and their young will die too? My young wife, but
one month pressed to my breast, would gladly perish rather
than have her husband a craven!'

"'We have no right to bring ruin on others, even though
they are our own wives and children,' the chief gently said.

"'But if they consent—nay, clamor to die rather than see us kneel to the white man?'

"'We should not place them where they are forced to consent,' the chief replied.

"For a long space there was the silence of despair around that camp-fire. At last another young man arose and said:

"'Let us take our wives and little ones and flee into the cañons of the mountains, and there defy pursuit.'

"'Such an attempt would simply result in instant death; for the white men, as I am informed by a scout, have placed sentinels in every direction,' the chief replied.

"'Then we can but die!' one said. 'We can but die!' his neighbor said. And this awful sentence passed around the little group, each man repeating it as his turn came, until it came my father's turn. All eyes were then bent upon him; for he, being the wise man of the tribe, was accounted able to free us from even worse difficulties than that in which we were then involved. My father rose, and shaking loose his long flowing locks touched with gray, as mine now are, fixed his piercing eyes upon us, and said:

"'We but lose time by repeating this wail. Fifteen days are allotted to us to find Long Knife. Is it the part of brave men to talk loudly and do nothing when the lives of their wives and children are in danger? Organize your scouting-bands, explore the rocks, come upon his trail, and bring the murderer back. He that finds Long Knife shall be the savior of his people!'

"Instantly we sprang up, ashamed of our inaction. The sun had been hidden for three hours behind the crest of the mountain, and no time was to be lost. The others went in parties of two and thee, but I preferred to go alone. So, kissing my wife and holding my children for a moment to my heart in what I, too truly, feared would be my last embrace, I started up the mountain-side. And as I walked the night came on, but at every footstep under the stars I thought of my loved ones, and whispered to myself the words of my father: 'He that finds Long Knife shall be the savior of his people!'"

CHAPTER X.

A VAIN SACRIFICE.

WHEN he had reached this point in his story the wise
man paused for a moment, as if to arrange his thoughts
before continuing. . I was conscious that the eyes of
Prairie Flower were turned up to me, and looking down
I saw that they were full of tears, and her lips were trembling, and such a look of unutterable sadness was upon her
face as I had never before seen her bright features wear.
I drew her close to me, so that she should not fear.

By this time the night had come down, and great clouds
were wheeling toward us from the south-west, massing
themselves into gigantic shapes, lit up by sharp lightnings
which shot within them. The noise of the distant thunder
sounded like the stampede of great herds of buffalo over
pebbled plains. The main storm passed far to the west of
us, but we got the flanking showers. The freshened breeze
swept by us, hasting into the storm-cloud, and causing
the aspen arbor in which we sat to tremble and rock as if
shaken by the hand of a giant. The gloom of the tempest, increasing the natural darkness of night, fell upon us
and brought us into trembling sympathy with the sad terrors of the wise man's story.

" I must now, my children," he said, resuming his narrative, " divide what I have to tell you into two parts, in
order to give you the story complete. I shall first tell
you what befell the people of our tribe whom we left in
our village, and afterward relate the adventures I person-
ally met with upon the mountains.

"You can easily imagine the anxiety with which those who remained in the village awaited the results of our search. As day followed day and no word was brought in that the criminal had been secured, the fear and apprehension of the people increased until it was the frenzy of madness. One ceaseless wail resounded in our beautiful village. Many of the women started out in hope of finding Long Knife themselves, and thus to save their babes from the bayonet of the soldier. Every child who was old enough to find or follow a trail took part in the search, until the soldiers who were stationed as sentinels around our village raised the alarm that we were endeavoring to escape in small parties to the mountains, under pretense of looking for Long Knife. Then the women and children were called in, and, having nothing else to occupy their activities, they prepared arrows for the hopeless conflict in which they now foresaw we should be called upon to engage. By day they toiled, and at night they formed a sad procession and passed round and round the beautiful spot where we had lived so long, exclaiming:

"'Ma-shán! Ma-shán! Another day has passed, another sun has set. Oh, our homes will soon be vacant! Ma-shán! Ma-shán!'

"At last the evening of the fourteenth day came. Every scouting party, as it came in, was anxiously questioned as to its success, and from each the dreadful news was learned that no trace of the criminal had been found. Then the wails of the women and the crying of the children increased a hundred-fold, for it seemed certain then that all must die. I had not yet come in. I did not reach the village for three days. But, my children, do not think me a coward, do not imagine that I left my wife and children to die, if need be, alone, until I relate to you what befell me in the mountains. What took place at the village was told me many months afterwards by one who was an eye-witness of the scene.

"A council was immediately held around one of the blazing fires. The chief called upon each party to report what efforts they had made, and with what success, if any, they had met. One after another arose and told how they had traversed the rocks, and penetrated the dark, deep places, and explored the cañons, and tramped down the wild grass in every high spot where a man could hide. They told of the agony in their spirits, and how they had made rocks which never before had heard the human voice resound and echo wildly with their wails. They told of lying down to rest when their steps wavered upon the paths from utter fatigue, and how they started up almost instantly again and pursued the search, chiding themselves that they had lost a moment of the precious time. They told of strange hopes that this place or that might harbor the criminal; of promises the night-winds seemed to whisper to their frantic hearts; of gathering breathlessly around some crushed flower, fancying it to reveal the sought trail, only to find that it had been trodden down by the brown bear. Whenever they saw a vulture or eagle hovering over a spot, however high and inaccessible, they hastened to it, hoping to find at least the carrion of the criminal; or when the stream at the depth of the cañon murmured as if clogged by some dead weight, they anxiously descended to its bank, to see if the obstruction were his body. And when the last sun had arisen they had turned their despairing steps homeward, ashamed to show themselves among their brethren, but still vaguely hoping that some other party had been more fortunate than they. Only one man could say that he had seen any trail that might possibly have been that of Long

Knife. This he had followed wild with delight and hope, until it suddenly ceased upon a high and barren rock, and, although he examined every sand-grain that rested upon its surface, that rock would hold forever the secret of where the murderer had gone, and would commemorate the slaughter of a race.

"When the last man had spoken, the chief slowly arose and said:

"'My children, the Dta-wá-e* of our people must be sung. The wave of ruin which has rolled over a land once ours and swept so many of a simple-hearted race away has at last reached our beautiful homes. The wild dove had hoped to save one little nestling out of so large and noble a brood, but this, too, must be sacrificed. And by whom is this last sad murder to be done? By a nation ignorant of Wakanda's ways, or careless of the pain of a human heart, or professing simply to be unlearned and savage? Nay! It is done by a nation boastful of its justice, its regard for the feelings of all, its desire to civilize our people—a nation shone upon by a free sun, fanned to sleep by free winds, and roared at by free waves and rivers—a nation favored and honored and blessed by the very liberty it denies to us. Long Knife ought to have been punished; we would gladly have seen him repay Wakanda with his life for the life he has taken. But why should our wives and little ones suffer in his place? But it must be. I would not unnerve you, my children, for the trial. We must die; see that ye die bravely. I have spoken.'

. "All eyes were turned upon my father at the conclusion of the chief's address, for to him they looked for advice when all other wisdom failed. He arose, shook out his flowing hair, and, looking slowly around on all the anxious faces, simply said:

* Death-song.

" ' Wait, my children, until Standing Elk returns.'

" He then resumed his seat.

" ' Truly!' the chief exclaimed, 'the brave young Standing Elk has not yet returned. He is fleet of foot and quick of eye and strong of arm; he may be the saviour of his people by bringing in the criminal.'

" ' You shall not see him for many suns,' sneered a young man who hated to hear me praised.

" ' What!' my father exclaimed, springing up, 'dare you say that Standing Elk will desert us in our sore need? Think you he has your heart, to stay away until the threatened conflict has passed? I will answer with my life that he returns before our last sun rises over to-morrow's peaks. Or if he comes not, some disaster holds him.'

" ' Peace! my children,' the chief said. ' We will watch here beside the embers of our last council-fire until the morning dawns. If Standing Elk does not then return with Long Knife, we will prepare to die.'

" All that night, while the pitying stars looked divinely down, they sat around that dying fire, speaking not a word, wrapped in the sad meditation of despair. The solemn, familiar peaks rose above them, and to their excited fancies assumed shapes of majesty or affright, became giants with stern faces and rugged arms and cruel clubs, or changed into fair fingers pointing them up to Wakanda as man's last hope. Every sound of the night-wind they listened to eagerly, hoping it might be my footstep. Whenever the loosened stone fell down the mountain-side they thought 'He is dragging the criminal after him, and will soon be here.' The stars wheeled away, and strange ones came up from the east to take their places, just as the red men had been pushed aside by the march of the white men; the planets set one by one behind the pine-trees, and the waning moon hid its scanty light from their

hopeless gaze. Still Um-pan-nez-zhe did not come. On
the high peaks to the west of the valley a faint streak of
light at last appeared. It was instantly erased by the hand
of night, and a deeper darkness than any that had rested
upon them came upon peaks and valley alike. Soon,
however, the light returned brighter than before, and the
spread of coming day began to creep down the mountain-
side into the valley. The day-birds opened their throats
for their song, the crushing of the sage-brush was heard·
as the bear hastened back to his den, and the pines began
to wave glad welcomes in the air to the approaching sun.
It was their last allotted sun, but yet Standing Elk did
not come.

"Then my father arose and said:

"'My children, some accident detains the brave Standing
Elk.   He carries the scalp of Long Knife at his belt, and
if a day or two could be granted he would be the saviour
of his people. But something must now be done. My
children, my locks are touched with gray and I have seen
the sun rise on many mornings. Hundreds of my people
and some of my sons I have seen shot by the white men.
Wakanda has given them The Book,* by the teachings of
which they have been made strong. He has not given us
The Book, and therefore we are weak. But how the white
men can use in robbing and murdering our helpless people
the strength they have derived from a book which teaches,
as we have been told, charity and brotherly love, seems
strange to me. I cannot understand this. The wild beet
lifts up into the air tender and tempting leaves, but its
root is full of poison. The white man is alike treacherous.
Every coming year adds to the snake of these cañons a
new rattle, and places fresh venom in its fangs. Every

---

* The Bible, singularly spoken of as *The Book* by all the Indian races.

year has increased the white man's loud professions to be
our friend, and at the same time made him more thirst-
ingly our enemy. I wish to die by the hand of the red
men. They may not know the mysteries of the white
man's religion, but are not rendered alike insensible to
the pain of a broken heart or the claims that the weak
may ever urge against the strong. My children, my
advice to you is: It is better for one to perish than that
all should die. Shoot me and lay my body at the feet of
the captain. Perhaps he will accept me as the criminal,
and have mercy upon our wives and little ones. I die a
willing sacrifice. Let my pale lips, when they cannot
speak, persuade you that Standing Elk remains not
willingly away, and tell him when he comes that his
father died gladly to vindicate his bravery.'

"'I repent already!' tearfully exclaimed the young man
who had cast suspicion on my courage.

"'Come, then,' my father said, 'let us go out into the
everglade where the crack of the rifle shall not reach the
ears of my children and grandchildren; there I will die.
Come, I lead the way!'

"One by one the warriors sadly and reluctantly arose
from the ashes of the dead camp-fire and followed my
father, who, stopping a moment as he passed through our
village, kissed the little ones of his family, took thee, my
little Prairie Flower, into his arms for a moment and
blessed thee, and then walked rapidly away. He led the
silent and sorrowful procession to a retired spot, where
the mountain's side had been worn away by a succession
of great torrents, and stationing himself on a mossy
bowlder, asked them to shoot. No one, however, had
thought to bring a rifle, as they were all so horrified
by the terrible idea of sacrifice. A messenger was dispatched to the village for the weapon. In the moments

of delay my father never trembled for an instant. His tall form and patient face and streaming white hair made a sublime picture against the purple and gray and green of the rocks behind him. The mighty mountains threw down deep mourning shadows to hide the scene from the pitying eye of the sun, the very eagle screamed with horror and flew away, and the wild birds in the bushes were dumb with awe !

"'Chief,' my father, said, 'the rifle is at thy hand; aim it as I have seen thee aim at the brown bear. I die to vindicate the bravery of my son ! I die to save the remnant of my people ! Wakanda forgive the white man ! Wakanda bless my simple-hearted race ! Wakanda receive me to his home ! I have spoken.'

"Thrice the chief raised the rifle to his shoulder, and thrice lowered it again. His hand trembled, his eyes were full of tears.

"'O wise brother,' he said to my father, 'I shoot but for thy sake and for that of my poor people.'

" He aimed the rifle once again and pulled the trigger. My father's brave heart was pierced. His gray hair streamed among the moss upon the boulder.

CHAPTER XI.

AN EMPTY SUCCESS.

"MEANWHILE, my children, what kept the brave Um-pan-nez-zhe upon the mountains? Why did he not return as the saviour of his people, dragging Long Knife behind him?

"I had not the slightest idea where I should be most likely to find the criminal. But I knew that in the horror of his remorse he would seek the very wildest peaks, and frequent the deep caverns which yawn in their sides, where the scorched pine, blasted by the lightning's stroke, lifted itself into the night akin to itself for blackness, and suggested to his mind a grim image of his own ruined life. I knew he would crouch under overhanging bowlders, and hide behind dark young pines; and would spring up at the slightest noise, glare fiercely for a moment, and then wildly, around; and then start like the hounded deer away and away through the darkness. I knew that if I could find his trail I might track him by the bloody prints he would leave of feet cruelly torn by the sharp rocks, by the scraps of deer-skin that the brambles in his flight would tear from his garments, by the very bending of the flowers and wild grasses away from his path on both sides, as if they had shrunk down in terror and hate when he had passed wildly by. Yet I knew that he would not go too far away, that a strange fascination would attract him, at still moments, to creep near the scene of his crime; that in the darkness or in fits of fevered sleep he would see the shining of the murdered man's face, and those pallid

lips would call him so sternly that he could not refuse,
and that silent finger would beckon him so commandingly
that he must obey. I knew that thus he would continu-
ally hover near, and yet not too near, the white man's settlement, now approaching it stealthily in the dead of night,
and now running wildly away again ; now coming so near
that from his rocky hiding-place he could see the smoke
of their fires resting on the distant hillsides, and now
dashing fiercely miles and miles and miles into the silent
hills; now groaning madly, rolling on the ground, that
he had done the deed, and now springing up with clenched
fists and blazing eyes, thirsting to do the murder over
again and ten thousand others like it. I knew that even
the cañon-stream could not alternate so quickly between
insane dashing and idiot quietness as he, and if I should
come upon him in his quieter moods I might take him
alive, but if when he was fierce with madness and remorse
I must kill him. And, as I searched, these and many
other thoughts went through my excited mind.

"But how could I kill him ? Never had my hand slain
human being, and what would make this deed the harder
was that I had known Long Knife well. Had he not been
a member of our own tribe ? Had we not slept by the same
streams, and eaten by the same camp-fires, and hunted
on the same rocks ? Had we not obeyed the commands
of the same chief, and when we both were children had
we not sat together at my father's feet and heard his
words of wisdom ? Yet when I pictured to myself what
he had done, and how his deed had hung a spear over our
whole tribe, and how my very wife and sweet children
were concerned in the doom, I felt that I could do the
deed. The more I thought of this as I struggled on over
the rocks, the more I was sure I could kill him. Was he
not virtually the murderer not simply of the white man

but of our tribe and my dear ones as well? Yet at other
moments I pitied him. At the back of all the difficulty I
knew the white man stood, with his sham professions of
law and his smiling hypocrisy and his cruel deceits. Long
Knife was only the instrumental cause of the doom that
rested on our people. Still, he had known how unjustly
the white man holds the tribe responsible for the crime
of any of its members, and knowing it had not hesitated
to commit the deed and bring down upon us the doom.
However unjust, and shamefully so, the white man might
be, Long Knife was the immediate, the nearest cause of
the difficulty, and as I brooded more and more over it I
began to hate him. Yes, I hated him. And in my hate
the pride of my race blended, and the love of my wife and
the joy of having sons, and all these made me hate him
the more. I transferred all the traditional scorn I had of
the white man to him, who was at least the instrument by
whom the stronger race could inflict all its cruel injustice
upon us. I hated the white man in him. I hated him
more in the morning than I had done in the evening, and
more in the evening than in the morning. The flowers
which bloom in such prodigal splendor and multitude
upon the high mountains stared amazed at me as I passed
exclaiming, 'I hate him! I hate him! I hate him!'
But I crushed the flowers down, so they should not shame
me out of my hatred by their large and beautiful eyes, and
I hated him all the more because he had caused me to
make such destruction of lovely things.

"Meanwhile I never for a moment relaxed my agony to
find his trail. The wondrous beauty of the scenery around
me claimed not a single look. The morning dawned, and
was amazed to see that a red man could be out on the
mountains and not be lost in rapture at the splendor of
its coming. The evening went to sleep, and with its last

peeps of light it wondered that I should turn my back
upon it and not admire its radiance by word or look. But
I had eyes for the grass, the sage-brush, and the flowers,
only to see, if I might, where Long Knife had gone, where
he had rested, where crouched for a moment, and in what
direction hurried away. The days were coming and going,
the nights were hurrying, the fate of my people was being
decided, and I must not rest. My brain was on fire with
hope, and yet I was filled with a constant dread that I
should not succeed after all. Some strange thing told
me that if any one should save my people it must be I. I
knew, as if by a revelation from Wakanda, that the scout-
ing-parties would not find Long Knife, that I must never
rest, never stop for sleep, never delay even for eating, if I
hoped to avert the horrible doom. Such wild roots as I
could catch up while I walked I ate hurriedly, and I bent
at every spring and rill that I came upon and tried to
quench my agony of thirst. But still my fever burned
more wildly than before, and still I hastened hither and
thither, wherever a man could hide, saying madly to myself, ' I must find him! I must have his blood!'

"So the days passed. Sometimes I feared that in the
greatness of my agony I would not number them aright;
but I found that my very anxiety and distress, being so
frantic, prevented me forgetting even for the slightest
moment what day it was. My memory of little things
was so vivid that I could recall every circumstance that
had attended my first, second, third, or any day that I
had been upon the search; and so by arranging the
transactions of the several days before my mind I could
confirm my count. Thus the tenth sun rose as brightly
as the others had done, and the eleventh, and they set
again,—without leading me to the criminal's hiding-place.

"Just before the setting of the twelfth sun, the sky.

which had been remarkably clear and beautiful, became
suddenly overcast with great clouds. They came sweeping up from the valleys just beyond the range on which I
stood, and, parting now and then to circle a high peak,
they would come together again nearer me and career on
wilder than before. I watched the coming storm changing its hues from gray to brown, from brown to scarlet,
and from scarlet to black, and I thought what a mighty
and portentous type it revealed of the doom that was
sweeping upon my race. I tried to think that Wakanda
guided our dark destinies as surely and easily as he did
those apparently lawless masses of heavy vapor, but in
the maddened state of my mind the thought either would
not possess me or gave me no courage. I tried to look
up into the heavens as the bright flowers around me did,
as brave as they, and as trustful that out of all this
tumult and night the refreshment would come and the
morrow dawn again; but I could not. Soon the thunder
became more fearful, the lightning darted hither and
thither among the rocks, and the great, heavy drops of
the coming rain began to fall among the pine-cones. The
breeze freshened moment by moment; the loosened stones
fell with a thundering crash into the valley, three thousand feet below; the roar of the storm, hastening up to
its full fury, smote me as with heavy blows; and the
swollen stream, near at hand, raged and hissed so as to
be heard above all the tumult. You cannot imagine, my
children, how fierce the lightning is in a mountain storm,
and how full of it the air becomes. It seemed to me that
day that the whole mountain was one mass of forked
flame: the rocks were glowing with it, the pines were
wreathed with it; the aspens, girded with it, forgot to
tremble. I knew it was certain death to remain where I
was, and although I valued my life little in itself, yet,

because of the deed I felt I must accomplish, I esteemed it dear, and so sought refuge under a large boulder which seemed firmly attached to the mountain-side. From this safe retreat I looked out with wild admiration upon the storm, and, feeling it terribly in sympathy with my passions and moods at the moment, knew something of my old enjoyment of the wild elements.

"There I sat until it must have been midnight. Suddenly a flash of lightning, brighter than those that were constantly shining, lit up the dark entrance of a cavern just on the other side of a little ravine before me, and I saw what seemed a human face. I started wildly to my feet, awaiting the next bright flash. It came—yes! O Wakanda!—it was he—Long Knife! I could see him crouching away from the storm, shivering whenever it thundered, and holding his eyes against the lightning. Awfully haggard and careworn he looked, and for a moment I pitied him. But only for a moment. After that I hated him far more than ever. He had not seen me, and I hoped that by coming suddenly upon him, when he was so terrified by the storm, I might take him prisoner and deliver him to the white men, leaving them to take his life.

"Full of this purpose and wild with hope, I came out of my retreat and began eagerly to skirt the ravine so as to reach him. The storm was wild enough still to conceal the noise of my footsteps, yet I stepped with great caution and cursed every twig that snapped under my feet. I no longer thought of any danger from the lightning, and although it buried its forked burning tongues into the soil beside me once and again, I did not even shudder. My whole soul was filled with one desire, and I had thought for nothing else. I had much more difficulty in getting around the ravine than I had anticipated; but at last, after the greatest struggling over slippery rocks and through muddy thickets, I approached the spot where he lay. The bank overhung him so that he was not visible to me, or I to him, and therefore I determined to creep to the edge of the bank, stare down into his frightened face and demand his surrender. I crept noiselessly forward. I held my breath. Every muscle and nerve of my body was drawn into one agony, and I felt that if I did not soon clutch the criminal my whole being, with one snap, would die. I reached the edge of the bank, peered cautiously over, and there he lay within three feet of me.

"My lips were just parting to speak, when, taking down his hands from his eyes, he turned his haggard face up and saw me. Oh the wild look in those staring eyes! Oh the deep agony upon those purple lips! With one cry of terror, such as the wild beast at bay might make, he sprang twenty feet sheer down the side of the ravine, and before I recovered myself he was out of sight in the storm. I had not the despair to make me take the leap after him, and by the time I had gained the spot where he had alighted he was nowhere to be seen. It was impossible to follow his trail in such a night, although I could scarce bring myself to believe it; but feeling sure that I could overtake him now that his trail was found, I returned and took shelter in the very cavern that he had crouched in.

"How slowly the hours passed, and how I filled them with moans and cries, you can easily imagine. At the first glimmer of early light I was standing on the spot where the deep indentations in the soil and gravel showed he had struck the earth after his leap. Then began the terrible chase. There was something certain before me, and the thought gave me almost the bear's strength and the deer's endurance. I knew that I was far swifter of foot than he, and his start could not be very great, as he must have been delayed by the storm of the night. How I could picture him rushing with frightened face through the storm, turning to see if I were at hand, trembling at every sound, falling prostrate in his too great haste, and springing up again with wilder energy than before!

" He took a course toward the upper rocks, hoping perhaps that I would lose the trail when the grass and underbrush ceased. But I believe my intense passion would have helped me to read his footprints on solid and smooth rock. I followed him as the she-wolf follows her victim. All that day and all the succeeding night, which was bright and starlit, I followed him. Sometimes the trail would be indistinct and I would lose many precious moments ; at other places I could fancy the point he wished to reach, and by a shorter path I could regain what I had lost. Once I saw him, pushing his way up and still up, panting for breath in the thin air and casting frightened looks behind ; but a huge rock hid him from my sight again.

" On the morning of the fourteenth day I saw that the path he had chosen would lead him to a wide table-rock at the very summit of one of the highest peaks of all the Rockies. From this rock there was only one way of ascent or descent, and that was the very ridge we were then advancing upon. I knew that in a few half-hours Long Knife would be brought to bay, and then the dread and deadly conflict between us would begin. Inspired with a new courage, I pressed still more vigorously forward, and passing round the corner of a great boulder I saw him. Yes, I saw him! He had gained the table-rock, and now knew that his escape was impossible. Oh, never shall I forget the spectacle he made, wild with remorse and fear, standing alone on that mighty peak, while beyond him nothing could be seen but the deep blue of heaven! When he saw me he wrung his hands in the most dreadful manner, and began to heap curses upon my head. I was rejoiced to see that he was not armed, and thus I regarded him as my prisoner already. After the first shudderings of fear had passed over him he awaited me, perfectly calm, and I could see by his clinched teeth and resolute air that some stern purpose was in his mind. When I came so near to him that my voice could be heard I cried:

"'Surrender to me, Long Knife, and I shall do thee no harm!'

"'No harm!' he said, glaring down upon me, 'who can do harm to a man hunted by conscience? But take this, thou boaster, for thy pains!'

"With these words he suddenly bent to the earth, caught up a huge stone that lay at his feet, and hurled it down the narrow path toward me. He flung it with so true an aim that, though I sought to avoid it by springing aside with all my agility, it struck me upon the ankle, mashing the bone. I felt at the time but slight pain from the hurt, but oh! through my whole life there has been a bitter aching of soul because of it.

"'Ha! ha!' Long Knife exclaimed, 'how feels the brave Um-pan-nez-zhe now?'

"'Strong enough,' I cried, 'to take thy scalp!'

"'That thou shalt never do,' he replied. 'I shall die at no man's hand. I perish upon Wakanda's rocks. Alas! that my life should be so soon blighted! Alas! for the youth of the noble Long Knife! Alas! that his eyes shall never more rejoice at the coming of the morning or gaze at the setting of the sun! But I will die bravely! I hate the white men, and I curse the red. Enemy of all, I shall crave pardon of none. I die thus freely, and I conquer as I die!'

"With these fearful words, chanted in a mournful strain, he cast himself headlong from the rock where he stood into the awful abyss below. I saw him shoot like an arrow through the air, and as he 'fell only one wild scream escaped his lips. Several awful seconds were consumed in his fall, but at last I saw him strike the cruel rocks, four thousand feet below, where he lay motionless and lifeless. Alas, poor Long Knife, how terrible was thy fate! Thy bitterest enemy, who tracked thee as if thirsting for thy blood to the last hiding-place thou couldst find, bows pitying before thee!

"It was only when I began to descend to him that I realized how seriously my ankle was injured. At first I could walk without any great difficulty, but the pain increased with every step and soon became unbearable. I sat down beside a little stream that raged across my path, and stripping off the inner bark from several aspens that grew near, I bound up my aching limb in them, after having soaked them in water. Then I was able to proceed My anxiety to have his scalp gave me strength; and at last I had descended to the spot where he lay, a tangled mass of human flesh. Oh! how I pitied him! If he had allowed himself to be guided by my father's principles of wisdom, and borne anything rather than kill a white man, he might have been among our best warriors. But here he lay, hated alike by the white men and the red, because passion instead of wisdom had controlled him. But I knew I must not delay, and hastily tearing from him his bloody scalp, the only one I ever took, I left him to the eagles who, having scented a feast from afar, were already circling in the air above him.

"It was now noon of the fourteenth day. I knew not how far I had wandered from our village, and only that sun shining above me, and another, were allowed me for the return. But holding aloft the bloody prize which I believed would save my wife and little ones from death, I started. The pain in my ankle made my progress very slow, and I was frequently compelled to stop and bathe it in the streams I crossed. The agony I endured upon this journey only Wakanda knows. The physical pain I suffered was as nothing compared with the deep distress that fed upon my mind as the wolf-cubs feed upon the deer's heart. What if I should be too late after all? I thought. How far could it be to our village? Would my crushed ankle allow me to make the trip in time to save my people? These and a thousand other thoughts and misgivings passed through my mind. The weary hours of that afternoon passed while I dragged myself along, and the dark moments of the succeeding night became things of yesterday. Still I plodded patiently and painfully homeward. The last sun arose, and still there was not one in all the wilderness of hills that rose around me that I could recognize. The terrible conclusion flashed upon my mind that I must have gone many, many miles in my eager pursuit of the criminal, without noting the distance; and only by the most agonizing efforts could I hope to reach our village in time to avert the slaughter.

"Oh, how I prayed for strength! Oh, how I cursed the stone that had crippled me and prevented me being the savior of my people! Now I would cast myself upon the ground in hopeless despair, thinking that all my efforts were useless. Then I would start wildly up, chiding myself for the precious moments lost through such cowardice, and thinking that the least I could possibly do was to spend the very last minute in earnest, although it might be useless, endeavor to reach our village. In the moments of my deepest distress I would throw the scalp of Long Knife upon the ground and stamp upon it in fury. Then

I would catch it up and hurry away. Oh, how I envied the eagles their wings, and the antelopes their speed, and thought, itself, its power instantly to fly to the point it desires to reach!

"Thus passed the last day allowed to us. I wept long and bitterly when I saw the fifteenth sun sink behind the foot-hills. Its dying moments were just as I had often seen them, the beauty of the crimson clouds was the same; but never, as it seemed to me, had so much depended on a sunset—never had it sealed so many dooms. I thought of my faithful wife and my beautiful children. Perhaps they would blame me for remaining away, thinking that I had deserted them to their fate. This thought almost maddened me. But, on the contrary, I dared at moments to hope that some kind plan of Wakanda would delay the slaughter and I might still arrive in time to save my people. Encouraged by this thought, I would advance more rapidly than before, although much of the way I was compelled to hop upon one foot, and the pain in my swollen ankle almost made me wild. Thus the nights and days passed—hopelessly, painfully passed. The sixteenth sun was no more, the seventeenth followed it, the eighteenth and nineteenth were things of the past—and on the evening of the twentieth day after the decree of the white man had been read in our camp, I stood in the gateway to the valley in which our village was built. Just before me was a large rock projecting out into the valley, and I knew that when I had passed that all the humble homes of my people would be in full sight. But I feared so much that the slaughter had been made that I dared not pass that rock. I stopped and listened. No happy laugh of child, no shout of youth, no voice of man, met my ear. All was silent, save that I heard the flap of some bird's wing as it hovered near the ground.

"'O Wakanda!' I cried, 'has the dreadful doom come upon my wife and babes?'

"Frantic with fear, I burst round the rock, and what a sight met my gaze! All our beautiful homes were burned to the ground. The bodies of my people were scattered upon the bloody sward. As I advanced I frightened off a flock of crows and vultures who were fattening on cheeks I had kissed and hands I had held in mine. I went, trembling like an aspen-leaf, among the terrible collection, recognizing here the chief and there a brother and there a friend. In their hands they still grasped their weapons, and on their pale lips was the scowl of battle. The blood was scarcely dry in their terrible wounds, their useless weapons had not begun to rust, and I knew that the day before must have been that on which the fatal conflict had occurred. Oh! to think I had been only so few hours too late to prevent the taking of so many precious lives, which all my tears and my most passionate cries could not now recall from the silence and coldness whither they had gone!

"'At least,' I said, mournfully musing, 'my noble people died bravely defending themselves and their little ones against the whites.'

"Nowhere could I find the body of my noble father; the cause of his absence you know, my children. And for a long time I could not find thy mother, my Prairie Flower, though my brave sons were lying dead where they had fought and fallen beside their chief. At last in a little copse which grew near the spot where my once happy home had stood I saw thy mother lying. Her breast had been pierced by a bullet, and her folded hands showed she had died pleading for her life. Beside her dead body I threw down the scalp of Long Knife, stamped and spit upon it in rage, and exclaimed:

"'Was it for this, O Wakanda! I traversed the mountains—for this I scalped the Long Knife? Was it for this I have suffered agonies that man never felt before? O Wakanda! O my noble wife! O my brave sons! Ma-shán! Ma-shán!'

"I fell helpless to the earth, and had almost sunk into insensibility when I was startled to hear the feeble cry of an infant. Wondering much whence it could come, I started up and hastened toward it. From a box which lay not far from thy mother's side the wail had risen, and turning the rude hiding-place over I drew thee forth, my Prairie Flower, wrapped in a bright scarf that I had given thy mother on our wedding-day. Thou didst smile at once and weep, to see my face, and hugging thee to my heart, I looked up to heaven and said:

"'O Wakanda! I thank thee! I can still live and still forgive!'"

CHAPTER XII.

BLINDFOLDED JUSTICE.

WHEN Standing Elk had concluded this part of his story he paused because of very emotion. His eyes were blinded with tears, and the deep wrinkles on his cheek ran full of them. The tears of an Indian warrior, and of an Indian wise man, must be called forth by some great sorrow indeed—they are the very weightiest that fall. Little Prairie Flower, seeing her father weep, stole to his side, since there she believed her true place and office to be, laid her head upon his shoulder, and wiped away his tears with her long shining hair.

While the wise man's story was being told, one after another of our people had gathered round my aspen arbor to hear it, so that now a large number were crouching on the ground on every side, thrilled with his tale and sympathizing with his woe.

O mighty Secretaries of the Interior! O noble Commissioners of Indian Affairs! O learned Senators and Debaters! O people who boast of your equal laws! O fathers who are proud of sons, and mothers who love babes! O young men and women who weep over imaginary tales of woe—would you not have pitied us had you seen us sadly crouching there, the poor remnant of a once proud and powerful race, bemoaning much the ruin that had fallen on our people in the past, but bemoaning more the sad prospect that our time to bear the white man's unpitying blow might soon come? Ours was a real fear, ours was a real despair. The uncertain light of the night was just beginning to break through the clouds which were scattering after the storm, and the weird shadows, chasing each other across the prairies, passed over our spirits as well. And the dread uncertainty in our hearts was far greater than any gray darkness of a stormy night could ever be; for when such strong enemies were against us, and when they had such an awful hold upon us as the threat against our wives and children furnished them with, how could we hope long to enjoy the freedom so dear to us, and live in the homes we ourselves had built? We felt that, as there was no law to which we could appeal, as we had no friend stronger than the white man, all we could do was to turn our petitions to Wakanda, whose ears are never closed to the wail of distress, no matter what the color of the lips whence it comes.

But the story of the wise man was not completed, and therefore I said to him:

"Noble father, did not the white man accept thy father as a martyr substitute?"

At this question the sorrow of Standing Elk broke forth afresh, and I heard the soothing voice of my little Prairie Flower whispering to him:

"Dear father, do not grieve that you failed to save my mother. No one who knows the pain that delayed thy return could possibly blame thee or fail to admire thy wonderful strength and courage in struggling forward at all. Wakanda I know forgives thee, and my mother, if she knows all, as thou hast taught me she does, forgives thee also and loves thee but the more."

"I weep not, my child," he said, "for what I have told you, but for what I have still to tell."

At these words a moan passed round the group that listened. Could he have more dreadful things to recount?

Had he not reached the depth of the white man's perfidy?
What sadder thing could he relate than the dreadful story
he had already told?

When he could command his voice sufficiently to
resume his narrative the wise man said:

"To me the saddest part of the story is the scorn that
my father's poor remains met with from the white men.
I have told you how gladly he laid down his life to vindicate my bravery and save his people.   They lifted up his
body from the rocks where it had fallen, the green moss
clinging to his gray hair as they carried him, and while
yet his body was warm they laid him at the feet of the
commander.

"'Here is thy satisfaction!' they said.

"The commander was friendly to the red men, as so
many of the white man's officers and soldiers have been,
and wished to save us.   Therefore he said:

"'It is well, my friends.   You have done nobly, and the
Great Father will certainly not forget you.'

"But standing near, there was one of those wicked
white men whom no words of hatred and cursing can
forcibly describe aright—a man who coveted our land,
and for years after the fatal slaughter I am to describe
lived on the very spot where our village had stood; a man
who boasted of his scorn of all decency and law, and who
had openly desired for many months to ruin our people.
This man, rising with great show of justice, said to the
commander:

"'This is not the criminal, sir!   This is not Long Knife,
as you very well know.   If you have regard for the opinion
the Great Father has of you, you must carry out his orders
and make war upon this tribe.'

"'How is this?' the commander said to those who had
brought my father's body to him.

"They then related to him the whole story. They told him how anxiously they had searched; how they had held a council in deep despair; how the brave Standing Elk was still upon the hills and might any moment return with the criminal, for, they said, he never comes empty-handed home; and how they had watched for me the whole night through. They told him, with tears, how my father had offered to die to vindicate my honor and save his people, and how with sad hearts they had done the wise man's wishes.

"'This is truly a pathetic story,' the commander said. 'I must send word to the Great Father and get his orders in the matter.'

"'Will you tell him the whole story?' they asked. 'How we hunted long and painfully for Long Knife, how Standing Elk is still away, and how his noble father died?'

"'Yes, I will tell it all,' he answered.

"He sent the story over the white man's talking wires, and after two days an answer came which, with a few short words, sealed the death-doom of nearly all our tribe. The words of the Great Father were grand and boastful, but they were words of murder. I do not know how the message was expressed, but the meaning of it was, 'Make war upon them. The dignity of the white man must be preserved.' Oh! would it not seem a grander and more enduring dignity to have had charity for a helpless race, and to have refrained from the unprovoked murder of helpless babes and women? Have the white men no thought of the consequences of the crimes they commit against us, which sooner or later will overtake them though they are the most powerful race upon the earth? And perhaps these consequences will be all the more deadly and ruinous because the heads upon which they fall are proud and lifted high.

"You have beheld out upon the prairie, the slow but steady rise of white vapor curling to the skies, and although each little mist thus formed seemed slight and powerless, the aggregate of all when joined in the black, dense cloud could sweep whole villages away, and pour streams of heavy rain upon the land, amid thunderings which will not cease, and terrific blinding bolts of lightning which strike the highest objects first to the ground. Have the white men no ears to hear and no hearts to dread the many moans and cries and prayers that, vapor-like, are rising to heaven, to pour a dark and mighty vengeance on their heads when the cup of Wakanda's forbearance shall be full and overflow?

"The first notice of the Great Father's answer was conveyed to my poor people by the hasty riding of one of their scouts into the village, crying:

"'The soldiers are upon us! The soldiers are upon us!'

"This was, as I had conjectured, on the nineteenth day after the decree had been read to us, and the day before the sad one when I returned to our village. During all this time the people had anxiously watched the rocks above them, and the upper parts of the valley in which they lived, hoping that Standing Elk would come with the scalp of the criminal.

"When, however, the scout rode in shouting these fearful words, all hope of life deserted them. The moans and wails that had resounded through the camp instantly ceased, and in a silence more terrible than the greatest tumult could have been they prepared to die. Hastily catching up their weapons, the warriors took positions of safety behind boulders and trees, while the women and children with the greatest bravery remained at their sides. My noble sons attended the chief and fought with him during the conflict.

"The soldiers, numbering twice as many as our warriors, marched up with their banners flying and their drums sounding, as if they were performing some great act of bravery, and when within two lariats' distance they poured in a merciless volley upon our people. Thus the unequal contest began. Our warriors defended themselves bravely, until every bullet had been shot and every arrow used; then, having kissed their wives and hugged their little ones to their breasts a moment, they started up and cried:

"'Ma-shán! Ma-shán! Alas! for the freedom of our race. Alas! for the glory of the red man. We die! we die! Unjustly and shamefully we die! Ma-shán! Ma-shán!'

"Making this cry for home and liberty, they rushed toward the white men that they might die the more speedily. There was a volley. And when the smoke cleared away, scarce a score of all my noble people were left alive. These were allowed to escape. But the glorious sun, going to rest that lovely evening, looked down upon a scene of bloody horrors which has never been surpassed in all the dreadful history of tyranny. And this is simply one out of many wholesale massacres which stare the white men in the face. The papers in all the Great Father's cities, I was told, gave a most false and bitter account of this conflict, representing our poor people as refusing to yield up the criminal, charging us with an attempt, at the beginning of the battle, to creep upon the soldiers to slaughter them, and praising the commander for his great bravery. We had no means to deny these statements, and thus the honest-hearted among the white people were deceived, and the base schemers who had caused the murder were shielded and admired in their treachery to secure our lands.

"When I had found thee, my Prairie Flower, in the hiding-place where thy poor mother, with her last failing love and strength, had placed thee, I fled with thee from that fatal spot as swiftly as my injured ankle could bear me, and hastened to join myself to Eagle Wing's band, whither also the few other survivors had naturally gone. I pray Wakanda that the lust and avarice of the white men may never attack us here, and that living peaceably and wisely until our end shall come, we may then rest undisturbed among our fathers upon yonder hill. So, Prairie Flower, thou hast the story of thy mother's death, and thou, Wolf Killer, hast in the same sad recital an illustration of the dreadful slavery we are in to the white man, and of the galling thongs he binds us with, by holding the innocent among our people responsible for the guilt of the criminal."

The night was far advanced when the wise man spoke these concluding words, but so thrilled were we by his story that not one among all the listeners showed any tedium or desire to go to their rest. The tops of the mighty pines and cottonwoods, under which our homes were built, began to rustle and murmur their midnight music, and the roar of the river, never ceasing in light or darkness, seemed doubly distinct now that the myriad noises of day were hushed. My mind was throbbing with feverish excitement, and though my heart ran alternate currents of submissive fear and revengeful hatred, as I thought how real and bitter the slavery was that ground us down, still I hoped that somewhere in this awful night there was a glimmer of hope for the red men, and therefore I said to the wise Standing Elk :

"My father, surely this case you relate is an extreme one. No one touched by the least feeling of human sympathy, which all hearts must possess, and even the Great Father's too, could possibly order a repetition of such a barbarous outrage. And in the instance you mention, he

must have been deceived by the falsehoods you have re-
ferred to. Tell us, my father, your sad story is a bitter
exception, is it not, to the general treatment the red men
receive from the white?"

"My son," the wise man gravely replied, "the holding
of the innocent among us responsible for the crimes of
the guilty is a definite policy, adopted deliberately by the
white man's government, defended by his statesmen,
clamored for by the multitudes, demanded loudly and
fiercely by his public journals, and repeated as many times
as there have been years since first he made profession
of loving liberty himself and giving it to all. I cast my
thought over the names of all the proud tribes which
once possessed this wide land : where are they this silent
night ? Silent as it ! Not one single tribe among the
whole multitude but has been butchered and destroyed,
either wholly or in part, by the carrying out of this terrible law ! Yonder river flows not more constantly within
its banks than has this stream of unjust and unmerciful
slaughter poured through the homes of our race !"

"But," I asked, "might not the white man find some
excuse for this cruel dealing with us from the fact that it
would be exceedingly hard to find an Indian who has committed a crime, unless the tribe were held responsible?"

"The white men make the most of this plea. But, my
son, it does not make right the cruel wrong. In my
younger years I made a visit to the city where the Great
Father lives. One night while we were there, a murder
was committed in one of the low streets. The next morning I walked out and saw many great houses where the
rich and learned people lived, and I thought to myself:
How would these proud men and women feel if some great
king, much more powerful than they, should send a vast
army and demand that this murderer be delivered to him

in fifteen days, or he would kill them all and burn their beautiful homes to the ground? They would answer the king: 'We did not do the murder, we are not guilty, and you must not kill us.' But the king would answer: 'The murderer has not been found. In this great city with its many streets and alleys he is very likely to escape, and this excuses me for dragging your wives and little ones from your comfortable homes and putting them to a shameful death.' They would answer the king: 'Before our laws, and before your own, every man stands alone. If the murderer can be found he ought certainly to be punished, but that he cannot be found gives you no right to kill the innocent.' And the king would say: 'I care not what your laws hold, and as for my own I can regulate them to suit myself. I am far stronger than you, and thus I can and will have the blood of your warriors, nay, also of your wives and children.'

"These thoughts, bitter indeed, but it seems to me just, passed through my mind as I walked that beautiful morning before those splendid mansions, some of them far higher than these tallest cottonwoods, and the conclusion I reached was this: It makes all the difference in the world whether arguments are directed against ourselves or against those whom from childhood we have hated and despised. In dripping places, near our rocky springs, there grows a plant whose pounded root drops into one cup health and stimulus, and into another poison and death. Thus a policy which is outrage and ruin to us seems to the white man necessary and right. But if they were to change the cup at their lip for ours, how bitter and poisonous the draught would seem!"

With these sad words the wise man became silent. A subdued moan passed round the little group of listeners. For some of them knew by experience, and all could guess,

how terrible and fatal this law is to our race. For many
minutes they all sat mute and despairing upon the ground,
and then, one by one, they silently arose and went to their
homes. I held Prairie Flower to my side, fearing that
some power might be near to snatch her away forever.
Oh! if I could but write down upon this page the horror
and despair and the many intangible emotions of bitterness and dread that throbbed within my heart as I felt my
bride's soft touch upon my hand and warm breath upon my
cheek, and thought how some white man might, before
my eyes, insult or maltreat her, and that I could appeal to no
law for protection,—could not even strike the foul villain
to the earth without bringing disgrace and ruin upon my
whole tribe, I am sure real sympathy would come into
your hearts for us, and in your eyes tears of real sorrow for
our woes! How can it be, I thought, the mere shade of
one's skin brings upon him such deep and irremediable
woe! My thoughts were again interrupted by the voice
of the wise man :

"My children, I have told you my story. You behold
me, a bowed and broken man of many years and many
sorrows. In Wakanda's Home, but only there I fear, will
the white man learn that the despised Indian is his brother,
and might, had he been blessed and encouraged by just
laws, have become the helper and equal of the more
favored race. There I shall soon be. You remember the
scorched and blackened elm-tree that stands alone upon
yonder hill. It has proudly suffered many lightning-
strokes and waved through many prairie-fires, but now
every branch is gone, the mere stump remains; yet at
morning and evening the glory of coming or departing
day rests in a glory of beauty upon its head. It has by
patience conquered. Only thus can any man triumph
over his destiny. At the foot of the scorched stump there

grows one little elm-sprout, slender and beautiful as a ray of light, and in that sprout the old tree shall live again. I am that blackened elm-trunk, standing upon the hill—"

" And I," little Prairie Flower exclaimed joyously, "am the twig? Nay, my father, I am a strong tree, to hold thee and comfort thee in thine age!"

" Bless thee, my dear. Thy mother and I shall live again in thee. And it may be that the elm-sprout I have spoken of may be saved from the fires by which the old tree was blackened. So I pray Wakanda that in the greater wisdom of the white man a protecting law may be given to you both to save you from the woes your parents have suffered."

CHAPTER XIII

KIND FACE AND GRAY COAT.

THERE was a shriveled little Frenchman living near our reservation, whose heart was always warm toward us and whose hands were always full of gifts for our necessities. He dwelt in that most singular species of domicile called by the Western people a "dug-out," because mostly underground. In fact, the Frenchman's home was simply a cellar hollowed in the side of a hill, with a roof of plain pine boards. It had but one room. Along one side he had built a narrow berth of rough boards, covered with army blankets, whereon he slept. At one end there was a large fireplace dug into the hillside, with an opening above for the escape of the smoke. A rude table and a couple of camp-stools composed his furniture. Here he had lived for many years, and strange stories were in circulation among our people as to the secret of his thus being content to dwell away from civilization.

In appearance he was attractively comical. Short and thin and misshapen, he yet impressed one as possessed of wonderful nerve and agility. In fact, few of our young men could outrun him or match him in strength. His hair was long and curly, falling in white waves upon his neck. He wore a heavy mustache and what he called an "imperiel." When in his ordinary gait, he advanced by means of a curious springing hop which invariably sent our younger people into fits of laughter. His hands were small and beautiful, and he always wore gloves upon them. Of their whiteness he was very proud. He had the strange habit of drawing his right glove off and putting it rapidly on again while conversing.

His expression of face was the most singular mixture of grave roguishness and real kindliness that I have ever seen upon a human countenance. The wrinkles about his eyes seemed to play with the several emotions and passions. There was something exceedingly attractive in his smile, and his coming among us was always the signal for boisterous merriment. Because of the gentle, humane expression of his face our people had given him the name "Kind Face." They had given him also a place in their hearts, and always reserved for him the warmest corner around our camp-fires.

It is the greatest mistake to suppose that the Indian does not appreciate fun and humor. It would be hard to find a spot where mirth and gladness are better loved than they were in our simple cabins and upon our torch-lit play-ground. The Indian is quick to observe the play upon words, keen in his enjoyment of a skillful repartee, and alive to the humorous in everything. It is true we do not exhibit much laughter before the white people, but it is only because we shrink from their ridicule.

One evening, as dear Wágh-ta and I sat in my aspen arbor, the cry went up that Kind Face was hopping toward us. A troop of children ran out instantly from every hut, to go forth to meet him. They shouted and screamed and laughed, caught up handfuls of the fresh grass and tossed green wreaths of it into the air, and in every way attested their joy. Kind Face saw them coming and his face at once became one great twinkle. Onward the screaming company swept, and just before they reached him he dodged suddenly toward one side and started in his sidelong canter across the prairie with the whole noisy troop at his heels. He made great show of endeavoring to elude them, of being captured solely by their superior speed and endurance, and of being led much against his will into our village. We watched the sport with the greatest amusement, and the faces of even the sternest warriors relaxed into smiles of interest and pleasure.

The chase thus happily consummated, Kind Face, having greeted us all heartily, seated himself beside the fire of pine-boughs that crackled and blazed before the arbor. The conversation turned upon the harvest of corn our people had reason to expect, the growth of the cattle, the happiness of the young members of our tribe, and kindred topics of wild life. While thus engaged word was brought to us that Gray Coat and another white man were approaching, and we had just time to flee into our haughty pride—the last piteous resort the white man has left us —before they were with us.

"Good-evening, noble Eagle Wing," the comfortable agent said to my father; "my friend here is anxious to come into personal contact with you and your people so as to learn something of your customs and manners before returning East. And I may venture to mention that it lies in his power to benefit your tribe largely, munificently indeed, if it should be his most excellent pleasure so to do."

"Ahem!" replied the white man to whom the agent had turned with a pompous wave of the hand. "I may further say that I have the honor to occupy a seat in our National Congress, as senator from a neighboring State, and, most excellent Eagle Feather,—ah! thank you; yes, Eagle Wing, to be sure,—I may remark that I am chairman of a committee sent out for the express purpose of examining, and reporting upon, the exact condition of affairs among our Indian wards."

Wágh-ta and I, to whom his words were perfectly understood without an interpreter, were not a little amused by his grand airs and swelling manners.

"Where are the other members of the committee?" innocently inquired the wise Um-pan-nez-zhe, who was of our number.

"Well—ah! to tell the truth, they were so greatly pleased by the entertainment afforded by the agent that they were unable to tear themselves from his wine-decanter."

"Think you they can report intelligently of the Indian's necessities and wishes by inspecting the bottom of wine-glasses?" inquired Kind Face.

The senator looked down at the little Frenchman as if one of his great glances were certain death to all triflers, but made no reply.

Chairs were produced for the visitors, and when they were seated a great number of our people gathered round to hear what should be said.

"Ahem! tell me," the senator demanded with a majestic wave of his hand, "tell me without reserve what your tribe most wishes and most needs."

"The protection of just laws," my father answered.

"The what! Do I understand you? The protection of law? Why, who disturbs you? Does not the agent defend you?"

"Any one may rob us who wills. My child may be murdered and I cannot have the offender punished!"

"It is true, ahem! that our Indian policy is as yet imperfect, and some cases of violence may escape their proper punishment. I have heard rumors that this is the case, but have had no direct testimony of the fact."

Our good Kind Face was always strong in our defense, and while the senator had been speaking I had noticed that his right glove was coming off and being thrust on with uncommon vehemence. This was the usual signal of combat with him, and at this point he exclaimed:

"Any Indian can give you cases. The official reports of the agents are full of them. Just a few months since a member of this tribe was hired by a white man to chop wood for him in a secluded spot within a forest. The Indian was an honest, hard-working fellow, and we all respected him. As he did not return at the time expected, I went with a few of his friends to ascertain the cause of his delay. We found the poor fellow lying across the log he had been splitting, his heart pierced by a rifle-ball. It was winter and there was snow upon the ground, so that we could track the murderer from the cover where he had done the stealthy deed to his home. We endeavored to have him punished—we tried to have him indicted as a disturber of the peace, if nothing more—but, according to the most wise statute of your government, "No Indian can sue, or be sued, or form a party to any suit in a United States court," and we failed. That murderer is boldly living to-day within a day's ride of us, and there is no law by which he can be punished."

' Be calm, my friend," the senator complacently said, "You seem to be a man of sense, and as you can understand me, and speak to me, in English, I do not object to having a few words with you. It is true that the ward-policy, if I may so call it, of our government is liable to the abuse you mention. But I fancy the Indians would not be better off if they were placed under the protection of the law and forced to support themselves. The Indian is lazy and indifferent—I can speak unreservedly since I speak in general terms—and is constitutionally opposed to self-support."

"Pardon me," Kind Face replied, as the glove came off with a jerk, "you are either ignorant or grossly misinformed."

"I am thoroughly conversant with the condition of our

Indian tribes, as I am chairman of the committee I have mentioned," the senator haughtily replied, tipping backward in his chair.

"You must know, then, that out of 275,000 Indians in this country, 157,000—more than half—wear citizens' garments. You must know that there are 219 churches among the tribes, with an aggregate membership of 30,000. You must know that of the 70 tribes mentioned in a recent official report, 22 are stated to be entirely self-supporting. You must know that of the remaining 48 tribes, 44 are reported by the agents as able and desirous to support themselves if the government would only grant them the high privilege. Out of 70 tribes, therefore, there are only 4, according to the testimony of your own official records, which are not abundantly prepared for self-support."

"I speak on general principles," grandly said the senator.

"So do I," returned Kind Face with warmth. "You must know that the Omahas, numbering about 1100 persons, cultivate their farms with singular fidelity; the beautiful slopes of their reservation are crowned with comfortable frame dwellings, and the few tepees you still see in the valleys would speedily be displaced by houses if the Indians had any assurance that they will be allowed to remain where they are. The Winnebagoes are better farmers than some of the surrounding whites, and have a large sum in the hands of the government in the form of a loan, as they think, the interest on which, however, they can only with the greatest difficulty obtain. This tribe, by frugality and thrift, has become wealthy in spite of the greatest obstacles any community of people has ever been obliged to contend with. Years ago they resided in another State. They had their farms nicely cultivated, and their stock, of all descriptions, was numbered by the hundred. They were happy, peaceful, wealthy. But by order of the government they were taken to St. Louis, thence transported on flat-boats up the Missouri to a most barren spot in Dakota, where, among the sand-hills, without shelter or implements, they were left to their fate. The government agents promised to drive their stock overland from their old home to the new reservation, but to this day they have not seen a single head coming to them over the hills. After surveying the sand-hills, and becoming convinced that no support could be wrested from them, they worked their way down into Nebraska, and having transformed a region of wild soil into farms it was confirmed to them as a reservation. And now in your senatorial wisdom you are threatening another base robbery of them by means of a removal to the Indian Territory. And look around you. As you came up I was talking with this industrious people as to the harvests they expect to gather. They have nearly 1000 acres under cultivation ; they count their cattle by the score. Many of these young people can read and speak the English language far better than I can.

"In addition to all this," continued Kind Face, taking a pamphlet from his pocket, "I will cite, with your permission, the words of the agents themselves in respect to the good character of the Indians." He then read as follows :

"'The Ottawa and Chippewa Indians are naturally honest and scrupulously conscientious in keeping their word, and expect the same scrupulous exactness in the fulfillment of all engagements made to them, especially by the government.

"'G. W. LEE, Mackinaw, Mich., 1877.'

" 'Less crimes have been committed by them the past year than by the same number of whites. I have not known a drunken Indian upon the agency during the year.

" 'J. H. WILBUR, Yakama Agency, W. T., 1877.'

" 'I believe it can be shown that no Indian tribe in which education and Christianity have been introduced have given our government any trouble by war.

" ' R. H. MILROY, Agent, W. T., 1877.'

" 'The Sabbath is generally regarded by them as a day of rest, and more strictly observed as such than by the white settlers in the frontier towns. No intoxicating liquors are used by the Indians on the reserve.

" ' E. H. C. HOOPER, Sisseton Agency, Dakota, 1878.'

" 'Considering their location, it has been a subject of remark that no crimes have been committed by them against the whites or among themselves for the last three years.

" 'THOMAS S. FREE, Sac and Fox Agency, Iowa, 1878.'

" ' Situated as they are, in a flourishing farming community, they have become well informed regarding their relations to the whites, and have been very peaceable and quiet. No crimes have been committed, while they have advanced in the knowledge and disposition to labor, and have made many friends. Nearly all of the able-bodied men have been employed during harvest, receiving good wages, and make good laborers.

" 'THOMAS S. FREE, Sac and Fox Agency, Iowa, 1878.'

" 'The Santees are nearly all professors of religion. There are six places for worship, which are generally attended on First day.

" 'ISAIAH LIGHTNER, Santee Agency, Neb., 1878.'

"'They say that they have been faithful on their part in complying with their promises and obligations to the government, and intend to continue to be so; and they ask a reciprocal compliance on the part of the government with its promises and treaties with them. They are often disturbed by rumors and probabilities of changes, either of their homes or their management, and they feel that either would be great injustice, especially without their free and unenforced consent. They are quick to discriminate between justice and injustice, and they say they want to live in undisturbed peace on their own rightful possessions, and in friendship with their white neighbors; which is certainly asking no more than a generous and just humanity would accord to them.

"'JACOB VORE, Omaha Agency, Neb., 1878.'"

"I must insist that I speak generally when I say that the Indian character is worthless," responded the senator.

"Let us broaden our survey, then. One of the ablest presidents the Mexican Republic has ever had was a full-blood Indian. It was under his far-sighted statesmanship that Mexico threw off the yoke of Rome which had been weighing her people down in ignorance, superstition, and vice ever since Cortez subjugated their ancestors. Thus an Indian is the combined Washington and Luther of Mexico, and I say, All honor to him! To go a little farther back, the history of Tennessee is most suggestive. The first party which in the old days, before the Revolution, fought as a party for the liberty of the United States, being worsted in their untimely attempts, fled to the wilderness, were cordially received by the Cherokees, and from them obtained the tract of land which now blooms as Tennessee. To go still farther back: when the eloquent young clergyman, Roger Williams, was driven out of Plymouth Colony because he had forecast the religious freedom for which 'this nation is now distinguished, who received him with open arms? All the world knows it was Canonicus, the celebrated Narragansett chief, who, with a charity as pure as the new-fallen snow over which the young clergyman fled to him, bade him welcome to his wigwams and council-fires. Thus an Indian gave the first countenance and afforded the first harbor to the idea of religious toleration in the United States!"

"I fail to see how all this affects the working of the committee of which I have the honor to be chairman."

"I thought you demanded that I should show you, on general principles, that the Indian character is not utterly worthless. Similar facts of a far more convincing character are to be found nearer home. So far back as 1839 the Osages showed their great desire for civilization by requesting agricultural implements, and by special treaty they were promised them ; but in 1870 the government by a public statute acknowledged that it had disregarded the treaty for thirty-one years, and appropriated $20,000 to repair the loss. In 1868 the Sioux, supposed to be the most untamable of all our tribes, demanded that a teacher for every thirty of their children, and missionaries to teach them of The Book, should be sent among them. Spotted Tail, who is held up as the "chief of red devils" by our public prints, said recently to the Secretary of the Interior : "I want God's Word taught to my people. I want to be allowed to employ honest lawyers to plead my cause." This same bloodthirsty savage sent word down to this tribe not long since that his people were anxious to learn how to till the soil. Twenty of our young men started toward his home to give his people instruction in the matter. But they were arrested at command of Gray Coat, your "agent," and sent back in disgrace to their homes.   Thus has the government, through its agents, interfered with the progress the Indians are anxious to make toward civilization and self-support.   These Indians before you were compelled, last season, to cut their wheat with butcher-knives because the Indian Department would not grant them reapers and thus aid them toward self-support.

"Allow me to refer to my little pamphlet again :

"'They hear of Indians at other agencies receiving them, and they are constantly asking me, "Why cannot we have them?" And when I urge them on to work, their reply is: "How can we work without anything to work with? Give us what we need and you will see what we can do."

"'H. E. GREGORY, Agent Lower Brule Sioux, 1877.'

"'There have been no agricultural implements here in season for use, except two old ploughs.

"'GEO. W. FROST, Crow Agency, Mont., 1878.'

"'It is the avowed policy of the government to make the Indians self-supporting; and yet I am left without the means to make the initiatory steps for the furtherance of that policy.

"'W. V. RINEHART, Malheur Agency, Oregon, 1877.'

"'My resignation having been tendered some time since, I avail myself of this opportunity to say that while I have not at any time claimed to have sought or accepted an Indian agency for motives of philanthropy, I did wish and believe that I could be instrumental in doing them good. I supposed that all agencies were located on Indian reservations; that more or less farming was done; that there were schools connected with them, and all reasonable effort made to civilize, educate, and Christianize the Indian.   Instead of such influences and opportunity for usefulness I found my agency located in a Mexican village, more than fifty miles from a reservation ; and the Indians, when visiting the agency, exposed to all the most demoralizing influences. I have, of course, been disappointed in my expectations.

"'S. A. RUSSELL, Abiquin Agency, New Mex., 1878.'"

"I repeat my assertion of the worthlessness of Indian character," said the senator with an august wave of the hand, "and I further remark that, by his love of blood-shed and robbery, the red man has forfeited all claim to our consideration."

"That the Indians are in many instances treacherous and revengeful I do not deny," answered Kind Face. "But that they are worse than a corresponding number of white people would be, under similar circumstances, I am far from admitting. Let a certain class of white men be treated with outrage, perfidy, robbery, and ridicule, for a long succession of years ; let them grow up in the knowledge that they are ground down by a stock company of those who are being enriched at their expense ; let them see their holiest affections disregarded, their dearest relatives murdered ; let them live in constant dread of being removed by a brutal and murderous command to the Land of Fire, which is literally the land of Death—and they would be either more or less than human if they did not resent such treatment. The Swedes are a patient race, and the Germans are slow to take offense ; but how long do you imagine either class would bear to have the nearest Englishman or American enrich himself from their barn-yards and stores, avail himself of their best land and their purest daughters, and hide his villainous deeds under high-sounding professions of 'ward-policy' and senseless sneers as to Swedish or

German worthlessness? How long, think you, would any class of white people bear such unjust treatment as I find written down in my little pamphlet? Another case or two may be given as most wholesome reading:

"'A party of Texans, under the pretext of searching for horses stolen from them by the Indians, were shown by my direction through the Indian camps; but they were, as they say, unable to find any of their horses. The next night they surrounded the weakest camp, fired on the Indians (fortunately without effect), and drove off all the horses they could collect (thirteen), the others having scattered during the firing. This raid was allowed to go unpunished.

"'F. C. GODFREY, Agent Apaches, New Mex., 1877.'

"This is a very interesting case, as there is much discussion at present in regard to the cruelties practiced by the New Mexican Indians against the whites. Who will write a history of the long years they patiently suffered before resorting to arms? But here is another point:

"'It is not the fault of these Indians that they are not to-day self-supporting. They have been left by the paternal government without a home, and compelled to become wanderers, by being driven from place to place, when they have attempted to locate and cultivate the soil. They have, through me, been for almost four years *begging for a home*—a place where they could farm and have schools for their children. It has thus far been denied them.

"'S. A. RUSSELL, Abiquin Agency, New Mex., 1878.'

"'The state of disquiet among the tribes north of us has not been participated in by the Klamaths. They have their own grievances, which are serious, and a great deal of patience and forbearance on their part is shown. They claim that "there are lands offered for sale and purchased and occupied by white settlers which in reality belong by treaty to them, and it is injustice to deprive them of these lands." '

"'J. H. ROOCK, Agent Klamaths, Oregon, 1877.'

"'With few exceptions they are a quiet, peaceable, well-disposed people. Quarrels and contentions among themselves are infrequent, and not a single instance has come to my knowledge of violence or crime committed by them against the person or property of the whites settled along the borders of their reservations, or even against the squatters, who knowingly, and in defiance of all rights and justice and even the authorities of the government, have encroached upon, and taken possession of, their most fertile lands.

'" J. B. ABBOTT, Los Pinos Agency, Col., 1878.'

"'Large trespasses have been committed, from year to year, upon these lands, to which the attention of the proper officers has been called; but still the work of robbery and destruction goes on unchecked.

"'GEO. W. LEE, Mackinaw Agency, Mich., 1878.'

"'The Indians are much discouraged by these raids, and seem to think too little effort has been made to recover their property.

"'P. B. HUNT, Kiowa and Comanche Agency, 1878.'

"'The white settlers alluded to in my first Annual Report still remain on the reservation, being located on their several claims, increasing their stock and improvements, and, of course, still further encroaching on the Indians' rights.

"'JAMES I. PATTEN, Shoshone Agency, Wyoming 1878.' ·

"And, in addition, I can say that in a comparison of Indian cruelty with white cruelty the shame must be upon the pale cheek.   Save in dime literature, and in sensational falsehoods for the columns of partisan papers, there is no recorded case of Indian massacre which will outcolor the cruelties the whites have frequently practiced against the red men.   Since the Pequot Indians were starved to death on Block Island—the white men having stolen away their canoes—hardly a year has passed without a scene of outrageous cruelty, in which the Indians are the victims. Just a few years since, the farmer hired by the government to teach the Pawnees how to till the soil superintended the raising of a large amount of grain, the Indians doing most of the work.   When the crop was harvested the farmer claimed it all as his share and had it secured in granaries.   Then came on the long, cold winter with its dreariness and hunger.   The Indians, having trusted to the promise of the farmer that they should have this grain for support, had made no other provision for winter, and soon were literally starving.   They went to the farmer and begged piteously for some of the corn for which they had labored.   They pointed to their starving wives and children.   They were refused.   When in the extremity of their distress some of them ventured to go to the granaries to take a little of the corn, the farmer, standing in the doorway of his house, coolly shot them down.   A 'red devil' was never more cruel than that."

"They might have applied to the agent."

"Truly; but the winter would have been consumed waiting for your National 'Circumlocution Office'—known as the Indian Department—to take action, even if the agent had been willing to intercede for them.   The Utes waited more than a year for provisions that should have been sent to them, and the country knows the dread result. The agents in these cases, and in all cases, are so impeded by the regulations of the Indian Department that they cannot act upon kindly sentiments toward the red men, even should they entertain them. It is a public statute, I understand, that no agent shall visit Washington to intercede for those under his charge, on penalty of instant removal, except upon special invitation of the Indian Department."

"There is one circumstance," the senator remarked, shifting his position as if he had just thought of a way out of all difficulty, "in the warfare of the red men which has always had the effect to prejudice my own mind, and the minds of many of the chief thinkers of the country, against them. I refer to the cruel practice of taking scalps. Ugh! Ahem!" The latter exclamation uttered apologetically to his own dignity.

"Even in this particular," Kind Face replied, "the Indians have been surpassed by the white men. At one time the most Christian commonwealth of Massachusetts offered a large bounty for every Indian scalp secured. And when they were not forthcoming in sufficient quantities, the bounty was sevenfold increased. And it is to be noted that this bounty was offered for the scalps of women and children as well as men, and to encourage the cruel practice in times of peace as well as war. The Indians with all their cruelty never countenanced a worse barbarity than that. There are many other cases of the same character. One is historic. Soon after the terrible massacre in Wyoming—"

"Ah! yes, a case in point!"

"Soon after this massacre, which, as you will remember, was instigated and conducted by the white men, a British general stationed at Detroit issued a proclamation that a rich bounty would be paid for every scalp laid at his feet, adding significantly that no reward could be expected for the taking of prisoners alive. For this infamous transaction the Indians well called him 'The hair-buying general'! In each of the English appropriation bills for the war in America dated from 1775 to 1778 there is an item for 'scalping-knives.' The practice of scalp-taking has not been as distasteful to all white men as it is to you."

" You are so evidently a partisan in this matter," broke in the smooth voice of the comfortable senator, "that it will be necessary for us to take your arguments with some allowance. You might explain to us whether you would wish an Indian punished at all or not."

"I would have an offender punished whether he have a white or a red skin. I honestly believe that the white officials, whoever they may be, who are responsible for the massacre of the Cheyennes at Fort Robinson, ought to be hung as much as any common murderer. That a man, or a few men, cause the death of from one hundred to one thousand persons and then call it a " Policy" seems to me an odd reason that they should go free, when he who slays one man is strung up. To my mind, also, they who insist upon the removal of northern Indians to the Indian Territory, knowing that they will die there like sheep, are simply murderers and cut-throats in wholesale. In the report of one of the recent Indian Commissioners I have found these words: 'Experience has shown the exceeding impolicy of removing northern Indians to the Indian Territory.' He then mentions that out of 2376 Pawnees removed to the Land of Fire, 800 died in two years. He states that the same death-ratio prevails among Cheyennes and Poncas, and remarks that this simply means the extinction of all northern tribes sent to that latitude. In the very next sentence after these bloody details are given, the Commissioner coolly says: 'In *this connection* I recommend the removal of all the Indians in Colorado and Arizona to the Indian Territory'! To my unofficial mind that seems a simple recommendation that some 20,000 persons be forthwith murdered by inches. I must not forget, however, that if a murder is called a 'Ward-policy' it is not a murder."

"You certainly must have intellect sufficient to observe," said the senator angrily, "that a government has the right to pursue certain policies, even though they be attended with some loss of life, when the ultimate object is of commanding importance. No one blames the general for the loss of life when liberty or honor is gained by the battle."

"True," said Kind Face, "but the object to be gained by the removal of the Indians is simply the enriching of the whites living in the vicinity of the reservations. This is the very grandest aim you can profess to have in view. In too many instances the benefit accrues to a few plotting individuals. The Indians are perfectly aware of the condition of affairs. They are conscious of being the victims in a great gambling system."

"To what do you refer, sir?"

"To the method of obtaining appropriations of Congress for the benefit of the Indians, upon whom the good seldom descends. From seven to nine millions of dollars are appropriated yearly for the Indian tribes, and it is quite safe to say that not more than three millions reach those for whom the money was designed. Let me show you a case before your very eyes. Just beyond this line of hills there lies a treacherous swamp, for which the Indian children have a singularly expressive name, 'The Eleven Hundred Dollar Bridge.' The secret of the name is this: Some years since the government appropriated

$1100 to build a bridge across this swamp so that the children, on their way to school, should not get their feet wet and take cold in the bleak weather. The money, however, disappeared in some one's pocket; the bridge was never built; and the children, as they trudge through the swamp, laugh as they give it the name I have mentioned. The agents among some of the tribes receive a salary of $1500, but in many cases the position is acknowledged by all concerned to be worth an even $10,000. For the removal of each Indian tribe from $25,000 to $45,000 are appropriated, the great bulk of which disappears in the pockets of those who conduct the removal and their coadjutors. A dying agent recently made a confession to a friend of mine that he had been concerned in two cases of fraud, while he had witnessed many others. The cases in respect to which his conscience was aroused were as follows: A prominent man, now residing in Omaha, received $7000 for ploughs which were never delivered to the indians; and a merchant in the same city was awarded a large sum of money for the breaking up of a certain tract of land for the Indians, when in fact not a single foot of turf had been overturned. The agent, who revealed these facts when dying, had certified to the vouchers for a monetary consideration, and the matter lay so heavily upon his mind that he disclosed it."

"It is unavoidable," remarked the senator, knitting his brows with the show of much wisdom, "that some abuse of contracts should occur in so extensive an operation as is the supply of the tribes. This, however, should not be laid up against the government or its policy."

"So far is robbery from being incidental to the conducting of Indian affairs," replied the sturdy friend of our race, "that it is the deliberate purpose of many who, from official position, should be above it. I happened a few months since to be traveling on the cars in company with a number of wealthy gentleman. One was a judge from Montana, another was from Kentucky. The latter gentleman was very anxious to learn from the former just how he had succeeded in making so much money out of an Indian contract the preceding summer. The judge was exceedingly communicative and, not minding in the least the presence of a deformed Frenchman, told the whole story of a gigantic robbery. 'You see,' he said, 'there was Mr. A. and Mr. B. of Iowa, Mr. C. and Senator D. of Illinois, Senators F. and G. of New York, and myself, in the ring. We took one hundred thousand dollars, went to Washington and made Christmas presents of two thousand dollars to some of the Congressmen. Then a bill was introduced by Senator D. of Illinois, appropriating one million dollars to certain of the Indian tribes— it was of course passed, for nothing can be more noble than our care of our red wards—and the contracts were awarded to us who stood in the background of the ring. The main condition upon which we received the contracts was that we should devote $200,000 for election purposes in the State of Iowa. We bought a supply of guns and ammunition, sent them out to our Indians, and instructed the agents to grant permission to the Indians to go upon a grand buffalo-hunt. They remained away the entire summer, and consequently we had to furnish no provisions for that period. We reported ten thousand Indians upon one reservation, when the actual number was about one thousand, and in all other cases the same liberal ratio was carefully observed. Then by skillful buying of damaged articles for a very low price, and selling the same to the Indians for a high price, we were able to get through the winter. When we came to square up accounts we had about an even $100,000 for each of the seven members of the ring.' 'But how did you manage the vouchers?' asked the uninformed Kentuckian. 'Vouchers!' exclaimed the judge in a tone of the highest disgust. '*Our* agents swore to them and *our* Indian Department audited them. What more would you want?' While the company indulged in a hearty laugh over the solving of the golden riddle, my heart was sore for the poor Indians."

Kind Face paused for a moment, and, the white men making no reply, there was a sad silence around our twilight camp-fire. Kind Face was gazing thoughtfully into the distance where the bluffs beyond the great river reared themselves into the sky.

"See!" he exclaimed at length. All eyes followed the direction of his pointing finger. "Behold that little speck, that dark spot, far, far away in the distance, rising slowly against the sky. Watch it; it grows somewhat more distinct; it is a slender line now against the evening sunset. Turn your attention now to the rocks opposite us where, every Indian child knows, is the nest of a brace of Washington eagles. By their keen vision they have long since discovered the speck and the line we have noticed. Behold! the male eagle with a scream springs up from the nest, soars with heavy strokes of his wings into the sky, and conceals himself at a great height. The line we have noticed comes nearer: it is a bird—a snowy brant—belated in its return from the uplands. He comes with great speed toward the eagle's nest. See! as he nears it the female eagle springs up, faces him in his flight and stops him suddenly. The affrighted brant, startled by the sudden appearance of such a terrible foe, pauses, wheels, circles aloft, trusting to his strong, lithe wings for escape. And he would elude his foe but that the male eagle, who has been watching the whole proceeding from his high station, now descends like a thunderbolt and attacks the brave brant from above. Oh! the eagles' eyes are fierce, their claws are sharpened against many a pine-trunk, their neck-feathers rise up stiffly with savage thirst for blood, their screams are wild and exultant; and the poor brant soon pours forth his warm blood to tinge his snowy breast. Most noble agent and senator, in this aërial combat, so unequal, so unsought by the victim, so unavoidably sanguine, I see a type of what is occurring daily in the constant struggle between the white and the red races. The poor victims in this larger battle simply desire to be left in freedom to fly unmolested where they will, to haste from their fields to their simple homes. In plain words, the Indians make but one petition of the Great Father— that they may have the protection of equitable laws; that their wrongs may be righted and robbery prevented.

"Let me read just two little sentences from my pamphlet:

"'Wish well to the Indians as we may, and do for them what we will, the efforts of civil agents, teachers, and missionaries are like the struggles of drowning men weighted with lead, as long as by the absence of law Indian society is left without a base.—*Bishop Hare's Report.*

"'It seems to me to be an odd feature of our judicial system that the only people in this country who have no rights under the law are the original owners of the soil. An Irishman, German, Chinaman, Turk or Tartar will be protected in life and property, but the Indian commands respect for his rights only so long as he inspires terror for his rifle. GEN. CROOK.'"

"By Jove!" said the senator, "it must be dinner-time; I was almost asleep."

Without another word, the white men betook themselves homeward.

CHAPTER XIV.

THE BRIDAL EVE.

"Good evening, young invalid! You seem to be taking it rather easy under this arbor, while your lazy brothers are pretending at least to work in the fields. Have you obtained the consent of my father to lie around and do nothing?"

The speaker was the dreaded Scar Face, who, a few days after the events mentioned in the last chapter, surprised me talking with my little bride under the arbor that my father had built for me.

"And who is this nursing you?" Scar Face continued.

"She is Prairie Flower, sir," I said, "and as soon as I recover from my wounds she is to be my wife."

In uttering the first part of this sentence I could not prevent my lips trembling with dread and anger; but I spoke the last words proudly, and yet hastily, that he might not presume that she was nothing to me, and try to win her away from my side. How foolish I was to suppose that he would respect the love we had for each other, I did not know until some days thereafter.

"By Jove!" Scar Face said brutally, "she has a pretty face and a neat form and a—let's see your foot, miss!"

But Prairie Flower did not move. She held her face down upon my shoulder and blushed in deep shame and indignation.

With a coarse laugh Scar Face passed on, turning, after he had taken a few steps, to shake his finger at Prairie Flower and say, "I will see you again, my dear."

For days I could not rid my mind of his rough and ribald expression of face, and by night I was haunted with a fear of some great disaster to come upon my bride. I saw his scarred countenance in everything about me, and when I heard a sudden noise I sprang up in affright, as if it were the scream of my Prairie Flower struggling in his grasp. But as he came not again, I by and by forgot his insult, and began to hope that he meditated no particular wrong against us.

Meanwhile the days as they came saw a great improvement in my strength, and before many had passed I was able to walk abroad upon the prairies. The main thought in my mind was my approaching marriage with Prairie Flower, the day of which had been fixed. The wedding customs of my people were very simple, the service beginning with the gathering of all the members of the tribe to a feast as complete as we had means to prepare. But if this feast lacked many of the choicer delicacies which go to make up a more civilized entertainment, it more than supplied the deficiency by furnishing the most abundant quantity of good will, the most extravagant joy, and the truest happiness. When the fire leaped up before which the savory antelope ribs were to be roasted, what delight there was! How the faces of the old warriors would relax into the pleasantest of smiles! How important and busy the wives were as they bustled hither and thither preparing the odorous coffee and seeing that the maize-cakes be not done too brown! How the sweet wild vegetables tempted us to attack them, and how fiercely we accepted the challenge when all was ready! How pleased and blushing the bride would be when she was placed at the head of the rows of hungry relatives and friends, prepared to do full honor to the feast! And if we had not the toasts and sentiments of the entertainments of otner races, we had at least warm expressions of affection, genuine wishes for the welfare of the married couple, admiration without hypocrisy, and friendship without jealousy.

After the conclusion of the feast, generous draughts were taken from the cool waters of the neighboring spring, and the company composed themselves to witness and partake in the remaining ceremonies. These consisted in the giving of presents by the bridegroom to the bride and her parents, the accepting of the bride from the arms of her father, and the triumphal march to the home where the wedded couple were to live. There were also songs and dances of children, and trials of strength or speed upon the play-ground, and matches between the best bowmen of the tribe to see which could shoot arrow after arrow into the sky and have the largest number in the air at any one time, the playing of pranks upon sly lovers whose turn to be married would next come, the wreathing of wild flowers and divers colored grasses into fantastic shapes, and such other spontaneous expressions of delight as a simple-hearted people love on a holiday to make.

There was another custom among us which could by no means be disregarded. The bridegroom on the day before the wedding was required to gather a large quantity of the most beautiful wild roses, with which to adorn the bride. When the day before the one set for our wedding had arrived, I started out, in obedience to this custom, to gather flowers, which, for beauty and fragrance, were to exceed anything my people had ever seen before; for, I said to myself, only such flowers could possibly be allowed to twine around my Prairie Flower's neck and rest upon her bosom. The morning was of that radiant brightness which dawns only, it seems to me, on wide stretches of prairie in high altitudes. The hills in the distance were just of sufficient height to vary the scene delightfully and to impress upon one the real loveliness of the grassy plain at his feet. With high hopes and bounding pulse I started out in my search, in full sympathy with all the happiness and beauty around me. Was not the next sun to see me wedded to my sweet bride? What then could bring me sadness? With her by my side I could be happy in any, the most fearful, calamities, I was sure. Do not these dear doves, that fly with whistling wings above me, get under the heavy pine fringes when it storms, and coo and love as happily as if no rain were pelting to the earth and no thunders were raging in the sky? Oh, if but my bride and I can remain together, even the white man cannot bring a woe upon us that we could not patiently bear.

But then the thought would come to me, What if my bride be wrested from me? What if Scar Face plots already to have her for his own base use? The thought maddened me, but the day was so fair, and my heart so light, that I laughed off my fears and continued my search.

Nowhere, however, could I find roses sweet or beautiful enough for my Prairie Flower. Every bush that I saw I eagerly examined; but, although there were many delicately tinted flowers full worthy to adorn a less shapely neck than hers, there was none that would not blush to a deeper red if placed near the cheek of my bride. I hunted every little defile where before I had thought the roses beautiful, but they all seemed to have faded since I saw them last, and I wondered that I had for a moment thought them worthy of her, So the day passed and the evening began to come down upon me, and I realized that I must soon make a choice. Then I regretted that I had not plucked such or such a flower that I had hesitated over. Hastily gathering my scarf full of those which were nearest at hand, I thought, " It is just as well : she would outshine the most beautiful rose that the sun and earth ever bore, and these that I have found, being of inferior shape and odor, will but make her superiority the more marked and her triumph surer."

Comforted by these thoughts, I hurried back to our village, which I reached just at dusk. Filled with my own bright thoughts, I did not notice that the first group of my people that I met looked pityingly upon me. I met another group, but when they saw me they whispered together and walked another way, so as not to encounter me. A third group I smiled upon, but they turned their faces away. "What is this?" I thought : "surely the people mean no insult to the son of Eagle Wing. Oh, I have it now : they do not wish to disturb me in my joy."

I soon saw one of the maidens of our tribe coming toward me. We called her "Swallow," and I knew that she loved me and thought hard of Prairie Flower that I had not chosen herself to be my bride. Her face was sad and tearful this evening, and as she came toward me I determined to soothe her hard feelings against us by showing her the roses I had gathered for my bride. I did not then know how hateful the finery and possessions of one woman appear in the eyes of her rival, particularly when they are the gift of the one they both love.

"See! dear little Swallow," I exclaimed, "see the roses I have gathered for my bride. Are they not lovely? Come, now—tell me if Prairie Flower will not be the sweetest rose of all the cluster?"

The little maiden would not cast a single look upon the flowers, but turned her eyes, full of tears, up to my very face, and said:

"Alas for thee! Alas for thee, Shá-ta-ga-dtá-tha!"

"What is it, Swallow?" I exclaimed. "Can you not forgive me that I love Prairie Flower—or has some calamity befallen me? Oh! it may be that. Tell me, is Prairie Flower safe?"

"I love thee too much to tell thee. Go to Eagle Wing, go to thy father! But thou mayst as well drop thy roses here!"

I let them fall at her feet and dashed swiftly away. Little Swallow seated herself amidst the scattered flowers and wept aloud that they had not been gathered for her.

My father was standing with folded arms at the door of our home when I çame up.

"What is it, my father?" I exclaimed. "Why do the people turn their faces away from me as I pass? Why does little Swallow send me hastily to thee for tidings? Is my Prairie Flower safe?"

"My son," he replied, turning upon me a look of the greatest sympathy, "thy time for suffering has come. Hold thyself proudly under it as becomes the son of a chief.'

"But is Prairie Flower safe?" I demanded impatiently.

"She is as yet, but I know not how long she will be."

"Thank Wakanda! the worst at least has not come. Is she at her home—is she sick?"

"Nay to both questions. This afternoon Scar Face—"

"Oh! oh! oh!" I broke in, "has that beast carried out his threat? Has he stolen her away?"

"He took her away. I know not where, I know not for what purpose."

"I know," I said bitterly. "O Wakanda! why could I not be spared this? All my bright hopes thus cast in ruin to the ground. My sweet bride torn from my arms at the very moment when she was to be fully mine. O Wakanda! Wakanda!"

I threw myself upon the ground, and my mother, who had stood weeping near, came and held my head in her lap.

"Be comforted, my child," she whispered. "No allurements of the white man can ever make Prairie Flower forget thee, and if her heart be still thine no wickedness that she may endure can make her unworthy."

"But she will suffer so! And oh! mother, I cannot kill him!"

Anger and sorrow combined to bring tears into my eyes, and by their flow I was calmed though not comforted. O mother, mother! how I think of thee now as I write and bless thy tenderness! How I bring back thy face and touch out of the darkness of death! thy warm kiss still lingers upon my cheek; thy words still thrill my heart; thy bending, beaming countenance is still a bright sky, a holy heaven, to me. Thou wert great when but one tear fell upon my cheek as the Sioux thrust their cruel arrows into thy side, but thou wert greater and more motherly when many tears of sympathy fell from thy eyes because the white man had stolen away my bride. O mother! earth has but one of thee, and even Heaven cannot supply thy place!

How long I remained thus upon the ground I know not, but suddenly the thought came to me that the wise Standing Elk would be able to give me the particulars of the stealing of my bride; and starting wildly up I was about to dash away, when my mother caught my arm and exclaimed:

"Art thou mad, my son? Stay with me! stay with me! Do not destroy thyself, for Prairie Flower will return and will weep much if thou art not here to welcome her!"

"I go to Um-pan-nez-zhe, mother," I said with forced calmness. "He can tell me all."

The night had now come on, and as I sped madly, reck-lessly toward the home of my bride, now so sadly empty, I blessed the darkness which hid me from the curious gaze of our people. I could see around the camp-fires groups of happy lovers who laughed and caressed each other as if my laden, beating heart were not nigh. As I paused a moment before such a sight, which by cruel contrast gave me a feeling of bitterness strangely sweet to my heart, I heard a soft step at my side, and little Swallow caught my hand in hers and said :

"O Wolf Killer, may not I comfort thee one little moment? May not I hold thy head upon my breast while a star twinkles once and delude myself that thou art mine?"

"Swallow, I can love but one!" I said, and dashed away. I did not hear her say proudly to the night :

"I *will* comfort him—in a way he little thinks of!"

I did not see her steal cautiously through our village and take her course toward the splendid home of Gray Coat, our agent.

As I neared the home of the wise man and saw it so dark and lonely I slackened my pace, feeling almost that I—even I—had no right to interrupt the sacredness of a father's grief. I crept so near that in the starlight I could see the old man pacing backward and forward, tearing at his long gray hair, and showing every possible sign of deep grief. He moaned and wrung his hands, and in pity for him I half forgot to grieve myself. At last he came to the door of his home and exclaimed bitterly :

"Look down, ye stars ! and see the deepest grief that even Um-pan-nez-zhe has borne. You have dropped dew-tears of sympathy upon me when I mourned for wife and father and friend; but these all died nobly and with no stain upon their names. But now, in my old age, my last comfort and joy is wrested from me to be disgraced and dishonored by the cruel Scar Face. O Wakanda, hast thou lost all pity for the red men? Hast thou forgotten us in our simple homes and turned thy thoughts upon statelier nations? Nay! I know that cannot be; but why, oh why are the Indians' hands so cruelly bound? O my little Wágh-ta, was it for this that thou wast saved from the death that overwhelmed thy mother? for this that I have tended thee so long and lovingly? for this my gray hairs have been preserved in many perils? I saw thy mother in thee; in thy ruin thy mother dies the second time! O my Flower, my Flower, torn from thy old father's arms and from those of thy husband, who shall bring comfort to us now? And I could not dash the foul villain to the earth! This arm, trained to defend thee, trained in so many battles to strike a killing blow, fell limp to my side when a brutal wretch tore thee away! Ah! were it not better for all my people to die rather than to see Prairie Flower disgraced? But no! I must not cause the death of the innocent. O white man, what cruel bonds you bind us with! O Prairie Flower, where do thy tears fall to-night? O Wakanda, spare thy feeble ones!"

When I could stand suspense no longer I rushed forward and cried:

"My father, what is this terrible fate that has come upon my bride? Speak! I can stand anything rather than uncertainty!"

He turned upon me a look in which sympathy appeared struggling with woe. And it triumphed, for with a great effort of will he subdued his moans, and becoming wonderfully—almost fiercely—calm, he said to me in a steady voice:

"My son, it may not be so bad with little Prairie Flower as I fear. Perhaps my sad experiences with the white men have made me too suspicious, and what may be but a temporary absence I have magnified into a permanent loss. Scar Face—"

"Curses upon him !" I could not help exclaiming.

"Came shortly after noon to-day, saying that his mother had commissioned him to select a waiting-maid for her from the most beautiful of our maidens. He had examined, he added, with a wicked leer, all that could lay any just claim to the title, without being satisfied, and as he had seen my daughter once before, he requested that he might be honored with a sight of her again. I tried to excuse her on the plea that she was not well, but he demanded —yes, demanded—that she should instantly appear before him. My fatherly love sprang into my arm, and for a moment I clinched my fist, half intending to strike him to the earth. He stepped back a few paces and drew a pistol from an inner pocket and pointed it at my heart. Oh! would to Wakanda he had killed me on the spot ! But he knew that he must not stain his hands with murder, and so he demanded, with curses, that Prairie Flower be given to him. I replied, as calmly as I could :

"' Scar Face, it is not fear of thee that prompts me to obey thy devilish command. It is because I scorn to do a wrong. If I should strike thee to the earth, as my hate of thee and love of my child prompt me to do, thou well knowest what a cruel fate I should bring upon the innocent ones in my tribe. I scorn to adopt the unholy selfishness of the white man. Thou dost take advantage of this unjust law which treats us all as guilty if one offends, and for a short time thou wilt enjoy thy brutal triumph. But mark the words of an old man : in no race can crime prosper, and the passion which now leads thee to outrage shall of itself lead thee to ruin.'

"There was no need to call little Wágh-ta, for the

moment she had seen the pistol pointed at my heart she had rushed forth, and during my speech to Scar Face had clung sobbing to my breast. I saw the base libertine's eyes gleam upon her in insulting admiration of her charms; I saw him close his rough hands upon her shoulders; I felt her tender arms clinging to me for protection, and I, her heaven - appointed protector, could not touch the villain with my finger. I heard her sob as he tore her away, and for the last time—yes, I am sure for the last time—I felt her soft breath upon my cheek. Mark me! Shá-ta-ga-dtá-tha, my mind is old and has attained the prophet's foresight. I can feel my soul snapping like a bow-string too tightly drawn, but there is a strange, wild music even in the breaking of it. I see that a great calamity approaches our tribe. A dark, a fierce cloud comes sweeping up toward us, and either in the blackness of the ruin it shall cast upon us, or before it comes, I shall be separated from my child so that from this moment I shall never see her again. O Wakanda! Wakanda!"

A solemn look of woe passed over the old man's face—the holy expression that all the prophets of my people have—and sinking upon the ground he covered his face with his blanket and relapsed into silence.

"Which way went they, my father?" I exclaimed.

But his ears were deaf to me as he swayed backward and forward in his hopeless grief.

"Speak to me, my father! which way did they take?"

Still the old man did not speak. Gradually he sank back upon the ground. I snatched the blanket from before his face, and saw that his eyes were glazing and his lips gasping for breath. He started up, and waving his arm with majestic grace, said with a rapt smile:

"Wife, I come! My noble sons, I come! Wakanda, I come! Wágh-ta! Prairie Flower, I—"

He sank down to the earth again. The wind in the pine-tops deepened into a moan. The wise, the noble Um-pan-nez-zhe was dead. O noble legislators and governors! O learned debaters and lawyers! O proud senators and statesmen! O most honored Great Father! O multitudes of unthinking people! heard you nothing in your happy homes that night like the snapping of a heart? As you read your papers next morning and saw the demand that this or that Indian tribe be exterminated for the crimes of a few—without which demand scarce an issue can be published—seemed there no voice in the air whispering, " Unjust! Unjust! Unjust!"?

I left the dead man where he had fallen, and stole away into the darkness. Clouds had gathered under the stars and were rolling up blacker and blacker from the southwest. I felt almost calmed as I walked along. A strange sense that the crime of Scar Face had been avenged in the death of Um-pan-nez-zhe came over me, so confused was I by the thrilling events a single day had brought about. It seemed to me that the glazed eyes and white lips and stiffening cheeks of the wise man were laying up a mighty claim against the white men in some sure place under the very eye of Wakanda, and that by and by our whole race would be benefited because of what we were suffering now. So I began to pity Scar Face, as if he had been foiled after all, and I painted to myself how his disfigured countenance would look, covered with blood and gashed deeper than before, lying under this brush or beside that rock, and in the thought I had a strange delight.

But when I realized that the bride who was to be mine on the morrow was in the clutches of a more savage brute than the wolf could ever be, I ceased to pity and began again to hate him. I called upon all the powers of the night and all the terrors of the storm to blast him. If any one had been crouching in the bushes beside which I passed and could have heard my wild ravings and seen the fierce hatred upon my countenance, he would have supposed that some demon had escaped from the place of his confinement and was wandering up and down the earth. I took no account of space, and though I impatiently trod upon miles of daisy-spangled sod, I was as unconscious of changing my position relative to what was below and around me as I was of shifting my place relative to the star-spangled sky above me.

"Can it be," I thought, "that this is the very prairie I wandered over, and these the very valleys I explored, only a few hours since, hoping then to secure roses beautiful enough to be allowed to adorn my bride? How different my feelings now! Then I was hopeful and happy; now I am brideless and despairing! Then I sought flowers to add to my joy; now I only desire to hide my grief! Then it was day; now it is night. Has the darkness come so soon to swallow up the sun-rays? So soon also, and so completely, has the night of heavy woe overtaken me and quenched all the day of my heart.

"Is it because we are poor," I continued to think, "that the white man denies us the protection of his law? But are there no poor ones in his great cities, no shriveled hearts in reeking places, no despairing wretches dwelling in dark, damp rooms, no souls to whom day brings no light and night no repose, no orphans longing for one touch of sympathy, and no childless parents weeping that misery and want have robbed them of sweet smiles and tender kisses? And if this great class of distressed beings are not debarred by their wretchedness from the protection of just and equitable laws, why should we be? Or is it because we are incapable of appreciating the white

man's civilization? But when has any one come to us
with charity and patience who has not been welcomed as
a brother and whose instructions have not benefited us?
When have we had an honest chance to become as the
white men, since so many of those sent to us prey upon
our substance and make return to the power that sends
them only by publishing the most extravagant falsehoods
concerning our cruelty and laziness? Are we not cruel,
then? Yes, in war with each other, or when crazed and
maddened by being driven from one home after another
and suffering insult, robbery, and outrage without limit at
the hands of the white man, we do try our best to be as
cruel as he—though we are not cunning enough or strong
enough to succeed. I have often been told that our more
favored brethren living far to the north of us, in a country
lying out of the Great Father's possessions, are fully as
intelligent as the majority of the white people, are in
many instances far better informed than they upon the
leading questions of the day, and are wealthy, industrious,
and happy, because they enjoy the priceless benefits of
legal protection on an equal footing with the whites. The
guilty are punished; the good are fostered : contentment
and prosperity are the result.

"Is it because there are too many people on the earth
that the white man thinks himself excused in destroying
our race as fast as possible? But would not Wakanda be
a better judge of the number that the world He has formed
is capable of supporting? And how can the white man
judge whom it would please Him most to see destroyed?
It may be that the judgment of the stronger race is at
fault in this matter; that He loves the simple-hearted and
feeble children of the plains as much as he does those who
have power to build gigantic cities and fill them with huge

rivalries and hypocrisies; and if this be the case, where comes in the unquestionable right to destroy our race as being the one which by all means should perish?"

These thoughts, though not in any connected shape, passed through my mind as I rushed frantically along. They were present, at one moment, in a mass, revolving, and rolling, and boiling, and raging there as if they had entered into a special conspiracy to drive me wild. Then one of these thoughts would take complete possession of me, chaining me, however, with not the less rigor. Images of my lost Prairie Flower constantly floated before my heated fancy, and her last words, coupled with her sweet looks and winning ways, were ever present to my heart. Oh! she was so much to me—can I believe that she is gone? Shall I never again feel her soft breath upon my cheek? I began to think I had attained the dead Um-pan-nez-zhe's prophetic sight, and, gazing into the darkness before me, I seemed to read that the sweet Prairie Flower should never be mine again.

This mood alternated with one whose chief desire was revenge. Why should I tamely weep when I had more than strength sufficient to strike Scar Face, who had brought all this woe upon me, to the earth? Again and again I resolved, as I walked along, to kill him. But at such moments the solemn voice of Um-pan-nez-zhe came whispering on the night wind to me:

"Bear anything—bear to see thy wife torn from thy arms—but never kill the white man!"

And these words seemed the more solemn and sublime now that the wise man was dead. Had he been living I know I should have rushed back to the mansion of Gray Coat, sought out his infamous son, and killed him on the spot. But the noble Um-pan-nez-zhe is dead, and his words are as sacred as his memory.

Then at other moments I would think, " What if Prairie Flower should come back to me in a few days—could I love her as I had done?" At first I almost answered " No !" but when I thought how helpless and innocent she was I stopped, looked up into the stars which were now peeping from the clouds, and resolutely said " Yes!" I could picture her as she would come. Oh, how sad would be her beautiful face! how disgraced would she seem to herself! how timid she would be lest I should not receive her as of old! how I would open my arms to her, and how she would weep joyously and sadly as she fell into them! When I thought of this I exclaimed aloud in the night :

"Come, my bride! my Prairie Flower! Here is a heart that will never do thee dishonor! Here is a breast that will always be warm to thee, and where thou mayst ever ·find rest !"

Startled at the sound of my own voice, I hurried on faster than before. What was my surprise when I came suddenly and unexpectedly upon a rude fence of willow pales stretching directly across my path! In my heedless wanderings I had described a circle, and now discovered that I had reached the fence that enclosed the beautiful grove where stood the house of our agent. Something impelled me to enter the enclosure. The mansion that our money had built loomed up grimly in the darkness before me, its successive stories and rows of windows and high porches and corniced eaves presenting to my inexperienced mind the most complete image of all earthly magnificence and wealth. I approached the building from the side. All was dark about it; neither in door nor window did the least sign of life appear. I crouched low in the underbrush, some of which was still allowed to remain in the grove, and crept cautiously toward the house. What I hoped to obtain I could not tell distinctly even to

myself, yet I dimly felt that it would be a relief to be near
my bride although I had no power to render her assistance. So I lingered round the house. In the barns I
could hear the baying of the savage hounds that Gray
Coat kept to defend his premises and hunt down the
unyielding among our people; but I feared not their
cruel jaws; to die so near to her would have been an
inexpressible pleasure. Round and round the house I
crept, now imagining that a face was peering out from this
shutter or from that upon me, now fancying I heard a
smothered scream as of some one—my bride, perchance—
in deadly fright. I wondered which window hid my
Prairie Flower from her lover's sight, and I wept to think
what a short distance there was between her falling tears
and mine.

By and by I grew bolder and came very near the house,
with the dim hope that at some corner I should hear her
whisper:

"O Wolf Killer! Wolf Killer! save me! Hold wide-
spread your arms and I will spring into them as I have
often done, as a child, from some fallen log or crumbling
boulder. Here I am! Save me! Save me!"

But no such voice I heard. The first gray streaks of
the coming day—that was to have been my wedding-day
—now began to appear in the east. The twitter of the
early birds resounded through the grove. I heard a shutter open in a distant part of the house. Certain I was
that soon I should be apprehended for prowling around
the premises of the agent, but even to save my bones from
the jaws of the blood-hounds I could not flee. Oh! another
moment might place my bride in my arms. Or she might
in the *next* minute need me so much—and what if I were
not here? For a time I seriously thought of confronting
the agent and demanding my bride, but I knew such a

course would be of no avail. Oh what should I do! what should I· do!

While I was gazing thus hopelessly at the great blank walls I felt a touch upon my arm, and turning I met the gaze of little Swallow. She beckoned me to follow her, which I was only too glad to do, as she seemed to promise some hope.

CHAPTER XV.

BLOOD-HOUNDS AND LUNACY.

IT was well that the little maiden had come for me, for I should never have been able alone to find my way out of the labyrinth of walks and drives, flower beds and garden plots, terraced lawns and shady avenues, with which the agent had adorned his luxuriant home, even if I had found in my heart the desire to leave my post of observation and make the attempt. But Swallow seemed to know so well what paths to take and what turns to make, that I followed her quite assured that she would lead me out into the prairie again, where I should be perfectly at home; but what was far more encouraging, her familiarity with the surroundings of the agent's house, together with a certain importance with which she set each little foot upon the ground, seemed to promise that she had some revelation to make in regard to Prairie Flower.

"Swallow, dear Swallow!" I said after we had walked some little distance, "what tidings of my bride? Will you lead me to her?"

"Hush!" she replied sharply; "do you not fear the hounds?"

As she spoke, their fierce baying broke out afresh, and this time I noticed with terror that the sound seemed much louder, as if the animals were nearer to us than before.

" But—" I began.

" Hush!" she said.

Down along the fringes of a spruce hedge—around a patch of sweet corn—up a narrow path in which the weeds were growing thick—crouching a moment under this vine-covered arbor while the milkman passes us and makes his way toward the house. The hounds were baying fiercely.

"Curses on the brutes! Shut up!" the milkman said. "They must smell Indian blood. Shut up, I say!"

Hurrying on again—along the fence of an enclosed pasture—past the stables, in which the horses are just noisily rising from their night's sleep, striking their hoofs against the sides of the stalls—past the very kennels of the hounds, which dash against their chains and foam upon us madly—down through the corn-lands, breathing more freely now—and at last out upon the glorious, glorious prairie—so we pursued our way.

"Swallow, tell me of my bride!"

"Hush! hush! On! on! The moment the hounds are loosed they will be upon our track. We must reach the little stream, and cross it and gain the valleys beyond, before we shall be safe. Should Gray Coat discover that you have been wandering like the wolf about his dwellings in the night, he would assume thy name—he would be the Wolf Killer's killer."

On and on—along this dry creek bed—past these blooming roses, such as were on this very day to adorn my bride—into this thicket to pant a moment and listen—scrambling down this bank and up upon the other side —through this patch of brambles which tear garments and flesh—pacing this level spot, unthinking of the radiant daisies crushed by our footsteps—hush! hush! away! away!

"Take up this pine branch and carry it with us," Swallow said as we passed one that had been rent from

the old tree in some great storm and swept alongside our
path. "We shall need it."

Away! away! the morning has fully dawned—yonder
is the sun—see how the dew-drops sparkle in its light—
not brighter they than my little bride's eyes—ah! not
more moist than her tears—away! away! the chains have
fallen from the hounds' necks. Hark! was not that a
deep bay?—and there is another!—away! away! has not
Gray Coat sworn that if any cursed red devils are found
stealing his vegetables or prowling around his chicken
coops, they shall die?—away! away!

There the hounds come. Hear their fierce bark; see,
even from this distance, their red jaws; mark the fearful
leaps they take, fully ten of our steps in one. Hasten,
little Swallow!—hasten, brave, sad Wolf Killer! See the
milkman, and the cowboy, and the gardener urge them
on—hear how they shout and laugh—rare sport, rare
sport—human game!—far better than antelope or grouse
—far better, ha! ha!

But they do not see *us*, we are hidden by this thicket.
No conscience in those cruel hearts; no feeling in those
mangling jaws; no law that all the high legislators, and
noble senators, and honorable Great Father, and govern-
ing people can grant to us now. Hasten! hasten! the
Horsetail or death—the Horsetail or death!

For the little stream we are straining to gain is called
by our people "The Horsetail," because of its foaming fine
white spray.

Now the baying is louder, fiercer, nearer, and the
laughter is pleasanter—ha! ha! noble statesmen, you
are joining in the chase. O dignified Secretaries of the
Interior! O pompous members of the Cabinet! I see your
eyes gleaming over yonder hill watching the lark. Come
on, patriotic debaters—on! boasters of "equal laws."

Ha! ha! how the learned editors scramble and jostle and stride — ha! ha! how the intelligent and truthful reporters drop pencil and note-book and join the hunt! Noble game, this! Only country on all the face of the earth in which you can have such sport: can't have it in Russia, the serfs are free; can't have it in England or Canada, the Indians enjoy the protection of law; can't have it even in the slave-hunting South of this same free America, for the blacks are at least allowed to *call* themselves citizens— slaves no longer. But an Indian may have stolen a potato or a turnip, which no white man ever does: therefore the Indian can't be civilized. Hunt him! kill him! Ha! ha!

Now we've gained the bank of the Horsetail.

"Quick!" panted Swallow; "tread with me upon the pine bough you have brought; place your moccasins beside mine upon it; bind bunches of the pine-fringe on your bare feet; set the bough adrift. So! Now for the other side!"

Oh! the pine fringes pierce our feet like needles; the current of the stream is fierce; the quicksands lurk slyly on every hand; the slippery rocks try to cast us into the waters. We gain the other bank; we press on through the long grass, crouching low that we may not be seen; moccasins of pine-fringe are not for swift racing, but they leave no trail-scent behind. On! on! on! until the baying of the baffled hounds and the curses of the disappointed cowboy and milkman die away in the distance, and we reach the shady valleys we had been longing for. Under a thicket of sumac we cast ourselves, panting, gasping. Our hearts throb wildly and our temples beat and rage. The lips of little Swallow are livid with fear and exertion; my own eyes I can feel bursting from their sockets; we are panting, gasping—gasping, panting—but oh! safe, safe, safe!

And I think of little Prairie Flower, sweet little bride of mine, pursued and hunted down by the hounds of lust and filthiness whose scent is unerring and devilish. Oh, in all the plains of human law, in all the fields of human charity, in all the green forests of pity for the feeble, is there not one little pine bough of mercy that can be thrown to her?

"What took thee to the agent's mansion?" Swallow demanded, breaking suddenly the flow of my thoughts.

"What wonder that I should find myself, without knowing how or why, near the spot where my bride is imprisoned? The mocking-bird hovers around the wicker basket where the Indian boy coops up her young, hoping to comfort if she may not rescue."

"But thou wert in the greatest danger, from which little Swallow—always remember it *was* little Swallow!—scarce rescued thee."

"Remember! Dear little Swallow, if I were not wedded in love to my Prairie Flower, I should hope to show my gratitude by shielding thee, as my wife, from every danger in the future."

I did not think how galling such words must have been to her.

Then I added, sadly musing to myself:

"Oh! I have shielded my true bride in a brave manner indeed!"

Meanwhile the breast of little Swallow was heaving as if some great storm raged within. Her eyes gleamed with some strange passion, her cheeks were hot with some great resolve; yet her teeth and lips were tightly set together as if she strove agonizingly with herself to hide her emotion. Her hands were clenched and she half started up upon her feet, but reconsidering her resolution she sank upon the ground again. Even in my own woe I noticed these singular evidences of some great struggle going on in her heart. I half thought her insane for a moment, but I did not conjecture the real cause of her agitation. I did not know it until many weary months thereafter.

"Listen to me, Wolf Killer," she said, when at length she had forced herself into a severe calmness. "Your bride is not imprisoned. She might return to you at any moment—if she would."

"Is she really the waiting-maid of Gray Coat's wife?" I asked, not at first catching her terrible meaning. "Then is she perhaps safe after all! O Wakanda! I thank thee!"

"I mean not that," Swallow answered fiercely. "She is not in a woman's service, but a man's; yet she might return to thee if she would."

"False! false! false!" I cried, springing up. "Little Swallow, I have honored and even loved thee, but if thou tellest me this horrible lie I will hate thee—I will kill thee! There is no law to prevent my killing an Indian!"

"But if it be *true*, will you love me still—love me more than before?"

This was said with the most piteous expression of pleading on the sweet upturned face of the girl.

"But it cannot be true!" I exclaimed. "If Prairie Flower were free she would come to me swifter than you ever saw wild dove wing herself back to her young. She must be imprisoned by the villain Scar Face!"

The pleading look faded out of Swallow's face, and eager hatred took its place. I had always considered the girl a child, as indeed she was in years, and I had considered her love for me as a childish passion which would soon pass away; but now before my very eyes she seemed to live several years in as many moments and to become a woman, with a woman's stern hatred when her love is refused. She straightened herself up, her lips trembling with anger, her eyes sparkling with it, her breast heaving with it, her cheeks as red with it as the sumac berries above her were red with ripeness, and shaking her tapering forefinger at me, she exclaimed:

"Thou hast treasured a love that was not thine; thou hast spurned a love that was. Shá-ta-ga-dtá-tha, thou knowest that at one time I was waiting-maid to the wife of Gray Coat. It was then that I learned the paths through which to-day I have led thee to safety. It was then that I became aware of the base nature of Scar Face, and when I knew that he was casting his eyes upon thy Prairie Flower, at first I shuddered, but at last I exulted. Yes, I exulted! For thou knowest little of an Indian woman's heart if thou hast not weighed the dark deeds she will do and the horrible thoughts she will entertain when stung by jealousy. I saw thee devoted in thought and deed to her. I hoped that if she were removed thou wouldst learn to love little Swallow. So I consented to carry messages from Scar Face to the bride, and she at first received them spurningly, then timidly, and at last gladly."

"Thou liest!" I exclaimed through my clenched teeth.

"He promised to take her to be his wife and to make a grand lady of her. This promise she joyously believed. When the moment had come for them to escape together, the Wolf Killer being away in search of roses—ha! ha!— she feigned the greatest sorrow, so as not to break the heart of her father, the wise Um-pan-nez-zhe."

"She has broken it!" I bitterly exclaimed.

"What! is he dead?"

"He is dead!"

I did not at the moment particularly notice the strange effect this announcement made upon little Swallow, who had not returned to our village since the previous evening and consequently did not know of the wise man's death.

But in after years I recalled the expression, half remorseful, half frightened, that passed over her face; and remembered how for some moments she seemed unable to resume her narrative. O Swallow! thou wast too young and too really good at heart to be a great deceiver, even though thy passion was great; but thou didst cruelly and bitterly succeed upon me, stunned by my own sad thoughts, that day!

"When they had gone," at length she resumed, "I waited to see if thine eyes would be tender toward me, and when they were not I dashed after the runaways, hoping to frighten them into returning by threatening to tell the plot to thee. I overtook them in the very arbor where we crouched hiding from the milkman this morning, and there I confronted them."

"O Wakanda!" I exclaimed, interrupting the narrator, whom I strangely, foolishly believed. "Spare me, Swallow! spare me!"

The little maiden regarded me anxiously for a moment, as if to see what impression her words made upon me, and then continued:

"When I demanded that they should return they laughed aloud, and your '*own* little Prairie Flower' said: 'Go and tell Wolf Killer what you have seen. Tell him that I love Scar Face and that the morrow shall indeed be my wedding-day. But I shall be united to a noble white man, and shall be a grand lady instead of an Indian's squaw.' This she said, and with another laugh they passed on. I lingered round the grand mansion the whole night, hoping that she might repent and come out to me when she knew the real character of Scar Face. That she did not repent thou thyself knowest; and while lingering to succor her I came upon her unhappy lover, and had the bliss of rescuing him from a fierce and bloody death."

"Swallow!" I cried, grasping her hand with a passionate strength that must have made it ache, "wilt thou swear before the great Wakanda that thy story is true, and that these were Prairie Flower's words?"

"I—I—but why should I swear it? If I had told thee a falsehood would I not be willing to twice perjure my soul to uphold it? Take my word, or go on in thy ridiculous deception, and when thy bride comes back to thee accept her as she is!"

"I believe thee!" I moaned. "Why hast thou cruelly saved me from the jaws of the blood-hounds to be devoured by this fierce agony?"

Let no one think me easily duped and worthy the scorn and contempt of all strong hearts, until he has placed himself in the physical and mental condition to which I had been reduced—until he has wandered though a whole despairing night upon the prairies, racked by every fear and persecuted by every doubt, and until he has measured that strange jealousy of which the loving heart is capable, which often assumes the garb of humility and prompts one to believe, on any evidence that seems at all adequate, that the object of his love loves him not. O my Wágh-ta! my bride! in my heart of hearts I knew even at that moment that I cruelly wronged thee, yet maddened by uncertainty, deep in the raging currents of despair, which are colder and fiercer than the swirls of the Missouri, because thou hadst been torn from my arms, I persuaded myself that I believed her—I thought I believed thee false.

Again the pleading, loving look came into the eyes of little Swallow, and turning a frightened, flushed, piteous face up to me, she said:

"Dost thou not yet love me? Wilt thou but whisper once in little Swallow's ear ' Khta-we-tha?' " *

* I love thee.

" Love thee ? No !" I cried, casting her from me. " How can I love one who confesses to have helped to rob me of my bride, and who exulted to know that she should be won from me ! I would kill thee, but that thou hast told me certainly of my—of Wágh—of *her !*" For the first time her name was bitter upon my lips, and I gnashed my teeth in rage upon her as if I were the wolf himself and not his killer. But ah! my little Swallow, my dear little Swallow, now, many years after that morning under the sumacs, I do love thee ; I understand the strange attempt thou didst make to win my heart ; I treasure thy memory next to the love of sweet Prairie Flower herself ; and if the angel into which thou hast been transformed could pass by me as I write, I would kiss and weep upon the hem of its garment !

When I had thus madly repelled the deluded little maiden, I turned from her and rushed wildly away.

Away ! away ! away ! wading rivers—stumbling through bramble patches—panting in shady nooks a moment— lapping water from the spring (oh ! that it could cool my soul !) tearing blindly through forests darkened by heavy night—starting at shadows, and yet hoping for danger and praying for death—afraid of the sound of my own footsteps, and yet heeding not the crackling of the underbrush as the black bear plunged through it. On ! on ! on ! unresting, tottering, scrambling, racing, despair-ing—vainly striving to get rid of myself by fleeing from place to place ; pausing upon beetling rocks that over-looked the shining, surging river, and trying passionately and with tears to cast myself off, but held back by some tormenting power. On ! on ! on ! the days chase the nights, and the nights chase the days, and both chase me —the howling hours hard at my heels—dreams, phantoms, memories, shadows, noises, fears, join in one yelling pack and between all horrid barks and bays cry, "We'll have him down! we'll have him down!" What I thought and fancied only Wakanda will ever know. The only rest I had was when a storm was raging. Only in the contortions of wrestling clouds, and the thundering stampede of the buffaloes of the air, and the flashing of the lightning—which is so vivid itself that no likeness can be found for it —only in such turbulent commotions could I find any companionship. I would stand on some little ant-mound or tree-stump in the prairie, and fold my arms when the rain began to fall, and smile when the lightning played around my head, and the fierce voices of the storm roared and laughed at me; and when the wind would come to batter me from my perch, I would brace myself against it and sneer in its teeth; and when the storm was full and wildest I would open my arms to take rain and lightning and thunder and tempest into them and greet them as my brothers.

When the storm began to fail I sadly watched it depart as if it were the one great comfort of my life. And when it was gone and.the sky became clear, all my passion and fear and misery came back upon me a hundred times fiercer than before, and leaving my blessings upon the stump or ant-hill where I had enjoyed one little moment of repose, I would start my pained, bleeding feet upon my hopeless, aimless journey. Through the hissing wet grass—over the tree-trunks hot yet with the lightning stroke that felled them to the earth—through the swollen muddy creeks, from which the very frogs spring up with the swiftness of deers to join the chase—away! away! away!

What years I lived in those few nights and days! What .agonies I suffered! I hated the day for its brightness and the night that it was not gloomier, but I hated the day more than the night, and grew so much in my detestation of it that soon I had to lie under thick bushes all the hours that the sun shone, and cover my head with dirt to keep the light from driving me mad.

I though always of my Wágh-ta—my poor, deluded little bride. My years had had but one passion, but one happiness—my love for her; and now that she had left me I was more deeply despairing than perhaps I should have been had not my life been so retired and simple. I would catch myself, as I rushed along, thinking of her sweet ways and soft breath and wonderful eyes. Then I would fiercely try to forget them. And I would nerve my poor, frantic brain to see if I really did believe what Swallow had said. *Was* Wágh-ta false, or had she been torn away against her will? Was I Wolf Killer at all? Was this agony real, or did I but dream? And I would dash headlong into a bunch of wild blackberry bushes to awaken me.

Whither I went I know not. I paid but little attention to the scenery, yet even in my frenzy certain vivid pictures of the country I passed through fixed themselves in my memory, as the images of a horrible dream remain in the mind after the day has come. I know that the country I traversed became more broken day by day; the settlements of white men, by which I would creep fearful and breathless at night, became fewer and fewer; the prairies gave place to the hills and the hills to the mountains. The great gray rocks under which I would now cast myself when utterly fatigued were seamed and ridged with purple and scarlet, knotted and twisted into all fantastic shapes, and scarred and chiseled by the cold storms which dashed daily over them. These scenes reminded me painfully, and yet with a tantalizing pleasure, of the story the wise Um-pan-nez-zhe had told us of his boyhood's home; and by consequence they brought before me—as everything I looked upon seemed sworn to do—the face of my poor bride.

These wild scenes acted upon my mind just as the storm did—they awed me into calmness, and in their rugged grandeur I felt that I had sympathy and brotherhood. I thought much of what Standing Elk had suffered in just such scenes, and I grew strong in the fancied presence of his example. I blessed him again and again for what he had been to me, and I blessed Wakanda that the wise man had died unconscious of the shame that rested upon him. I had no curses in my heart to heap upon Scar Face even, although I moaned day and night, "Wá-gha! Wá-gha!* How dreadful is thy power! How helpless is our unhappy race in thy grasp! No law, no hope! Wá-gha! Wá-gha!"

Wandering aimlessly among these great hills I came one evening upon a little lake, whose waters were so blue and beautiful that it seemed as if a part of the deep sky had fallen down and been caught and retained within the rocky fingers of the banks. My mind was now so calm that I could enter, with something of my former enjoyment, into a contemplation of serene beauty, and so I sat down upon a mossy boulder to survey the scene at my leisure. On one side of the lake the mountains rose rugged and precipitous from the very edge of the waters, while on the other side there was a little stretch of level sod which gradually dimpled into hills and broke into towering crags. The lake itself was so clear that I could see the bright-finned trout sporting unmolested in the deep places, idling under rock-shadows, or proudly exhibiting their crimson spots to their mates. The shadows of the hills seemed to float upon the surface of the waters

* "White man! White man!"

as if they feared to pollute the pure depths. Near the
farther bank a flock of wild ducks fed among the ripples,
and now and again expanded their bright wings in the
sunlight. The distant murmur of irrepressible brooks
hasting toward the lake mingled tauntingly with the
hoarse growl of the larger stream that was forced to leave
that quiet resting place and begin its weary journey
through the haunts of men. The fern stalks along the
banks waved their fronds sleepily; the fringy mosses
rose and fell upon the miniature tides that put into the
tiny bays between the pebbles, and the rows of white
flowers seemed like a troop of fairy antelopes that had
come down to the water's edge to drink, and, charmed by
the loveliness, had neglected to depart.

It was all so beautiful and restful that for the first time
since my sad loss I could think it all calmly over. How
strange it seemed that such heartless passions and fierce
agonies could be in a world where the lakes were so still
and the flowers so lovely. Were not these holy scenes
mingled with the unholy for the purpose of pointing the
sick heart to the better world beyond? I leaned my hollow cheek upon my thin hand and brooded for an hour
over this thought. The fire of my passion seemed to
have burned out, and it was with a strange feeling of relief that I found I could not awaken a single bitter thought,
although I summoned before my mind all the persons by
whom I had been wronged. I could even speak the name
of my lost bride, and when I found that it was not bitter
upon my lips I repeated it over and over—" Wágh-ta!
Wágh-ta!" And speaking that sweet name I fell into a
gentle sleep.

When I awoke it was high noon of the next day, and
the first object that caught my sight was a white man sitting upon the root of a tree scarce five feet from me. His

head was down between his knees; with his hands he was
tugging at his curly black hair; his clothes were rent and
cut as if his journey had been as long as mine; streaks of
hardened blood scarred his hands and naked feet and haggard face; and his wild eyes were glaring upon me in a
look of the most terrible longing and desire. At first I
half suspected that this was one of the horrible creatures
which had been pushing their leering faces into my dreams
and dogging me with phantom feet, but all doubt of his
real existence vanished when the man with foaming lips
hissed these words:

"Ha, ha! I have found you—horrible, ungainly, devilish
reptile that have been riding on my back all these years—
I have found you! I was watching you all the long night,
and while the morning came, and didn't I draw a rattlesnake over your lips to awaken you, and you kissed it as
if it were your bride? Ha! ha! You've been down to
Boston, have you? And did you see the treasurer of the
'Non-Interference Missionary Band of Hope'? No! you
didn't, didn't, didn't—he's here; your favored eyes behold
him. But I'll have your blood—it shall trickle through
these fingers—you are mine, mine, mine!"

Unable to stand his horrible jargon any longer, I began
to rise from the ground, when, with a piercing scream,
which was half a laugh as well, the bloody creature sprang
upon me with the strength of ten buffaloes and hurled me
back to the earth, I clutched him with my arms, and we
tugged, twisted, wrestled, now one having the advantage,
and now the other, until, with a scream wilder and shriller
than the largest eagle could have made, he caught me in
his arms as if I had been a babe, and plunged with me into
the lake.

CHAPTER XVI.

LITTLE SWALLOW TAKES THE TRAIL.

WE must now return to little Swallow, so that you may have the whole story in your mind as we pass along. Many weary months had passed before I fully knew what thoughts throbbed through her busy mind under the sumacs that morning, and what brave deeds she performed to help and save my bride; but as I do know them while I write, it will be better for you to learn them now.

When I turned from Swallow and rushed so wildly away she followed me with her eyes, in which the piteous pleading was mixed with a look of deep disappointment. She had played a desperate game, and now that she had so plainly failed to gain her object, she saw how foolish and wicked the whole attempt had been. Mournfully she called upon me to return, extending her arms toward the path I had taken, and weeping hot tears of repentance; but either I did not hear her voice or I would not obey. Standing for a few moments in this attitude of guilty despair, she at length sank down upon the ground and covered her head with her blanket.

"Woe! woe! woe!" she moaned, rocking herself from side to side; "would that long since I had sung my Dta-wá-e!* Would that I were dead! How could I so wrong thee, Wágh-ta! how could I so blast thy life, my noble, generous Shá-ta-ga-dtá-tha! Why did my lips speak such falsehoods when my heart loved so well? And why

* Death song.

did the brave Wolf Killer mention the name of the dead
Um-pan-nez-zhe? O wise man! wise man! How poorly I
have kept thy teachings, how shamefully I have forgotten
the sacred reverence in which thou art by all my people
held! And thou art dead too! Upon thy pale lips and
stiffened cheeks did I dare to heap falsehoods? What is
life to me now? Without the love of Wolf Killer and
with this great shame resting upon my heart, it were far
better to die." As she thus mourned she saw at her very
feet a poisonous root, one bite of which would tear soul
from body; and she instantly resolved thus to die. Then,
as is our custom in the face of death, she broke out into
her death song: "Farewell, O glorious, glorious sun! I
look forth upon thee even from my agony and remorse;
I look upon thee for the last time. Farewell, O swelling
prairies and shining river and blooming flowers! ye are
all so far purer and better than poor, unhappy Swallow,
that I leave you unstained in your loveliness! Now I am—
but am I, ready? Shall I eat this root—this little root
that my hand so easily holds, and die? Let me think, O
my pounding heart! Would that be bravest and most
noble? What will Wakanda say to me when I appear
before him? How will the wise Um-pan-nez-zhe weep for
me! Nay! nay! I will live. 'Tis cowardly to take one's
own life when so much ought to be done. I will face the
injury I have wrought and repair it if I may. Up! up!
I will hasten to Wágh-ta and save her from the cruel
clutches of the white man. O Wolf Killer! I have tried
two means of comforting thee, one by proffered love and
one by bitter falsehood. I will try another—I will save
thy bride. Love and hate have failed, unselfishness may
succeed !"

With these words she sprang up, and tearing the bandage
of pine-fringe from her bleeding feet, started upon her

noble mission. Jealousy had been conquered or forgotten in the fierce struggle she had had with remorse; and now her whole soul was absorbed in the desire to repair what her misguided love had wrought. And hers was a noble soul truly. She was one of those strong, self-reliant little bodies, who, having adopted a wise course of action, pursue it to the end. And if, as in the case of Swallow, such a strong nature is apt to fall into errors or even misdeeds, it is the quickest to see the fault and the wisest to undo it. She had a remarkable store of that womanly faculty which reveals, as if by inspiration, what is to be done and the right time for doing it; as indeed had been shown in our race with the bloodhounds that very morning. Blessings upon thee, little Swallow, as thou art crossing the Horsetail again with bare and bleeding feet, and retracing thy steps toward the beautiful mansion of the agent, searching for my love!

The wise little maiden presumed that Scar Face had poor Wágh-ta in some place of imprisonment which was not far from the mansion of his father, and yet outside of the building itself. She understood the singular desire of the young man that the good opinion his mother had of him should not be altered by any knowledge of his misdeeds, and therefore she argued that he would be very secret and watchful in his present scheme. She thus came to the conclusion that Scar Face would consume some time in the pretense of gaining Wágh-ta's real love by a hypocritical offer of his own, so that his shameful crime should not be talked of among the Indians, and thus reach his mother's ears. Thus she would have opportunity to find the prisoner and help her to escape. If worst came to worst, Swallow resolved to notify his mother of the whole transaction, and thus use her influence over her son to make him desist.

Revolving these thoughts in her mind, the self-reliant girl made her way toward Gray Coat's home. Her service with the wife of the agent had been so long and so recent, that all the employés knew her and allowed her to come and go as she pleased. Even the tan-eared bloodhounds opened their sleepy eyes for a moment, and then closed them again when she passed their kennel, as if they were satisfied that she had a right to tread upon the sacred ground they guarded.

As Swallow thus gained the garden on this eventful morning she met the milkman going toward the barn.

"Helloa! Swallow, is that you?" he said condescendingly. "Come back to visit us again? You came too late this time, my dear. We had some grand sport this morning chasing one of your worthless race."

"Did you catch him?" asked Swallow, and for the life of her she could not keep a sly twinkle out of her eye.

"No! Drat it all, we didn't!"

"Niver ye moind!" said the Irish gardener, who now came up, and resting on his spade joined in the conversation. "It's me op*ine*-ion that we'll have another whirl at 'em some of thim foin mornins. To think of the biggars crapin' around an honest man's house whin he's a slapin' away as paceful as a kitten! It's me op*ine*-ion that we ort to nip 'em in the bood, it is."

Little Swallow's blood was up, so turning her flashing eyes upon the foreigner she asked:

"And how long have *you* been in this land of liberty that you have learned to judge other people, in true American style, without a hearing?"

"Nigh onto a twelve mun', me leddy. And I'm purty well plazed wid all I see, 'cept that the abrigoinal savages ort to be anni-*high*-letted. It's me op*ine*-ion an honest man 'll niver get his rights till the rid divils are gone."

" And what are your rights, noble sir?"

" Hundred and sixty acres o' land all paid for, but now occupied by the Injins, and no sass from youngsters!"

" And what are *our* rights, noble sir?"

" You haint got none to spake of."

" Ha! ha!" said the milkman. " He! he!" said the cow-boy, who had pushed his speckled nose into the group.

Encouraged by this flattering reception of his eloquence the Irishman squared his elbows, tipped his hat upon the side of his head, and having spit once or twice upon the ground as if in deep thought, resumed the attack as follows:

" Look'ee, me gerrel. It's me op*ine*-ion ye've niver been to Ne-York harbor, hev ye? Well, in a prominint attichude in said harbor, there's goin' to be a jegantic statute of Liberty, holdin' in her moighty hand a torruch, out to sea, to loight me honest counthrymen to the broad shores of this land of the free and hum of the brave. And we're a comin', too. And you red-skins is a-goin'. And that's all there is about it."

The brave little maiden turned her brave look upon them all and answered:

" It seems very strange that while the most ignorant people of the world can come to this land, and claim and receive equality under her laws with her greatest states-men; the poor Indians, who have always lived in happi-ness and freedom on this very soil, are put under the meanest whim of the most evil man. The torch-light you tell of may welcome your countrymen; we do not com-plain of that. But I think some of its light might shine toward the red man, who owns the land that you are pushing him out of."

" Ha! ha!" said the milkman.

"Ho! ho!" said the gardener.

"He! he!" said the speckled-nosed cow-boy.

Then the three profound statesmen stepped aside and allowed the Indian girl to pass.*

Without heeding their sneers the brave Swallow made her way to the mansion of the agent, with the vague purpose of finding Scar Face and watching him until he should slip away to the prison of little Prairie Flower, whither she would follow him, and do what she could to defend or even rescue the captive. In the spacious reception-room of Gray Coat's residence she found the agent and his wife and son pleasantly conversing upon the events of the day. The lady, with whom she had always been a favorite, gave her a kind welcome; and little Swallow, taking a station behind her chair, prepared to profit by any hints that Scar Face might drop in the conversation as to the place in which Wágh-ta was concealed.

"Are you sure," the lady said, resuming their conversation, "that it was a thief whose track the dogs caught and followed this morning? Have you missed anything from the premises, or was anything disturbed?"

"What object, dear mother," Scar Face answered with the greatest reverence, "could any of the red heathen have prowling around our dwelling if it were not the hope of securing plunder? And why did he flee so swiftly from the hounds and plan so skillfully to escape, if he did not feel himself guilty?"

"But why, dear husband," the lady said, without seeming to notice the arguments of her son, "is it necessary to keep such cruel and unthinking instruments as these hounds with which to execute justice? They are just as

* The attentive reader will discover that this scene in the garden is simply a shorthand report of one of the recent debates in Congress (somewhat condensed).

likely to fall upon and strangle the innocent as the guilty, since you teach them to follow every Indian's trail. Why could not culprits, if there be such, be brought to punishment in some more equitable and humane way?"

"My wife," the smooth voice of the comfortable and hearty agent replied, "it would be very hard to find an Indian who is not in some manner and degree a culprit, so that the hounds can scarcely do any great amount of injustice, even though their jaws close upon red throats indiscriminately. Besides, in this wild country this is all the law we have."

"It is all the law *we* have," exclaimed Swallow from behind the chair, unable to keep silence any longer. "And let me tell you, Gray Coat, it makes all the difference in the world whether you are before or behind the bloodhounds when they are on a trail. If you could hear them after you just once, you might have a different opinion of the justice of this kind of 'law.'"

"Come, come!" exclaimed Scar Face sneeringly, "we have a legislator here."

"But, little Swallow," the agent replied, in his smooth tone, "since the Great Father has seen fit, in his wisdom, to deny you the protection of our national laws, is it not best to submit?"

"Our unhappy race, as a race, can but submit; but we as a tribe," said Swallow, with a heaving breast, "have one—and but one—hope of succor."

"What is that?" laughed Scar Face.

Turning her steady eyes upon the young man the maiden slowly replied: "It is in the kindness and grace of thy sweet mother's heart, which surely cannot see the innocent oppressed!"

With these words Swallow knelt at the lady's feet and hid her face in her garments. With a laugh which sadly professed to be careless the young man went out and up the broad stairs to his own room, and his father, with a hearty, comfortable step, passed into his office on the other side of the hall. When they had gone Swallow dared to look up, and she saw that the lady's eyes were full of tears.

"Is there need, then, of my interference to prevent thy simple-hearted race being wronged?" the lady asked.

"Thou shalt see, dear lady; thou shalt see!"

And without trusting herself to say more, lest in her excitement she should reveal the crime of Scar Face prematurely, Swallow rushed from the lady's presence. She was sure that the young man had meditated, and perhaps accomplished, a cruel purpose, and though she did not hesitate to reveal her suspicions to his mother on his account, or from any felt probability of their being ill-founded, she still wished to spare the lady until she discovered that her interference alone could save the unhappy Wágh-ta.

After this singular but eventful intervfew Swallow hastened to the quarters of the female servants below to inquire, as cautiously as possible, so as not to arouse a dangerous curiosity, if Wágh-ta had been brought to the mansion at all. Her suspicions were fully sustained and justified by the intelligence, obtained after the most careful questioning, that not one of all the servants had seen the missing girl upon the premises. In some secret prison the sweet Prairie Flower drooped, and there was nothing now for Swallow to do, as she thought, but to watch the only hall by which Scar Face could escape from his room, and when she saw him issue forth, follow him, and thus learn the whereabouts of the captive. Taking her station therefore at a window in the servants' quarters where she could command this whole passage with her eyes, she made herself as comfortable as possible for a watch that might, as she correctly surmised, last for hours.

While Swallow is thus watching I must recall one little incident in her life showing how firm of nerve and strong of purpose she was. One day, when she was a little girl, a troop of us had gone away upon the prairies in search of plovers' eggs. We boys having our moccasins and the girls their scarfs full of them, we sat down under a clump of bushes to rest and count our treasures. Little Swallow having been among the most active of us all was soon overcome with fatigue, and sank back upon the grass as if to sleep. When we had gone on with our sport for a few minutes, my attention was suddenly arrested by the horrified look upon the face of one of the other girls. She had clasped her hands as if in agony, her lips were trembling and pale; and her eyes, starting from their sockets, were turned upon Swallow. I followed the direction of her gaze, and saw the cause of her horror. Creeping across Swallow's tender bosom was a huge centipede, whose sting we all knew was a painful and instant death. Swallow, who was now wide-awake, saw her danger, and instantly comprehending that her only safety was in perfect silence and repose, she moved not a muscle, allowed not a nerve to tremble or a cord to tighten, while the horrible and deadly creature crept the full breadth of her bosom and across one beautiful arm, imprinting with every one of his hundred steps a burning, festering, though not a deadly, sting. This ordeal was the harder that we had seen but few of these creatures around our homes, and its sudden appearance, if not its terrible nature, must almost certainly have startled a less firm person into a movement or exclamation that would have been instant death. Of such sterling courage is an Indian maiden capable !

The long afternoon passed as Swallow sat patiently
at the servants' window, and the twilight began to hide
slyly among the trees, yet there were no signs of the
coming forth of Scar Face. The maiden watched until
her eyes ached so that she scarcely could see at all, and at
every sound which might by any possibility be a footfall
she started nervously, as she might have done had the
sudden wail of the panther issued from behind a neighboring rock.

When she had given up all hope of being successful in
her plan, her attention was arrested by the shuffling step
of some one approaching from the wild woods which
grew around the cultivated lawn before the house. A
narrow path ran through these woods, almost concealed
by the heavy overhanging underbrush and lower tree-
boughs. Swallow fixed her attention upon this path and
soon saw the leaves and brush waving, and then they
were parted, and a wrinkled faced, grizzly-haired, and
brow-bent woman stepped forth. She was apparently
very old. Her limbs trembled with feebleness as she
shuffled along, her cheeks were sunken and pale, and her
eyes, although strangely wild and bright, looked forth from
beneath brows which made the fierceness of her glance
the more appalling. As she walked along she mumbled
and cast a wild glance about her, as if she were engaged
in some hellish work of witchery. She was such a wretch
as in the simple legends of my people is supposed to sit,
naked and horrible, upon the rocky edge of some high
cliff, presiding, with a demon's glee, over the bursting of
the blizzard-hurricane, and laughing horridly so as to be
heard in the pauses of the tempest when the wind sweeps
a toil-made village into a moaning ruin. Swallow instinctively determined that this horrid hag had something
to do with the imprisonment of Wágh-ta, although she

could not imagine from what dark abode of sin such a foul creature could have arisen, since during her whole service with the agent's wife she had never seen this person about the house. As the woman opened the gate and came into the lawn, Swallow became strangely excited and could scarce restrain the fierce desire to burst from her hiding-place and grapple with the hideous accomplice of Scar Face, as she already regarded her. But knowing that the safety of Prairie Flower depended on her discretion and presence of mind, the little maiden wrapped her blanket more closely around her, and, still barefoot, stole cautiously forth. Hiding under the dusk shadow of a flowering bush until the woman had passed, she fell into her path and began the stealthy tracking of her steps. Swallow thought of the bloodhounds, of their pertinacity and endurance, and determined to be like them, as now she had taken the trail.

The woman shuffled toward the kitchen, and as she disappeared through the lighted doorway Swallow discovered that she carried a basket under her ragged shawl. Hastily running forward and concealing herself behind the kitchen porch, the little maiden overheard the following short conversation.

"What do you say you want?" asked the servant-girl.

"I want the pastries and the goodies and the vittels as the young master ordered ye to git for me," said a whining voice, which Swallow supposed was that of the hag.

"What do you want of such good things as these cakes and puddings and pies?" said the girl.

"Don't ye suppose I likes de*lick*acies as much as any un?"

"Where do you live, Aunt Mollie, anyway? Why do you skulk around in this way? Why not come and live

with the other white folks here—there are few enough
of us—and rest your bones on a decent bed, instead of
wandering around through the woods and sleeping at
night on the damp leaves—as they say you do? You
only have one life, and you ought to make the most of it."

"Ah, bah! Gim'me the vittels and the goodies as the
young master ordered, and mind yer own business—that's
what *I* say."

"But, Mollie, we girls all pity you. In the bottom of
your heart isn't there one bit of womanly feeling—one
wish to live as others do?"

"Come, come, gal! Does yer think there is no fun but
to live in grand houses? Does yer think the only thing
worth doin' is to tread carpits and sleep in beds? Oh, ye
don't know what Old Mollie lives fer—ye don't know that
a woman's love when turned bitter is stronger than when
it was sweet. Ye never saw the bright pictures in a
snake's eyes shinin' in the night—ye never tasted of the
honey there is in a groan. Oh, ye don't know what life
is, gal! I hate men, and I hate women, and when I kin
do an ill turn I do it. That's me!"

"You're too old a woman, Mollie—"

"Mind yer own business!"

After this amiable dialogue there was a silence of a few
moments as if the servant, unable to influence the woman
to a more sensible course of life, were filling her basket
with the provisions demanded. Then the woman came
forth, and glancing stealthily around, as if she feared pursuit, took her way toward the path through the woods in
which Swallow had first seen her. The little Indian
maiden followed with a soft step and a beating heart.

After crossing the lawn and entering the woods, Old
Mollie increased her gait as much as her feeble limbs
would permit; but the spry little Swallow had no diffi-

culty in keeping as near her as was prudent. The stars peeping silently down between the leaves afforded a holy light 'which seemed to the meditative maiden sadly polluted, in being used by Old Mollie for such unholy purposes; and so she determined to redeem back the bright radiance to Wakanda, by using it in designs of rescue, as well. Oh how neutral seem Wakanda's benefits, that man may stamp them with the image of angel or of devil, as he please! The path wound down into a thickly-wooded defile, and at right angles crossed the dry bed of a small stream. Up this pebbled water-course the old woman unhesitatingly took her way, evidently understanding every inch of the ground she trod upon. The darkness was heavier here, the stars being hidden, and the shrubs and branches of near trees overhung their way so that they were often compelled to creep in order to make any progress at all. Swallow found it necessary to keep within a few feet of the hag, lest she should lose her in the darkness. She was so near that she could hear the old woman's mumbling, which never for a moment ceased, and in the silence and gloom sounded weird and awful enough.

"Pretty thing to be a doin'," she grumbled, "packin' goodies to a squaw! And I has to pet her up, has I, and tell her how good and noble the young master is? Pretty thing that he couldn't find a white gal to love. Sort o' novelty in this doin's, I expect. H'm! To make me foller and lead around this away. Pretty thing this."

In little Swallow's heart was a strange mixture of grief and gladness when she heard these words—grief that one bearing a woman's shape could be so debased by sin as to cherish such an unwomanly hate and so cruel an ambition —gladness, because her words implied that the woman was leading the way to the prison of poor Wágh-ta. And

so indeed it proved, for they had not gone far before Old
Mollie stopped suddenly, seemed to listen intently for a
moment, and then producing a bunch of keys, placed one
in a lock the bolt of which flew back with a screech.
Swallow could see nothing, but she heard a door open and
the scraping of a pair of heavy shoes upon the step.
While she was puzzling her little brain, for the best course
of action to pursue, a light was suddenly struck within
the hut which the woman had evidently entered, and
streaming through the still open door, and the wide
cracks between the rude boards of which the building was
composed, shone brightly upon the maiden.   Fortunately
Old Mollie's back was turned toward the door, so she did
not discover the startled little spy ; and Swallow springing
lightly aside, hid in the bushes that were nearest at hand,
where she could see all that passed within the hut without
being seen herself.

A brief survey revealed that the building was simply
a shed which had been occupied by the workmen while
constructing the agent's mansion.   It had evidently been
removed by Scar Face to this hidden spot, that it might
be used to carry out his sinister plots.   The hut contained
a rude table, a bed, and a few chairs, upon one of which
sat the unhappy Wágh-ta in agony and tears.

"Come, honey," mumbled the old woman, as she placed
her basket upon the table. " Come, and jest taste the
goodies and the vittels as the good young master has sent
ye.   Dry yer eyes, honey, for many is the nice white gal as
would like to be in yer place, my larkie. Come now, and
don't pout no longer."

Swallow saw the wretched captive lift her head indig-
nantly as if to reply, but having no heart even for scorn
she let her chin fall upon her breast and betook herself to
the sad refuge of tears again.   Her beautiful hair fell over

her shoulders, and as she wept she might have been taken for that benign and lovely spirit who, in the simple legends of my people, is contrasted with the storm-witch, and who is represented as sitting among the highest tassels of the birch-tree, sifting her tears through raven tresses, when the evening shower weeps in the sky.

"Come, honey," Old Mollie mumbled as she took the eatables from the basket; "dry yer eyes, now; there's a larkie. Don't you know as the young master may catch you any moment in them ways! Oh! he's a noble, fine un, he is! Generous and—a—thoughtful, and—a—fine! (Curse it! Old Moll's mouth ain't for sweet words!) That's what he is. Come now, eat a slice of this cake. He put it into the basket for ye himself. Try a bit of this lamb, 'tain't no tenderer than his heart."

And the old wretch chuckled as if the wit in her last remark pleased her not a little. She evidently was priding herself that she was admirably fulfilling her young master's directions to present his character in the most favorable light.

"And see, honey," she went on, with a grin of satisfaction. "Here is some bread as is light as a feather, but no lighter than *his* sperrits. You knows who I mean by *his*. And here's a napkin. Now, don't that show him kind and—a—noble and—a—fine, to send a napkin? Come honey, fetch yer chair. The young master as is so fine wants ye to eat and be happy and well. Come now!".

Wágh-ta looked up through her tears, as if to make a scornful refusal, but seeing the door standing open and the old woman busy with her preparation of the rude meal, she seemed to catch a hope of escape. She made one or two nervous, irresolute steps from her chair, and then, with the frightened cry of a hounded fawn, sprang toward the door. But the old hag, although she shuffled awkwardly along a footpath, was quick enough when occasion demanded, and now, with a sudden bound, she caught the poor girl before she could reach the door, and flung her violently upon the floor.

"Escape, will ye? I rather guess not," the woman hissed.

"Foul wretch!" the unhappy Wágh-ta exclaimed, lifting her stunned head from the floor. "Is there no womanhood left in your hard heart? Do you love to see one of your own sex maltreated and outraged; and is your highest joy to help on such cruel work?"

"Come, honey; work yer jaws on some of this yere vittel, and not on empty air."

"Oh! for the love of Wakanda, for the love of thy mother, for the love of thy childhood memories of modesty and peace—oh! for the dear sakes of these, save me from this cruel man! Let me escape to my people, or kill me here at thy feet; but save me from this awful fate. Be a woman for a moment. Be merciful!"

"Come, honey, this yere won't swallow no longer. Lay to on your vittel or you won't get none, I can tell ye. After all that the fine young master has sent ye too—how ingrateful ye be! Now look at ye!"

The heart-broken maiden was truly a sight to look long upon. Crouching upon the bare planks where she had fallen, holding her bruised head in her hands, weeping for deep shame and despair, she was the picture of abject woe. Little Swallow, seeing her thus, forgot all her jealousy in an instant, was absorbed with a real and passionate pity, and could scarce restrain herself from dashing in upon the unfeeling jailer, to strike her to the earth. She was sure, in her rage, that she had strength to do it. But she could not tell how near the cruel Scar Face might be; he might be lurking on the other side of the hut, she thought, or in some nearer bunch of bushes; and thus she considered that patience would be more likely to succeed than rashness. And thinking thus she sank back into the shadow and strove to be calm.

"He, he!" chuckled Old Mollie at length; "if ye won't eat the goodies, I must lay to myself, for it would be a pity to waste such de*lick*acies."

And as she greedily munched the food spread before her, the woman never ceased to mumble to herself: "A sob wipes lots out. A earnest beg wipes more out. A ruined soul wipes most out. That's Old Mollie's mult'-plication tables—that is!"

Speedily the dainties disappeared down her hungry throat, and when the last crumb had gone, she arose and having cast one stealthy look upon poor Wágh-ta, who had now crept painfully back into the corner, carefully closed and secured the door. In another instant the light went out, and Swallow could hear something moving and rattling on the hard boards across the doorway, as if wretched Mollie were laying herself down to her amiable dreams. Oh! as I write can it be that among the white race there are hearts as cruel, and once innocent lives as seared and blasted, as those of Old Mollie were!

CHAPTER XVII.

THE PERIL OF PRAIRIE FLOWER.

AFTER waiting until every sound had subsided within the hut, and having allowed sufficient time for the inhuman jailer to become sound asleep, little Swallow stole cautiously forth from her hiding-place under the bushes. Her heart was too brave to be frightened by the sharp bark of the wolf prowling along the slopes of the defile in the depths of which the cabin stood; or by the melancholy wail of the wild-cat, sounding like the moaning and praying of an Indian child over its mother's grave at night. She feared far more the lawless hand of the white man. She trembled to think that Scar Face might be watching her as she had watched his accomplice, and she knew that he might with impunity shoot her down in that lonely solitude—indeed that he need not for a moment fear that he would be punished by the United States law, though all the judges and lawyers of the land should hear of it. She therefore picked her steps very cautiously to the corner of the hut where she knew the wretched Prairie Flower was crouching, and stooping down she listened intently to discover whether the captive were awake or not. Low sobs and struggling moans reached her ears from within the hut, mingled with the more distant heavy breathing of some one in deep sleep. Swallow thus knew that the maiden was awake and bewailed her sad lot, while the cruel woman slept; and therefore, placing her lips close to one of the cracks between the boards of which the hut was built, she whispered softly, as if it were only the night wind blowing:

"Wagh-ta wá-spa!" *

The sobs continued—the sweet night-wind bringing hope and tidings of love was not yet heard.

"Wágh-ta wá-spa!"

"Ka-gah?"† was the inquiring and anxious whisper that came from within the hut.

"It *is* a friend, sweet Prairie Flower. It is thy little Swallow, who knows of thy sorrows, and now having found thy place of sad confinement, but waits to save thee."

"O sweet Swallow, what of my Wolf Killer—what of my brave, noble-hearted husband? Is he well? And my father, the wise Um-pan-nez-zhe? Mourn they for the wretched Wágh-ta?"

O poor little Swallow! How thy heart was rent by these questions! How the old love came up, and how the strange, strong jealousy tempted thee to try another falsehood, to put down thy rival and gain thy love! But how bravely thou didst crush down the tempter and cling to thy noble, unselfish purpose!

"When last I saw them, they mourned for thee," Swallow answered.

"And were they well?"

"When last I saw them, they were well."

Oh what a tempest of contending passions raged in the heart of little Swallow! Love for the absent Wolf Killer, determination to persevere in her pure purpose of saving his bride, the old jealousy and hatred of a rival, and the fear that if Wágh-ta should know of her father's death and her husband's insane flight, she would in utter despair take her own life, and then Wolf Killer would charge the deed upon her.

"But why came not Wolf Killer with thee to help in saving his bride?" whispered Wágh-ta.

---

* Gentle Prairie Flower.   † "Is it a friend?"

Again the old temptation came up in her heart, as the misty shadow of a demon rises out of the reedy swamp, and she almost spoke the words, "He is false!" which she well knew would end the happiness, and perchance the life, of the captive. How easy, the tempter said, now to gain all the love and joy for which thy soul panteth! Speak the sentence—the three little words— they may after all be true; speak them! Then Wolf Killer is thine!

She looked up into the midnight stars which had now swept into their places and were shining divinely down upon her. Shall she speak the falsehood; dare she, in the face of the stars? Is not this the very light which but now she was to redeem from unholy usages?

"Dear Swallow, are you there? Why did not Wolf Killer come with thee?"

"Did you speak, dear Wágh-ta? I was looking at the heavens. He could not come with me—he tried to, but the bloodhounds were set upon him."

"Oh, he is safe—tell me he is safe!"

"Yes, he is safe, but might not have been, had he come farther. I was well known to the hounds and the employés of the agent, and so could come without harm or suspicion. And Wágh-ta—he—he—loves you as ever."

The stars, as she glanced up now, shone brighter than she had ever seen them do before, and twinkled cheerily of all the honor there is in an honest conquest of self, and seemed to throw down golden wreaths of praise for her brave and truthful words. She had redeemed back their light to God.

"It is better thus—it is better thus," whispered Wágh-ta.

"Let him be safe, whatever befalls his unhappy bride. If he but loves me I am content."

" But, Wâgh-ta, did Scar Face use violence in bringing thee thither ?"

" Think you I came willingly ?"

" No ! no ! but did he use physical force ?"

" Threats against my noble father, whom he might have ordered to be shot, were the inducements he offered. He cruelly taunted me with the Indian's want of legal protection, and charged me, as I valued my father's life, to make no disturbance and occasion him no trouble. Still I had died in sight of our peaceful village, even though it had caused my father's death as well—for the wise man would have preferred that to shame—had I for a moment supposed that his promise to place me in his mother's service was a lie. The first I thought of any personal cruelty was when I was given suddenly into the clutches of Old Mollie, who dragged me hither."

" Hush ! Wâgh-ta," whispered Swallow from without, " I hear a man's footsteps coming up the dry bed of the stream."

" Alas ! it must be the cruel Scar Face. O Wakanda, spare thy child !"

" Here ! Wâgh-ta, I slip my hunting-knife to thee. Take it, and defend thyself. I go to thy Wolf Killer. We will come to save thee."

" Oh, tell him Wâgh-ta says ' Khta-wé-tha '* to him a thousand times—let him hear her say it in every evening wind that whispers, and every wave that sighs."

At that moment a heavy knock was heard upon the door of the hut, and the voice of Scar Face exclaimed :

" Here, Old Moll ! wake up, you lazy fossil, and let your young master in."

At the tones of his dreaded voice little Swallow sank

* " I love thee."

down lower into the shadow of the hut. On a moment's
reflection she changed her purpose of going in search of
Wolf Killer, rightly deciding that her presence might be
needed there, and that the mother of Scar Face would be
by far the best ally in case any help was necessary. She
therefore found a place where she could hear all that was
said within, and she hoped that she could also see what
took place when the lamp was lit.

"Comin', master—comin'," said Old Mollie, as she
scrambled to her feet. "Who'd suppose my noble; fine
young master would 'a come this time of night to see his—
Comin', master, comin'!"

The light was at length lit, the rude door flung open,
and Scar Face, much the worse for liquor, stalked heavily
into the room. He threw his hat down upon the table,
planted himself upon a chair directly in front of the corner where poor Prairie Flower still crouched, and gazed
insolently into her beautiful face. The wretched girl,
presuming that her only safety lay in as haughty a de-
meanor as she was able to summon to her aid, now arose
with the greatest dignity, and folding her arms upon her
bosom with that queenly grace and nobility that are
natural to a true woman in every sphere, gazed unawed
upon the leering face of her drunken captor. It was the
mystic strength of purity and truth matching itself against
the power of infamy and lust. In such a contest the
feeble are strong and the mighty become weak. Scar
Face felt instinctively that between him and the fair
Wágh-ta there rose an invisible wall which he could no
more break over than if it were of leaping fire. Still he
hoped that he had one weapon in his possession which he
had but to wave over that wall and it would fall in cold
ruins upon the earth.

The fox of our prairie hills has a passion for the human

face. Often have the mothers of my people found the animal crouched upon the ground before their babes that were sleeping, swinging in the lower tree-boughs. The wild eyes gleamed passionately upon the little quiet hands and nodding heads; the lips of mock fierceness were parted, trembling with some strange desire ; and the nostrils moved and sniffed as if the sweetness of the child's breath were fascinating odor to them. The animal, at such times rooted to the spot as if by some most mysterious passion, could only with the greatest difficulty be driven away, and sometimes even would be content to die rather than forego the strange pleasure it enjoyed. It was with some such fascinated look that the man gazed upon my tearful but haughty Wâgh-ta.

"Well, my dearie," he at length exclaimed, endeavoring to assume some dignity, "has Old Moll informed you of my sincere and fervent love for you? Has she told you that I desire to make you my lawful wife? The noble white brant will ally himself with the little red thrush, There's a sentiment for you, Moll," he added, aside, to that worthy, "that would do honor to one of the cussed red orators, hey?"

"That it would, young master, that it would. As I knows anythin', that it would!" mumbled the literary critic appealed to.

"And I want to know, dearie," continued Scar Face, "whether you are sensible enough to become my wife willingly, or shall I be forced to execute the intimations I have made as to the life of the wise Um-pan-nez-zhe?"

Ah! here was the weapon which was to beat down the wall, and place my lovely bride in the brute's possession!

"Scar Face," exclaimed Prairie Flower, with all the prairie-fire angry heat blazing in her eye, "I despise thee, as thou well knowest, and I defy thee to do what thou darest.

In spite of all thy plotting and all the cunning of thy villainous assistant there, I have seen one of my people who will do all that mortal can to save me from thy cruelty or to punish thee by the white man's law if any harm is done me or my aged father!"

"Ha! ha!" laughed the man, "the white man's law! Have I not been telling you that that law takes no notice of the redskins? The Indian has never even been recognized as a person by our law. The white man's law, indeed! Do you not know that the red devils have often appealed to it and never for a moment been heard?"

My poor Wágh-ta knew this only too well, but in her despair had piteously appealed to the law, vainly hoping that her persecutor might not recognize how useless the appeal would be.

"Don't you remember the shooting of White Feather?" sneeringly continued Scar Face, evidently relishing the hopelessness his words were forcing upon the maiden's heart. "I will tell you about it, if you forget. Two chums of mine were riding toward the reservation, to make me a visit, and met the young imp you called White Feather. Do you remember now, hey? One of the white men bantered the other to shoot this specimen of your filthy race, and a revolver ball was sent crashing cleanly through the Indian's body. Do you remember all this? Ah! I see you do. And you know how your people sent a delegation to D—— to have the young men punished by the white man's law that you speak of. Were they punished? Ha, ha! The constable could not even arrest them, although he saw them almost every day. They spent a happy summer with me, and returned peacefully home." *

Poor Wágh-ta knew too well that his words were true,

* An actual occurrence.

and her head fell down upon her breast in hopeless fear—
not for what the villain before her could make her suffer,
but for the dreadful fate and infamy he could bring upon
her father's head.

"But I will not argue with such as you," exclaimed Scar
Face angrily, "and I have thoughtlessly said enough to
show you that I have no real love for a vile Indian. You
know my purpose. Submit, or by all the powers in hell
or heaven, your father shall die ignobly and painfully.
Yes, now I think of it, I will practice upon him some of
the tortures that your hellish race have inflicted upon the
whites."

"The noble Um-pan-nez-zhe," exclaimed Wagh-ta,
proudly lifting up her head, "can die without a groan.
He dies gladly to save his daughter from the taint of
shame."

"It shall not save you," fiercely returned the man.
"Already I have the half-breeds of the tribe, whom you
know to be in my employ, informed of the part they are
to play in my little drama. They will spread a more
damning report of your shame than could ever otherwise
be concocted. Submit, or your father dies, and dies of
shame and sorrow for his daughter's ruin."

With these words the man sprang up and shook his fist
savagely at the wretched girl, who, overwhelmed by the
accumulation of villanies and calamities, to which in our
simple homes she had been so unused, crouched down in
the corner, hid her face in her woven shawl, and sobbed
aloud.

"Submit!"

As he spoke the word a little figure stole in at the open
door, sprang into the space between the villain and his
intended victim, and lifting her hand in an attitude of
grace and dignity, said :

"Scar Face, thy devilish purposes are by the great Wakanda defeated! Wágh-ta, thy father is already dead!"

It was the voice of Swallow, who, fearing that the infamous scheme of Scar Face might succeed, had rushed into the room determined to rescue Wágh-ta by the revelation which she had previously in tenderness withheld. When, however, she had spoken these words, she darted past Scar Face and Old Mollie, who sought to intercept her, and was instantly lost in the darkness without.

At this dreadful revelation, made as by the sudden springing of a kind spirit out of heaven, Wágh-ta dried her tears with all an Indian maiden's fortitude, and rising caught from her bosom the hunting-knife that had been given her, and said:

"Wretch, there remains no harm that now thou canst do. Come but a step nearer, and I drive this knife into my heart. Thou sneerest! I know that would be but slight punishment to thee, but it would save the daughter of the dead Um-pan-nez-zhe from shame. O E-thá-di!* E-thá-di! thou didst call thy child a flower! Alas! the bloom of her youth is blighted before it is full-spread. Thou didst teach her many wise things and many cunning works; but now there remainest only the chance to use what thou didst show her of the blade's keen point! And thou art dead, my noble, wise father! How the stars must bend and weep above thy grave! Thy Wágh-ta weeps with them, O E-thá-di! E-thá-di!"

I can fancy how my beautiful, heart-broken bride looked as she spoke these weeping words. Her attitude, always full of grace, must now have been such as the bright spirit of the evening sunset assumes when she waves back

* "Father! Father!"

the dark clouds that seek to spring above the horizon to tarnish her loveliness. Her flushed cheeks and scornful eyes, turned full upon her tormentor, must have awed him into conviction that her threat of taking her own life was not an empty one. The heaving of her bosom must have shown the fierce tempest of anguish that raged within, and the knife gleaming over it must have revealed how gladly that brave spirit, rather than be defiled, would leap away through a dagger-wound into Wakanda's arms. Oh! I have loved her from our childhood, and in my fancy of her as she thus bravely stood before the evil man, I love her a thousand-fold the more.

The white man had often witnessed the calm courage of my people, and knew that the maiden would not hesitate a moment to plunge the knife into her heart if he gave her but that one hope of safety. Awed by Wágh-ta's queenly attitude, and half-stupefied with drink, he sank into a chair as if unable to determine what course to pursue. He seemed unwilling to press the maiden to suicide, but whether he was influenced by any lingering tenderness or nobility of heart, or merely by the selfishness of evil passion to preserve its object, I know not. For a long time he sat regarding her, his lips now and again parting as if he would speak, and then closing without uttering a sound, his expression of face being a singular mixture of dread, admiration, and wonder.

The effect of my poor bride's attitude was not less singular and marked upon the debased mind of Old Mollie. Here was a defiance of the power of man which coincided with her own ideas; and although the pleading of a broken heart could not stir her compassion, such an exhibition of spirit as this excited her regard. There had been some dark transactions in the poor woman's history which had imbittered her against the whole race of man, and when

he could be spited or agonized by the ruin of one even of
her own sex she scrupled not to lend her aid to the accom-
plishment of the sinister purpose. Yet when her lingering admiration of dignity and purity was appealed to from
the side of her hatred of man, as she imagined it to be in
this case, it was still capable of asserting a semblance of
its rightful power.

"This is gran'! this is gran'!" she mumbled. "Old
Moll ain't so far lost as she can't understan' what is gran'
and what isn't. The young master ain't no match for her,
nor Old Moll ain't neither. Them arms—them eyes!
Blest if she don't pay up heaps of Old Moll's score against
the whole pack o' men by jest a-standin' there. I almost
would save her yet because she does it. I almost would
help her agin' the young master yet."

It was singular to notice how the calm resolution of the
feeble girl conquered the malice of one tormentor and
overawed the passion of the other. For a long time
neither of the incongruous group moved or made the
slightest noise. Wâgh-ta still held her hunting-knife in
her hand, and stood, partly turned from Scar Face, proudly
looking down at him over her upraised arm. The white
man sat stupid and motionless in his chair, feeling himself strangely conquered by one who was to have been his
victim. Old Mollie leaned over the rough table, her hands
resting upon it, and stared in mute astonishment into the
Indian girl's face, subdued by the feeling that there were
ideas and emotions represented in that rough room which
she could by no means understand. Such is the power
that the spectacle of courage exerts over the human mind
—such the awe awakened by the conviction of the imma-
nence of death. It is the simple belief of my people that
when the Spirit of Death casts his shadow over an individual, although he be not stricken down, he is rooted to

the spot whereon he stands and is stiffened in the attitude he at the moment had assumed, whether erect upon the hill-top, or crouching in the valley, or sitting beside the camp-fire, and is not able to cast off the spell until a day and a night have passed. Such a spell, it seems, had fallen upon the group in the shed that sorrowful night.

And the spell might, perhaps, have continued through its allotted time, had not Wágh-ta at length conceived that Wakanda had cast this awe upon her captors in order to favor her escape. The instant she thought of this she made a second spring toward the door. Ah! thus the spell was broken. Thus the momentary kindliness in Old Mollie's heart was driven forth, and the old malice rolled back in bitter waves. Springing upon the little maiden before she could possibly reach the door, the hag bore her to the floor and easily wrenched the knife out of her hand.

"Number two, my honey," the woman said as she flung Wágh-ta into the corner again. "Old Moll guesses ye won't try to excuse yerself from us agin—else ye'll get a broken head. An' ye won't kill yerself so bravely, now that I've got the knife. Me and my young master ain't to be trifled with more'n once or twice, I can tell ye."

"No, we're not!" exclaimed Scar Face, who had now recovered his senses and was wild with rage. "Curses! curses upon you!" he yelled as he caught up a chair, wielded it above his head and sprang upon the girl. "I will teach you who you are defying. I will show you whom you despise. I will—"

"My son!" said a sad voice at the door. "My son! my son!"

Wághta lifted up her eyes and saw the mother of Scar Face standing in the door of the shed. Her hand was held by little Swallow, who had hastily aroused her from her bed, and conducted her with all speed to the rescue of poor Prairie Flower. Her face was pale but calm, and her sad, sad voice sounded like the moan of the night-wind.

Scar Face turned upon her, and at sight of her well-remembered features, his passion seemed to be whetted to insanity.

"God in heaven!" he cried, "how came you here?"

"My son! my son!" was all the poor mother could say.

He foamed, like a wild beast, upon her for a moment, and then with a half-cry, half-moan, as if impelled by some horrible spirit that could not be shaken off, sprang toward her, and with one blow of the uplifted chair felled to the earth the form that had given him life. The moment the blow was struck he came to himself, and, horrified beyond measure by what he had done, dropped the chair heavily to the floor and sank down over the prostrate form of his mother.

"O mother, mother! Forgive me—do not die—you cannot leave me in hopeless darkness!" he moaned.

"My son! my son!" the bloodless lips murmured, and the poor mother was dead.

When Wágh-ta stood irresolute in the corner where she had been thrown, Swallow crossed the room, caught her by the hand, and led her swiftly out. They paused a moment when they had gained the darkness of the bushes, and looking back saw the wretched murderer bending motionless over his mother's body; and the night wind as it freshened into the breeze which always heralds the morning on the prairies, moaned and sobbed round the angles of the shed and started away through the tangled bushes to join the ceaseless wail. As they stood listening, Old Mollie went stumbling and mumbling by them, hurrying as fast as her trembling limbs would permit from that dreadful spot. When she had gone the Indian girls took the opposite direction, and were soon lost from view among the sage-brush and hazel-bushes.

As I think of this escape of my bride from the clutches of the white man, I remember what I once saw upon the prairie near my childhood home. One winter day when the snow lay several inches deep upon the hills, I was hunting with my bow for a rabbit or quail, that my father might have a tender bit when he returned from more daring exploits. I had wandered into a nestling valley, in which grew a number of little clumps of wild-thorn and furze bushes. My attention was suddenly arrested by the shadow of a great bird upon the snow, and looking up I saw a magnificent dun-spotted eagle circling grandly in mid-air and evidently scenting prey. At length he paused in his flight, hovered for a moment upon his wide wings, uttered a scream of victory, and then dashed head-long into the center of one of the thorn clumps I had seen. As he struck the bushes a spray of light snow fell from their branches, and out of this spray sprang a little rabbit which had been hiding under the bush. The frightened creature dashed for his life across the snow and made good his escape, while the cruel bird, which had hoped to make a meal upon him, remained entangled in the thorns, his grand feathers torn and broken and his sharp eyes wild with pain; and the more he struggled to be free from the ruin he had wrought for himself, the thicker fell his blood-drops upon the snow. There I left him, thinking it Wakanda's will that he should thus of his own wickedness perish. Thus did Scar Face fall a victim to his own unholy designs. He thought, in the greatness of his strength, to make an easy prey of the poor Indian girl, but the Wakanda who can save a rabbit out of an eagle's claws, brought to naught his guilty purposes; and as his soul bled upon the thorns of unrestrained hate and passion, he had but himself to be angry with. And my little rabbit sped over the ground to me.

CHAPTER XVIII.

RETURNING REASON.

MEANWHILE upon the shores of that distant lake among the snowy hills were being enacted certain things that I should tell you of.

When I felt myself borne into the lake in the arms of the insane white man, I realized how futile would be any struggle against his superhuman strength. I therefore supposed it to be Wakanda's wish that I should resign myself to inevitable death. The moment we sank into the cold waters, however, I felt his fearful grasp relax, in obedience to that natural instinct of self-preservation of which the wise Standing Elk had told us, and which perchance is not totally lost even in minds the most completely shattered. Having lived since infancy upon the shores of the darkly flowing Missouri, and being as thoroughly at home in the water as upon the land, I instantly improved the opportunity of escape thus afforded, and by exerting all my power I succeeded in throwing the maniac off after a terrific struggle which beat the bright waters into such white waves as might have been found in the death-conflict of rival buffaloes.

Being thus freed, it was the work of a moment only to swim ashore, and when I had clambered upon the rocks again, I turned to discover the fate of the white man. The lake, like nearly all of those found in the mountains, had steep, rocky banks, so that the water was very deep only a few steps from the shore. In those clear depths the white man had gone down, and I could see the bubbles rising to the surface and bursting brightly there, just above where he was lying. I can even now remember that in some confused way those bursting bubbles on the bright surface above the secret slime where a life was going out seemed to my untutored mind to afford sad illustrations of how strangely joy and beauty could be so plentiful above and around me when my heart within was dying of pain and agony. But my main thought at the moment was for the perishing man—should I rescue him or leave him to die? Might not I avenge the ruin of Wágh-ta, and that without actually staining my hands with blood, by allowing him to remain as he was? The temptation came fiercely upon me, and I paced like a caged animal up and down upon the rocks. " No tree," the Evil Spirit said, "will ever tell of it in its rustling, no wave will ever whisper it, no eye but that of yonder eagle, which would gladly be a fellow in such sport, is upon thee. And then," it went on to say, " how can you tell that the insane man, even if saved, will not dash again upon you and succeed in taking your life! Is it not self-protection to let him die—at most is it not merely remaining passive and allowing him to perish in the ruin he has wrought for himself?" But at that solemn moment all the teaching of the good Wa-gá-za,* all the great words of the wise Um-pan-nez-zhe, all the impulses of kindness which are naturally in every heart, and all the strange awe there is in the feeling that the eye of Wakanda blazes out of the sky upon every deed. came down upon me, and I plunged into the lake. I know there are great papers printed every day for the white man which say that the Indian is incapable of an act of kindness; I know that the most cruel falsehoods are published, so that even the kind-hearted among our oppressors think we go to war many

* Missionary.

times when we do not; and I know that we have no means
of denying these bitter things, since no public prints herald
the red man's story. But I must write what is true, trusting that some day you will find it to be so.

By diving down into the waters of the lake, I was, at
last, able to catch the white man's sleeve, and so I raised
him to the surface and dragged him to the shore. I laid
him first upon his face, so that the water could run from his
mouth; and when he began to gasp and breathe, having
prepared a bed of the last year's pine-fringes under a
neighboring tree, I placed him on it as tenderly as a
loving son would care for a father. I found a strange
delight in tending him, for all my hatred had died out, and
I fancied I might come into deeper sympathy with *Wakanda E-zhi-ga** by succoring one who was helpless
and distressed. And as I stood beside the deep, bright
lake and saw the place where the bubbles had been bursting, I thought that the white man had not been deeper in
the waves than I had been in ignorance and sin when He
came to rescue me and my simple-hearted people.

It was several hours before he opened his eyes. I sat
and watched him, tracing the lines of pain and sadness in
his face, and studying the long, matted gray hair that fell
in heavy coils upon the pine-fringes. His face still retained traces of noble and ingenuous qualities, his forehead
was high and broad, and the more I noted the shades of
expression upon the features, the more thoroughly could
I believe him to have been, once at least, and before the
fierce fires of disease had burned out the powers of his
mind, a refined and honorable man. The Indian is made,
by all the training of the hunt, a close observer, and hence
I noticed, and with the greatest interest and amazement,

* God's Son.

that his face exhibited signs of pain and anger as he slowly recovered his senses, as if he would gladly have remained in the arms of a sweet unconsciousness.

Slowly and gloriously the mountain twilight came down upon us, and when its golden wings were just full-spread above the pine-tops, the white man opened his eyes and gently said :

"Where am I ?   What is it ?   What has happened ?"

"You are with a friend," I answered, "and you are very weak.   You must sleep if you can."

"Where is Ben ?" he asked.

"I have not seen him.   But he will soon come," I replied at hazard.

Then followed a long pause, in which the white man gazed calmly up through the pine branches into the stars, and I fervently and sincerely thanked Wakanda that the man's mind seemed to have returned to him again. The music of the night was just beginning to burst forth, and the scratching of the eagle's claws upon the purple rocks far up the peak entered, with the shrill cry of the stray wolf, into the harmony as if they had a part to play which could by no means be omitted.

"What is that sound I hear ?" whispered the white man at length.

"What does it sound like ?" I said.

"Like the running of the waters of the old mill-race at home over the dam of beech-logs."

"It is the wind in that pine tree standing there upon the rocks."

"But on this other side I hear a sound precisely like it —is there another pine in that direction ?"

"No, a mountain brook runs along there into the lake. The running of its waters over the rocks makes the same sound as the wind in the pine-top."

"How strange—and one seems to answer and echo the other."

"Yes," I said, "they are the voices of the Twin Brothers. Did you ever hear what my people say of them ? There were once two noble-hearted brothers, who were twins. They loved the same beautiful maiden, and she loved both so well that her heart could not make choice between them. One day the maiden was in the quiet woods puzzling her heart as to which she loved, when she heard their voices calling her, one from one side and one from the other. 'Khta-wé-tha!'* sang one upon the right hand. 'Khta-wé-tha!' sang the other upon the left hand. And their voices were so exactly alike that the poor maiden could not distinguish who was here and who there. Frantic with love and agony, she cried aloud : 'O Wakanda, tear my poor heart asunder, and give half to each of my noble lovers!' And there in the quiet woods the maiden died. The brothers were so smitten with sorrow that, upon their praying most earnestly to Wakanda, they were changed, the one to a noble pine tree, and the other to a mountain brook. And to this day the pine sadly whispers in the wind 'Khta-wé-tha!' while the brook moans the same, 'Khta-wé-tha!' and it is still impossible for a man, listening at a little distance, to distinguish which brother is singing upon the right, and which upon the left. So, white man, you hear to-night the music of the Brothers. And hearing it, sleep."

His heavy eyelids slowly and dreamily closed, and he slept. I covered him with my blanket, and, having built a fire against a fallen pine-log, I sat for hours and watched the light playing upon his pale face. I was calm and almost soothed from my grief. What strange power is

---

* "I love thee !"

there in an exercise of sympathy to allay the agony of sorrow; what spell is there in the doing of a kindness to one of our own nature that causes us to forget the gall in our cup and the aching of our heart-sore? That it is so, who that has suffered and has shown charity to the suffering can doubt? And that it is so seems to show me what great inducements the good Wakanda offers that man should more succor his distressed brother. As I thought much of this beside the glowing fire that night, it seemed to me that surely the white men could never have suffered much, nor ever have felt the pang of slavery and the bitterness of oppression; else they would more readily grant charity of speech, thoughtful patience, and brotherly encouragement and assistance to the red men. The waning moon looked down at me through the tangled branches as I thus thought, and it seemed to me that in its shimmering beams Wakanda was lighting upon me a smile of commendation and hope.

"Halloo, there, my friend!" suddenly exclaimed the voice of my charge.

I started—it seemed to me that I had not slept: but now the full morning had come; the fire lurked under a heap of gray ashes, just as the rising sun seemed to hide behind the dew clouds; the healthful fragrance of forest and flowered plain was fully abroad, and the august peaks reared themselves where heavy blackness had but now reigned supreme. I roused myself and went to him. He had raised himself to a sitting posture, and seemed to be suffering very little inconvenience from his temporary insanity and cold bath.

"Sit down beside me," he said, "and tell me how I came here? Where did you find me, and from what did you rescue me?"

"I found you about twelve feet under water in yonder

lake, and so you can easily imagine what I saved you from."

"In yonder-lake!   And how came I there?"

I related to him how I had awakened from sleep and found him glaring upon me. I repeated his words and described with what a mad rush he had run with me into the lake.

"Great God!" he exclaimed, "I must have been insane."

He relapsed into silence, and a strange look of chagrin and dismay came into his face. Is it regarded as a disgrace among the white people for a man to lose his mind? Among our simple nations one so afflicted is with the greatest tenderness nursed, and in many instances even regarded as favored by constant communications with the other world. And it is a singular fact, which may, perhaps, be partially accounted for by this gentle custom, that very few cases of violent insanity occur amongst us. There may be something—I do not know—in the dread a white man would naturally feel at the approach of this, to him, humiliating affliction, to spur the shattered mind to excess and ferocity.

"At all events," I replied, "you are well now, thank Wakanda! And while I am getting such food as I can, you had better rest on your bed of pine-fringes."

"But I am not quite right yet, it seems," he answered with a puzzled look. "Have I ever done you any kindness; do you feel under obligation to me, that you show me such attention? I did not know—I confess it—that an Indian would save the life of a white man when he had him in his power."

"There are many evil men among the Indians," I said, biting my lip that I might speak calmly, "who would not have saved your life; and the Great Father's people will not be convinced that we are not all cruel and revengeful. Would you like to be spit upon as a thief, because some steal who have a pale check?"

"Assuredly not," he said, "assuredly not. But it seems to me that the proportion of the evil-disposed is much greater among the Indian than among the white race."

"This is because you are always informed of the cruel acts of my people, while the many kindnesses shown to the whites, the frozen feet that are warmed in our tepees, the hungry tongues that are satisfied by our camp fires, and the brotherly words of welcome we give, find no report. The Indian is human, and no more. Touch his heart with kindness, and it will be kind; touch it with encouragement, and it will wish eagerly to become civilized; touch it with suspicion or coldness, and it retreats within itself; touch it with cruelty, and cruelty springs forth out of it. You have seen the flint arrow-heads our fathers fashioned—do you know how the hard stone was chipped so smoothly and beautifully away?"

"I do not, indeed; I believe the secret of this process is one of the deep puzzles of learned men to-day."

"It is a simple secret. A sharp blow upon the flint would either have broken the stone into shapeless bits, or called forth a spark of fire. So my people were accustomed to press the flint gently and patiently with small sticks of hickory wood hardened in the fire, and thus, by degrees, the rough chips fell away, and the arrow-heads were beautifully shaped and sharpened. The Indian's heart is flint. To shape it for use there must be no violence, but the most gentle kindness and patience."

Meanwhile I prepared such wild vegetables as I could find for our simple meal, and set them before the white man, who ate with much eagerness. They tasted sweet upon my own tongue as well, after a fast of many days,

and were strangely sweeter because I had the consciousness of doing what is right.

The white man seemed very feeble after the severe
strain he had been under, and so, after his hunger had
been satisfied, I busied myself in providing a softer bed for
him to rest on. When he was made comfortable, he said :

"Thank you, thank you, my friend. I am easy now.
Tell me of your own life ; how came you to be here among
the rocks alone ?"

Oh, how all the flood of sorrow rolled again upon my
soul when he asked this question ! It was some moments
before I could speak. At last, when I could command
my voice, I told him my whole life : of my love for the
beautiful Wágh-ta ; of our peaceful dwelling-place beside
the shining river ; of the evil man's plot against my bride ;
of how there was no law by which I could have the wretch
punished ; and of my wild flight across prairie and river
to the rocks. Again and again he interrupted me with
exclamations of indignation and wonder, and when I
ceased speaking, he cried :

"Do you speak truly? Is there a God in heaven?
Have the American people no fear of Him?"

"Wakanda lives," I said, "and He will avenge the
wrongs of his children. But oh! the smart is hot and
sore while it lasts."

"Is there a general desire on the part of the Indians
to secure the protection of our laws?"

"For twenty years the one petition of our chiefs has
been for tools and farming implements, missionaries and
leaders, a secure title to their land, the benefits of just and
equal laws, and then the high privilege of supporting
themselves."

"And has not this been acceded to?"

"Can you not answer that question yourself?"

Our conversation had consumed the whole day. The afternoon was now far spent, the twilight was hovering down.

"See," I said, "the evening nestles under the trees. Thus the twilight of our race has come. Thousands of our fathers have died and have left no seed behind them. They say we are dying out; and truly, under the present system of cruelty and exaction, it is so. But grant us the blessings you freely accord to the natives of all, other lands, and we should increase in numbers, our homes would resound to merry shouts of many little ones, and the voices of our young men would make our harvest fields resound. They say we are a weakly race perishing from the earth; but it is because when, by a cruel decree from which there is no appeal, a Northern tribe is sent to the Land of Fire,* scores and hundreds die of raging fever. In our own homes we do not die more rapidly than the whites. Can they excuse themselves for causing us to perish by sending out the cry that we are a perishing race? But, Wá-gha, the despised Indian race is leaving a mark on your history that can never be wiped off. If you could walk with me to some of the farms of the white man, I could show you a strange-looking gully, several feet in depth, running through the wheat and oat fields, and down the sides of the hills, coursing away in regular line for miles together. It is an old Indian trail. Once it was a mere path through the heavy grass and nodding dandelions. Over it the children raced in their play, the lover hasted to the trysting-place, the old chiefs slowly went to the council. But now the rains of heaven have worn it deep. The white man's grain grows in it and along its sides, but it cannot be hid. Under brilliant sun

* The Indian Territory, so called by the Indians.

or flickering moon, it still is visible as a scar upon the fair surface of earth ; and oh, what a pathetic story it tells of the sad difference between what once was and that which is ! Wa-gha, there is a scar upon your national history, showing where once the Indians lived and loved, but where now they are not. Under whatever light shines out of heaven, whether of justice or of mercy, it still is, and shall ever be, visible. Seek to hide it as you may under the fruit of your thrift, it yet remains, and is worn deeper year after year by the rushing greed of man. Wá-gha, I have spoken !"

CHAPTER XIX.

CHOPPING LOGIC.

WHEN I had concluded I sank down upon the ground overcome with emotion. The white man was about to reply, when we heard the voice of a man calling in the distance.

" That is Ben !" he cried, almost springing up in his excitement.

The shouts came rapidly nearer and nearer, until the sick man could answer them. Not sure of the reception I should receive from the approaching strangers, and being unwilling to force myself into their company as a witness of their meeting, I quietly crept a few steps away, and cast myself down behind a clump of young aspens.

" Halloa, Colonel !" exclaimed a hearty voice, "you've led us a lively dance through brush and brier this time, or I'll be hanged. Come to yourself agin, like a regular Methidist out-and-out prodigal, has ye ? Wal, ye see, I brings this chum of mine along in case of accidents. Wasn't no match for ye alone, not I, and that crack over the head ye gin me ain't wholesome to be repeated. Ye don't look just now as ye could break an ambulance wheel over yer knee—now, do ye ?"

With these words two athletic men came out of the twilightg loom and stood before the "colonel". The one who spoke was tall, long-armed, loose-jointed, but evidently of great strength. His face was, as nearly as I could discover in the imperfect light, genial and mirthful, and in his eye there were both the twinkle and the shining of a star. His hair and beard were of that vivid red color which always so amuses an Indian. His companion, or "pard," as the miner would say, was shorter, darker, possessed of a singularly grave and knowing countenance, much given to silence and tobacco. Both were dressed in deerskin pants and blue shirts. Upon one extremity they wore heavy boots, and upon the other the customary broad-brimmed hats.

They both shook hands heartily with the colonel, who seemed to regard them with mingled shrinking and delight. In answer to their salutations, he said to the one who had spoken:

"Sit down here, Ben, and tell me what has happened. Where are the mules and the ambulance?"

"Not if I knows myself," Ben replied. " I don't enter on no such excitin' yarn as that 'ar, until I've had a somethin' to eat. Jerry and I's hungrier than wolves—ain't we, Jerry?"

" That's our policy," responded that individual briefly.

"So," continued Ben, "if ye have anythin' to eat in yer pantry, Colonel, and will just trot the same out, we will sup'rintend the demolishin' of the aforesaid. Jerry, you produce the bacon and I'll strike a fire, and we'll see what can be had."

" That's our policy," again answered Jerry.

" Ye see, Colonel," said Ben in a low voice to that individual, "old Jerry ain't much to look on—now is he? But he's tenderer'n a woman. The first time I seed him was when I was laid up at Reno by a little scratch as I got from a feller's dirk knife one night a playin' cards. I hadn't a cent in the world, Colonel; my folks had all died back in Jersey, I spect, and the fellers jest chucked me into an old room and left me to die. Wal, Jerry come along alookin' for a pard. I wasn't a likely one—now was

I? But never'less Jerry tackled to me. I opens my eyes one day after I'd laid there more'n a week, and the first thing I sot 'em on was Jerry. He jest touched me with them hard hands—seemed to me it was my mother a-come to me. Oh, he's tenderer'n a woman, old Jerry is. He paid all my bills, gave the cuss as tickled me with his dirk a blasted thrashin', stuck to me in all our ups and downs, and here we be. An' he's awful wise, Jerry is. He can jest *smell* the gold, an' ef it hadn't a been for some of my cussed foolishness we would ha' been rich long afore this. When I passes over the range, * Colonel, I wants old Jerry jest to tech me with them hands o' his as the last thing, fer he's tenderer'n a woman, or *I'll* be hanged! But here goes for somethin' to eat."

"Ben," said the colonel, "there was an Indian boy here a moment since, who saved my life and has kindly tended me—"

"A Injun!" said Ben, stopping in the act of striking a match upon the leg of his deerskin pants. "Saved yer life! Tended of ye! Jerry, let's die! But 'taint much queerer 'an ye should tend o' me, Jerry."

"Yes," pursued the colonel, "and he will show you where our provisions are kept, and show you about getting the meal."

"A Injun! 'Show *us* about,' hey, Jerry? He! he! Prodigal ain't quite come back yet. But call him in, Colonel, call him in; we is two to one, and I guess we ain't afeered!"

If I could have fled without being seen and without the suspicion of cowardice attaching to me, I should have done so rather than face the rough strangers. This being

---

* "When I die." A most beautiful expression used by the miners. One side of the Rocky range is usually rough and rocky, but on the other side there lies a lovely Park.

impossible, however, I arose, stepped forward, and with,
out a word assisted in the gathering of wood and the preparation of the meal.   At first Ben seemed to regard me
with some suspicion, but as I made no formidable demon-
strations, we were soon upon the most familiar terms.

The simple meal over, the strangers lighted their pipes,
and casting themselves in an easy posture before the fire,
prepared for the description of the colonel's dark days.
I was surprised to notice that Ben, although apparently
of a generous and noble nature, seemed to have no appre-
ciation of the fact that his words cut the colonel to the
heart, for he related the whole transaction as if it were
the most natural thing in the world.

"Wal, ye see, Jerry, the colonel thar hired me to drive
him over to Camp Roe.   He had a ambulance and four
mules, and I was to act as guide, cook, driver, and entertainer.   Wal, we gets along very comf'table for a day or
two ; we passes smoothly over the range and comes down
into this yer valley at the lower end.   I notices one night
that the colonel don't sleep soun'.   I notices him a tum-
blin' and a turnin' and a gittin' up· to look at the stars,
and I ses to myself, 'Somethin' don't set well on his
stomach or on his heart, I dunno wich,' and let it pass my
mind. (List'nin', Jerry ?) Wal, the next day the colonel's eyes
was kind o' wild-like, but I didn't pay no 'tention to that.
Sez I to myself, 'It's because he didn't sleep none.'   Wal
I hitches up and we makes a start.   That was jest a week
ago to-day.   I was a drivin' along, cozy as a beaver on a
log, when—whoop! a crack comes onto my head as if a
boulder had fallen on it.   Sez I to myself, 'Guess I'll git
out and kinder reckon-nooter'—leastways, I suppose I
sez that, for the next thing I knows I'm a lyin' on the
ground.   The colonel didn't seem to care no more about
me ; so, to be on the safe side in case of accidents I jest

crawls quiet-like into a bush as was nigh. Whoop! ye ort to have seen the colonel then! He was gran', I tell ye! He onhitches the mules, gives them a lick with a club, and sends them off to grass. He slashes out the ax and whacks the old ambulance all into splinters in no time —piles it all in a heap. (List'nin', Jerry?")

"That's our policy."

"And then he sots fire to the whole outfit. Blazes! how it did burn—varnish and paint and leather and cushions and all. The Colonel was wild with the fun; he dances roun' and roun' it while it blazes, slings his hat and coat in when the light got sort o' low, and, bless my eyes! ef I didn't think once he was a-goin' to jump in hisself. But he didn't, as ye may jedge. When the whole thing was a heap o' hot ashes he wades into it, kicks the ashes and coals about like split, clappin' his hands and shakin' out his hair. Then all of a sudden he takes a start, and— whoop! away he goes pell-mell, and I gathers in the mules and takes myself back to cabin. Ye knows the rest —how we sot out to find him—and here he is."

On the conclusion of his singular narrative the rough frontiersman puffed away at his pipe with the greatest gravity, and seemed lost in some deep meditation upon the fragility of the human mind or some kindred topic. I looked toward the colonel, and though he said not a word, his face seemed very pale in the fire light. I pitied him. The red man can boast of but one sure possession —the power to thoroughly pity woe.

"Jerry, are ye list'nin'?"

"That's our—"

"I'm thinkin' of the Injun Question, Jerry. Somethin' in the *personal* surroundin's kinder suggests it, ye know. All the gran' men of the nation thinks of it, but they haven't their peepers right on the difficulty as we has here on the frontier. The nutshell of the whole matter is jest this: *the Injuns has got to go.* They has the best huntin' and the richest mineral on their reservations. They don't use the mineral—they don't know how to prospect for it, nor how to mine it. It ain't accordin' to reason, Jerry, that a civilized race should stan' back and not git rich because a oncivilized race has got the rocks and won't use 'em. It's jest the old story of the dog in the manger, as we use to hear tell of back on earth.* I fer one means to kick the dog out."

"That's our policy," said Jerry.

"But, Ben," said the colonel, coming nearer to the fire and taking a seat on a pine log, his earnest face showing that he had forgotten his own sorrow for the moment, in his interest in a great question, "does it seem to you fair that the possessions of the Indians should be wrested from them without a reasonable compensation? The land, with all its hunting facilities and all its mineral wealth, is at present *theirs.*

"Ain't no doubt on that, Colonel."

"And every department of our government has acknowl-edged the validity of the titles by which they hold this land. In the ordinance of 1787 the claim of the Indians to their possessions is distinctly recognized. It was reaf-firmed by the Emperor Napoleon at the sale of Louisiana, and our government entered no protest."

"That all may be, Colonel, but hanged ef I see yit that I must stand aside when I sees a fine lead of gold or silver because it be on a reserve."

"But you must have some authority to go on another man's property before it can be right to do so. There are just three ways in which a nation can acquire right to

* *i.e.,* in "the States."

any possession: it must be either by discovery, conquest, or purchase. You cannot for a moment claim that we have the right of original discovery in this case, for the red men held the soil when our fathers first found it; neither can you justly say that the Indian tribes generally have laid themselves liable to a war of conquest on our part; and it is only too well known that but little of the Indian's land has been fairly purchased from him. You're an honest-hearted fellow, Ben; you would not take a dime's worth of my property without paying for it; and you must know that we have no right to their possessions until we have given them a just equivalent. Now, have we?"

"Lookee here, Colonel," said Ben, crossing his legs and sagely winking to Jerry—who moved his lips as if he were repeating his favorite sentence by way of encouragement —"lookee here: is it accordin' to the rightness of things, now, that a infeerer race should occupy possessions as could be better used of by a supeerer race? Ain't it our dooty, so to speak (hey, Jerry?), to improve everythin' to the very best, like? You knows what I mean, Colonel, but I'se been so long a livin' 'out o' God's knowledge '* as I can't put it jest right."

"Yes, Ben, I know what you mean. And I confess that until the last twelve hours this argument, which is the only one that can be urged on our part, has seemed to me enough to warrant the driving out of the Indians. But I have had time to think it over, and I believe it to be simply a national quibble. For where is this law of superior right to stop? If you owned a farm, and I should become thoroughly persuaded that I could improve it to better advantage than you, could I fairly or honestly drive

* On the Plains.

you and your family away? If I had ten sons, and you had but one, I might succeed in thrusting you away, but would my robbery be excused by the fact of my claiming that I could make better use of the farm than you were doing? I imagine you would claim your privilege of growing either wheat or weeds, barley or sage-bush, as suited your pleasure."

"But ye see, Colonel, I ain't a Injun!"

"Is a *White*-wrong a *Red*-right?"

"Ye see, Colonel, ye hasn't lived with yer peepers open right *on* the Injun question all yer life, as I has. They *is* all so cussed! It ain't nothin' personal meant to present company, ye understand; but it's so. And we on the frontier makes every chance *count*, as we can git agin 'em—hey, Jerry?"

"That's our policy."

"Yes, Ben, and I am afraid many of the frontiersmen cannot resist the temptation to make false reports of Indian depredations in order to increase the strife between the races, and thus hasten the removal of the red men."

"Why, Colonel, ye *can't* lie about a Injun!" and then, after a pause, "He's so cussed."

"Still, Ben, I have it on the best evidence that last summer in this very Park an Indian was killed by a couple of prospectors; and in order to divert attention an alarm was raised that the whole Ute tribe had gone to war. The daily papers published thrilling dispatches showing up the revengeful nature of the Indians and telling how several battles had been fought, which had existence only in the vivid imaginations of the frontier 'pards.' The cry went up all over the country that the tribes must be removed, and many voices were for extermination."

During this conversation Jerry had remained perfectly quiet except when he uttered his peculiar expression, or made an attempt so to do. While these last few words were being spoken, however, he seemed to be enduring a severe attack of St. Vitus's dance, so restless and eager was he to have a word on the subject of discussion. At this point, therefore, he said:

"Ye see, Colonel, I has a Injun policy along o' the rest. I adwise that all the tribes be gathered in some spot—takin' care that it ain't whar there is gold—and about two barks of a dog* distant have a lot of forty-rod red-eye secreted in the sand. Then leave 'em to their fate. They'd find that 'ar whisky less'n an hour—steal a heap of it—drink 'it stiddy till they all stretched out—men, women, and children in a row—*de*funct. This proceedin' would 'complish three things: they'd be happy a stealin', they'd be happy a drinkin', they'd be happy a dyin'. That's humane, that is. And they'd die of their own fault. That's my policy."

Ben and the colonel laughed heartily at this. Realizing how truly the rough Jerry expressed the light valuation placed upon our lives by the border men, I was sad.

"But, Colonel," said Ben, "hain't the Legislatur of any State the right to hustle off troublesome customers? Hain't they the power to protect the peaceable citizens?"

"If I should grant this," replied the colonel, "it would still remain a question whether the Indians or the frontiersmen are the troublesome citizens. Am I not right when I say, Ben, that nine tenths of all the trouble between the races is occasioned by the greediness and encroachment of the whites?"

"I ain't agoin' to be a denyin' of it."

"And it seems to me, Ben, that God has given our nation many warnings that He will revenge the cruelty

* It is common in the West to measure all distance by the distance a barking dog may be heard.

wrought by us against His helpless children.   I call to
mind, at this moment, a very striking case.   Years ago
the Cherokees were wrongfully dispossessed of their land
in Georgia.   Time passed on, and one of the most terrible
battles of our late civil war was fought upon the very spot
where these Indians had once lived.   If you should search
through the whole South you could not find a tract of
country so devastated, so covered with graves, as that.
Does it not seem that God has thus exhibited his dis-
pleasure and vengeance against those who sought to profit
by the misfortunes of His simple-hearted ones?"

"Prodigal ain't quite come back yit—hey, Jerry?"

"And I also call to mind at this moment, Ben, a clause
out of the last will of Cortez, the cruel Spanish conqueror :
'It has been long a question whether we can, in good
conscience, hold the Indians in slavery.   This question
not having yet been decided, I order my son, Martin, and
his heirs, to spare no pains to arrive at a knowledge of
the truth on this point, for it is a matter which interests
deeply their conscience and mine.'   Thus does the most
cruel of conquerors shame our great government, which
offers to Hottentot, Kaffre and Turk the protection of
just laws, but holds the Indians, the original owners of
the soil we now possess, in a slavery which is as hateful
and loathsome as it is subtle and shameless."

"That decides me, Jerry, or I'll be hanged," said Ben
in a low cautious voice.   "Prodigal is way off—ain't come
back by a heap."

The night had by this time descended darkly upon us.
The fire of pine-boughs crackled and roared, sending up a
column of vivid sparks that widened out aloft into a tree
of fire.   Our faces were aglow with the light.   I sat where
I could study the countenances of my companions, and
while I felt how unjust was the settled hatred to our race

depicted on the faces of the two frontiersmen, I could not find any bitterness in my heart toward them as individuals. I simply regarded them as the victims of a long course of false training, as the representatives of a class in which love for gold has crushed out every noble feeling of human brotherhood. The face of the colonel was animated and kind, showing the depth and force of the noble current flowing beneath the surface. I recognized in him a true friend, and wherever he may be this beautiful evening as I write, I pray that the blessing of Wakanda may alight upon him.

"List'nin', Jerry?" finally said Ben, knocking the ashes out of his pipe. Without waiting for a reply he continued:

"The news from down country is rather encouragin' like. Eagle Wing's band are ordered to the Injun Territory."

"Where does they reside at?" inquired Jerry.

"'Bout two hundred miles down the Horsetail. That is the river as we last passed on the over side o' the Range —do ye notice?"

Out of the glowing fire-tree a spirit seemed to come and snatch me suddenly from a most beautiful land into a region of thorns and darkness. My own father's band ordered to the terrible "Land of Fire," which to every northern Indian is the synonym of fever and death! Had the impending stroke—the blow from which we had so long shrunk—fallen at last upon us? Must our beautiful homes and fruitful farms be given up to those who had no right to them—who had not toiled to make them charming? It was only the Indian's pride that kept back the groan that started to my lips when I heard the white man's words.

My blood was instantly on fire to rush away to my

people, aid them if we were to resist the cruel command, or, if nothing more, suffer with them and show the weak ones how they might be strong. I thought how much my father might need a strong shoulder on which to lean in this sad moment. I thought of my mother, who had saved my life at the risk of her own. I thought of my beautiful Wágh-ta. Perhaps she had come back to our home—had found her noble father dead and her plighted husband fled away, no one could tell her whither. She might need my protection, or at least my sympathy. It almost maddened me to think that she might be chiding me for deserting her in her distress, or imagining that I had met some cruel fate among the swelling divides or upon the rocks. The long arms of the rocking pines beckoned me away; the voice of the brook murmuring "Khta-wé-tha" urged me to all haste; the smile of my Wágh-ta shone among the aspens where lay the path to the Horsetail.

I looked at my companions. While I had been thinking these thoughts they had stretched themselves out beside the fire and were now fast asleep. "I can slip away," I thought, "without suspicion, and it shall certainly be without delay." I stood for a moment beside the slumbering form of the colonel, the only white man, save the Frenchman who dwelt beside our home, whom I had ever heard speaking a word in favor of my race. I called down all blessing and eternal love upon him as he thus lay with the fire-light flickering over his pale cheeks, and then, with a pang, as if I were parting from a brother, I turned away and followed the smile that gleamed among the aspens. I never saw him again. Who or whence he was, or what anguish of life lay behind his brief but terrible aberration of mind, I know not; but his heart was kind and he pitied our woes—may Wakanda bless him

CHAPTER XX.

PLOUGHED UNDER.

THE glorious night was just at its height as I started upon my journey homeward. In the distance I heard the bark of the wolf, and once at my very side my ear caught the purr of the mountain lioness soothing her young. These and other sounds of the night caused me neither to hesitate nor to fear. I had now a great purpose in view, and was nerved by the thought of it. By morning I had crossed the Range, and by the following evening I was far down the Horsetail, whose bank I knew to be my surest and easiest way.

At noon of the third day I came to the divide from the top of which I knew I should see our village. I crept breathlessly up its side. I stood upon it, and oh ! what a spectacle did I behold ! Two companies of the Great Father's soldiers were camped in the circular space in the heart of our village ; my father's people were all crouching in abject misery upon the ground in the center of the camp. Seated a little apart from them I could see my father and his main warriors, their bodies wrapped in scarlet blankets and their souls in bitter woe. Some of the soldiers were busily tearing down the homes which we had built with such pains and in which we had spent so many peaceful hours. The few articles of furniture that we had been able to secure were broken, thrown together into a pile, and just beginning to blaze above the torch applied by one of the white men. The woody fringe along the river bank where I had so often sat and mused with Wágh-ta; the shining stream itself, in whose waters I had so often fished and sported; the rain-washed hills beyond the river, upon whose dewy summits I had so often hunted the antelope and wolf— these well-remembered objects must have been just the same as of old, but oh! how changed and desolate and sad they seemed! Several of the houses were set on fire, that being the easiest mode of destroying them. As these flames leaped upward, spreading their forked tongues, and clapping their cruel hands together, and wreathing the dear homes in diadems of fire, a great wail came up to my ears from the miserable company huddled together on the ground, swelled into such mournful harmony as I have heard the tempest make in the sounding aisles of some distant forest, and as the shifting winds bore the wail to me I heard this sad word repeated: "Ma-shán! Ma-shán! Ma-shán!" *

I ran down the hillside and was allowed to pass the lines of the soldiers and go into the space allotted to my people. I came upon my poor mother first; her eyes were wild with agony and tears, and her long hair was matted and torn. She lighted upon me a look of love even from her sadness, and said passionately:

"My son! my son! Thou hast come to witness our disgrace, to share our fate."

"Ná-ha!† Ná-ha! At last I see thy dear face again. Has my Wágh-ta—my beautiful bride—returned?"

She answered me only with a moan. Well did I know her meaning; the one I loved was still away. My heart chilled and hardened in an instant. I was fiercely glad to die. Yet that I might not add to my mother's woe by allowing her to see my own, I turned away without another word.

* Home! Home! Home!　　　　　† Mother.

As I walked among that mournful company toward the spot where my father sat, I thought how the great world of society and government and wealth never for a moment stopped in its mad rush to think of what sad things are occurring out upon the prairies, of what cruel wrongs are being perpetrated in the holy name of liberty. I was in a strange agony because I could not lay hold of all the people of the world at once, stop them suddenly, keep them perfectly still, and force them to a fair and brotherly consideration of our sufferings.

My father was calm and stern. He saluted me simply with a slight wave of the hand, indicating both that I was welcome and that I should be seated by his side. For some time we remained in perfect silence, for no one could speak until the chief had been heard. At last my father said:

"The white men will soon be here. Build the fire for the last council to be held upon our own soil."

Some of the warriors arose to obey his command.

"Da-dé-ha,"* I said, "have we no means of warding off this terrible fate that threatens us?"

"Thou shalt see, my son, thou shalt see. The white men will soon be here to hold a council with us."

"But how long have the soldiers been here? How long have our people been exposed thus to the weather?"

"Four days. And they have given us no food, hoping to starve our people into consenting to give up their beautiful homes and go to the Land of Fire, to die."

"And what say our people?"

"They say, better to die under the old trees and beside the graves of our fathers, than in the land of the stranger."

"And had you any warning of the approach of this fate we have dreaded so many years?"

* My father.

" The soldiers found us gathering in our corn, and preparing winter-tepees for our cattle. They have driven away our cattle and taken our corn from us.

" Da-dé-ha ! This is robbery !"

" Nay, my son.   It is the policy of a great government, and cannot be robbery."

There was an intense bitterness in his voice. Oh! it made my heart weep to see my noble father so crushed and despairing. He was born to command, to lead his warriors against the enemies of his people, to stalk haughtily among the grand ones of the earth, to overcome the mighty game of the forests—it was terrible to see him crouching under oppression, ridicule, and woe.

At length we saw the agent and three other white men approaching us from the direction of Gray Coat's mansion ; and my father arose, placed his war-bonnet upon his head, and, thus prepared for the council, awaited their coming. The head-men of our tribe ranged themselves upon the ground behind my father. Behind them the wretched people—the weeping women and the starving children— gathered to listen, in the agony of despair, to the words spoken by the white men. My father folded his arms quietly upon his breast, and stood forth, like a mighty bear at bay, to defend his little ones. It was a noble, a pathetic spectacle, this last stand made by a once proud and powerful race against the slow, creeping advance of a pitiless, hypocritical, irresistible foe. The tender hearts that read these words in their luxuriant homes can by no means imagine how cruelly the Indian is bound, so as to make him the easy prey of scheming men.

Thus in perfect silence we awaited the coming of the white men, as if it were an attack of the Sioux. One of their number, a stranger to me, was tall and stately in movement, and elaborately dressed ; his hands were nicely

encased in gloves, and his nose was surmounted by a pair
of gold-rimmed eye-glasses. I afterwards learned that he
was one of the inspectors appointed by the Great Father
to observe how our tribes obey the commands of their
several agents. Another of the agent's companions was a
base man, despised by Indians and white men alike for
his many known acts of perfidy. The fourth member of
the group was an interpreter, who had been brought to
see that the interests of the government were not
endangered by any want of understanding between the
contracting parties.

While this company was approaching from one side,
I saw that Kind Face, our friend, was quietly slipping
toward us from the other direction. He was always alert
to be by our sides at a moment of need, and my heart
rejoiced when I thought we might have his assistance and
sympathy in the coming council.

. The inspector, upon coming up, saluted my father with
a stately bow, which was as proudly returned. The
council was properly arranged around the crackling fire
of spruce-boughs, and the conference was about to begin,
when the inspector observed the presence of Kind Face,
and, turning to the base man I have mentioned, exclaimed
haughtily:

" Have that white man removed from our council."

It was beneath the pride of a chief to make any plea for
the help of any one not of his own race, else my father
had requested that the tender-hearted Frenchman might
be allowed to remain. As he continued silent, Kind Face
arose, and, looking the inspector firmly in the eye, said:

"This day, I well know, shall witness the crowning
perfidy of the English against the simple-hearted red men.
I tell thee this—"

" Have him removed! "

"I tell thee this, self-seeking hypocrite, that had it not been for the service of the red men, thy Anglo-Saxon race had never possessed the American continent. It is matter of history that, in the colonial days of this nation, when the French were bitterly disputing with you the rulership of this vast continent, there came a crisis when the question trembled in the balance. The forces on each side were balanced: both parties knew that in the hands of the Indians the decision lay. My ancestors—I do not deny— used every method and means to obtain the friendship of the red men, but they failed. At this moment, upon which the destiny of America hung, the historic Six Nations of red men embraced the Saxon cause, and literally changed the whole civilization of America from French Catholic to English Protestant. Right nobly, indeed, have you rewarded your faithful allies! You have repaid them with smiles and promises, robbery and death!"

"Command the captain of these forces to remove this insane fellow from our brotherly council!" exclaimed the inspector in a rage.

"I relieve him of the duty," Kind Face replied. "I depart willingly. Farewell, Eagle Wing! Wakanda shall avenge the cruelty of this day."

These were his words—could I ever forget them? Having thus spoken, the noble-hearted man turned his steps toward his dug-out, and I never saw his face again.

The peace-pipe was now passed from mouth to mouth; but each one saw in the curling smoke that the ceremony was a needless and cruel protest. There could be no peace between the victim and the robber, the helpless and the spoiler.

When this formality had been completed the inspector arose with much importance, and having dropped his eye-glasses till they dangled from a cord about his neck, produced a paper from his pocket and gravely opened it.

"This paper," he said through the interpreter, "is the basis of our action in pressing the removal of this tribe to the Indian Territory. I shall first pass this document to the several chiefs and head-men present, and ask them to be kind enough to identify their marks upon it, and then I shall read it. Interpreter, be so good as to pass this to Eagle Wing, asking him if he signed it in presence of Gray Coat, as our good agent is known among the tribe."

My father took the paper and quietly handed it to me. I instantly recognized it as the petition drawn up at the suggestion of the dead Um-pan-nez-zhe, asking, as we supposed, that Gray Coat might be removed and we allowed to live in liberty. But as I now cast my eye over it, having learned to read the English language since the paper was written, I was amazed and horrified to discover that the petition really requested that our entire tribe might be removed to the Indian Territory.

"Da-dé-ha!" I cried, springing up, "we have been cruelly deceived. Thou didst dictate a plea to the Great Father asking that Gray Coat might not be allowed to throw us into slavery; behold! above thy name there was written a petition that we might be removed to the Land of Fire. Rise as a chief and tell us if we have not been shamelessly trifled with!"

"Young man," the inspector said when the meaning of my words was made known to him by the interpreter, "it is foolish for you now to attempt to influence your father to repent his deliberate action. This document has been properly attested by the agent, the trader, and the interpreter; it has been considered by the Great Father; and although the removal will cost him a vast sum or money, he has decided to grant your petition. The Great Father has no patience with those who do one thing to-day and another to-morrow. It will be necessary for you now to abide by your petition, and as the Great Father has in much tenderness provided a pleasant home for you in the Indian Territory, thither you must go."

"This action is outrageous, sir," I said in English to him. "The chiefs and head-men of my tribe never signed a petition to be removed. Think you it is like human nature to pray the Great Father to grant misery and uncertainty, sickness and death, in place of happiness and freedom, health and life? Will the deer beg that the fangs of the she-wolf may close upon her own throat and crush the ribs of her fawn? You have added lying to murder and theft, in this."

"I refuse to hear any one upon this question," said the inspector, "save only the chief. Let Eagle Wing stand forth and present any claims he may have upon the consideration and mercy of the Great Father."

The afternoon was now far spent. The coming twilight threw out patches of deep shadow in the valleys to herald the night's approach, and sent forth the soft winds of evening to whisper of its peace.

The chief slowly wrapped his blanket more tightly around him, lifted up his face to the sky for a moment of prayer to Wakanda, and then with many a gesture of dignity and grace spoke the last words of appeal that ever issued from his lips.

It may not be to you known that the Indian chief uses a language far nobler and more picturesque than that employed by ordinary members of his tribe. Hence it is that very few interpreters are able to give the full meaning of a chief's address, while in almost every case the beauty of metaphor and the passion of expression are lost. Every sentence contains a reference to some expressive sound or picture of the natural world, and thus it is difficult to retain the full sweetness and glory in a language less intimately associated with the voices of grove and prairie. I speak of this that you may not think my father's words unworthy of a chief.

"I am," he said, "like one with the heartache all the time. Through my soul rings the sad cry of the O-wé-we.* The homes that our fathers built, in which we and our little ones have in turn been born, are blown by a tempest upon the ground—not one of them could shelter a fox. Our lands, the Wâ-gha† says, must be given up to the scratching of the broad-winged crows and to the burrowing of the badger. And he asks what claims I have to urge that we may be allowed, through the condescension of the Great Father, to remain upon our beautiful farms. May I not first of all assert the claim that we have owned by the law of nature and the gift of Wakanda this land whereon our fathers have always lived? May I not claim that our title to these homes has been confirmed to us by many treaties with the white men, and that we have never broken the slightest stipulation or agreement? May I not claim that we have fought with you in your wars, and for you in our contests with the Sioux; that many of our race have suffered with you in your woes, and now wear the scars of the veteran in your service? And we have committed no crime. I have been told that by the white man's law no one can be punished until he has done wrong. We have never done wrong, yet we are punished. Have you two laws—one for the white man and one for the Indian?

"Look upon us—we are human beings. The one Father made the white men and the red men alike. Therefore

* The morning dove.   † White man.

we ought to be brothers. You say there are some Indians who are bad—and my heart weeps because it is true. But are all white men good? And that some of our race are evil-hearted seems all the greater reason that we who wish to do right should have strong laws to protect us from their malice. Do you forget that we are men? We love and hate, we suffer and weep, we must take care of our sick, and prepare for the winter and for old age, as the white men do. Look at us—have we not hands and feet, eyes and lips, just as you have? Are we not men? We are poor. Our clothes are torn and soiled. They are all you have left us. But we still are human beings.

"You say that the Indian is unsettled, that he loves to roam from place to place, after the manner of the lynx. This is false. No one loves his home and the grave of his fathers as the red man does. The ants would never leave their sand-hill if the rising wave of the ravine did not sweep against their home. The Indian would never desert his village if he were not thrust away by the foaming torrent of white men. He loves to roam the hunting grounds; but he comes back always to his home. We have two words in our language that are more sacred than any other: they are 'Wakanda' and 'Ma-shán.' We speak them together because 'God' gave us our 'home' and would not take it away from us. There is another thing that we have always possessed, and is so dear to us that we have found no word by which to speak of it.* It is freedom of choice—to go, to stay, to be ourselves, to have our own. What shall we do to show you that we love our homes above any other thing? Shall we range ourselves along the top of yonder divide and be shot one by one by the soldiers rather than give them up? Would you do that, my people?"

* The Indians have no word for *liberty*.

Asking this question, my father turned with a proud smile to his people. The silence of death hung over us; no one uttered a word; but our entire tribe, men, women, and children alike, arose as if by one brave impulse. Their faces in the twilight were calm and firm—they would gladly die with their native breeze fanning their cheek and their native skies above them. I am an Indian myself, and so it was natural for me to think that those faces, lit by love of God and home, were just as noble as they would have been had they been covered by a white skin.

"My brothers," my father said, turning to the white men, "we are ready for your command. Shall we die upon the divide? For the days the soldiers have been here I have seemed like one facing a great prairie fire. The sky is red, the grass is tall and dry, the wind is strong and blows toward me—I would take up my babes and run to save their lives. I have seemed like one standing on the bank of an overflowing river. The waves cry; they run fiercely toward us, and I would take my helpless people and flee to higher ground. But no place of safety can be found. And so I stand and face the fire—I plant my feet toward the flood—I am willing to spring into either, rather than give up the graves of my fathers and the home of my childhood.

"My brothers, the Indians must always be remembered in this land. Out of our languages we have given names to many beautiful things which will always speak of us. Minnehaha will laugh of us, Seneca will shine in our image, Mississippi will murmur our woes. The broad Iowa and the rolling Dakota and the fertile Michigan will whisper our names to the sun that kisses them. The roaring Niagara, the sighing Illinois, the singing Delaware, will chant unceasingly our Dta-wǎ-e.* Can it be that you

* Death song.

and your children will hear that eternal song without a stricken heart? We have been guilty of only one sin—we have had possessions that the white man coveted. We moved away toward the setting sun; we gave up our homes to the white man. Behold! he comes and bids us move again.

"My brethren, among the legends of my people it is told how a chief, leading the remnant of his people, crossed a great river, and striking his tepee-stake upon the ground, exclaimed, 'A-la-bâ-ma!' This in our language means 'Here we may rest!' But he saw not the future. The white men came: he and his people could not rest there; they were driven out, and in a dark swamp they were thrust down into the slime and killed. The word he so sadly spoke, I am told, has given a name to one of the white man's States. Wâ-gha, there is no spot under those stars, that now begin to smile upon us, where the Indian can plant his foot and sigh 'A-la-bâ-ma.' It may be that Wakanda will grant us such a place. But it seems that it will only be at His side. My brothers, Khé-tha-á-hi * has spoken."

The inspector seemed in nowise affected by these words. In reply he haughtily said:

"The Great Father has borne patiently with you in all your changeable moods. For four days he has waited that you might make up your minds to go quietly to the Indian Territory. He will wait no longer. To-morrow as the sun rises we will begin our march. The soldiers will see that no one lags behind."

After speaking these words he was about to turn away, when one of our young men, unable to curb his passion longer, started up, and pointing angrily toward him, cried in the Indian tongue:

* Eagle Wing.

"Thou shalt suffer for this! The agonies of the widow and the orphan have a weight in them that crushes down the soul that offends them."

A moment of confusion followed; our sobbing people gathered round the speaker; they swayed to and fro in grief; the soldiers rushed among them; there was a shot; the heart of the young man who had spoken was pierced; his blood gushed into the upturned face of an Indian child standing before him. It was impossible, in the commotion, to tell who had done the deed, or by whose command it was done. The soldiers afterwards said that, not being able to understand the words of the young man, they had supposed that he was threatening the inspector's life. This may have been the case. But our poor people only knew that our blood had been spilt, and catching up the warm body of our son, slain on account of the generous impulse of his heart against a great cruelty, we formed a sad procession and instantly repaired to the hill-top where our fathers slept. We laid him down upon the dewy grass, and oh, how his upturned face shone in the starlight!

My father gathered the people around him and told them all to kneel down there before the face of Wakanda while he prayed. This was his prayer:

"O Wakanda, the red man's only friend! Our hearts are broken, our eyes are heavy with weeping. Thou didst give us this Ma-shán; who shall take it away? Here we have lived in love of thy smile, here we have learned more and more of thy wishes, here we have heard of thy Son who died for the red man, and loves him all the more that he is helpless and distressed. Is it by thy wish that we must now go to the Land of Fire? Hast thou given the white man the Book so that he may become strong and oppress us because we are weak? O Wakanda!

Father of the Indian! soften the white man's heart. Let him love us as brethren. Forgive them that they despise and forget us. Make us strong to go wherever it is thy wish. I pray in the name of Wakanda E-zhi-ga." *

We arose with strong hearts.

"My children," my father went on to say, "the lips of this son, who lies dead upon the grass, have spoken a true prophecy. Wakanda will see that the cause of the weak prospers. When I think of what the young man said it seems to me that we have no right to be stubborn, and so be killed beside our ruined homes. That would be selfish. That would be to interfere with Wakanda's plan. He seems to wish us to suffer in the Land of Fire; we bow to that wish. When I was a young Wa-shú-scha † I would go into the woods to hunt. Sometimes after turning homeward I would think that the old trail leading back to the village was a hard one to follow. The rocks would seem sharp, and the briers would pierce my flesh. Then I would leave the trail and seek a new path for myself; but I always became entangled in stouter vines, the rocks were sharper and the swamp deeper, so that I was glad to find again the old way, in which my fathers had walked. My children, it may seem now to us that Wakanda has guided us into a dark, rough way. Remember the word of your chief—better to go forward than turn aside. Wakanda shall guide us—His way is the surest trail to Him."

Then my father gave directions for the burial of our dead. He was the last of our line that has, as yet, found sleep beside our sleeping fathers. We built the cotton-wood shed above him in the silence of overwhelming despair. Then, having formed a sad procession, we passed

---

* God's Son.   † Brave, or warrior.

to and fro within our guarded llmits, around the ruins of our homes, out as far as we could go into our fields, wailing our sad Dta-wá-e, while the pitying stars looked down, and the old trees wept the dews of sympathy. "Ma-shán! Ma-shán! Ma-shán!" we cried, and the divides echoed, and the hills. Away through cottonwood aisles that echo ran; it joined the ceaseless roar of surging stream. Shall it ever die?

The morning came and found us ready to leave our homes. Enough wagons were taken to carry the women and children. The men walked sadly and silently beside them. One company of soldiers preceded us, and the other followed. They hurried us forward with oath and insult and blow. The red men have at least this advantage over their white brethren—they never curse the name of Wakanda until they learn the English language. In our native tongues we have no word of cursing or blasphemy. It makes my heart shiver when white men take Wakanda's name in hatred on their lips, for He made earth, and air, and sunlight, and man.

At every bridge the captain counted our number to see that no one had escaped to crawl back to our wretched homes. If a child, forgetting for a moment the hopelessness of our woe, ran a few steps aside to pluck a withered dandelion or a bunch of buffalo grass, the soldiers would swear at him, and amuse themselves by throwing stones at his head while he scampered back to the line. It was not long before even the children realized the misery of our condition, and devoted what energy they had to enduring the severities of the march. All day we pressed forward, and at night, around such scanty fires as we were allowed to build, we wailed our sad Dta-wá-e for loss of home.

It was now late in the fall. The cold rains of that

period descended in torrents upon us.   We were provided
with but scanty protection from the severity of the weather.
To add to our discomfort we were allowed the very least
amount of food that would suffice to keep us upon the
march.   Under these circumstances, and considering how
sore our hearts were, it is not surprising that many of our
people became sick.   In a few days they began to die.   A
hasty hole was dug by the soldiers for those who were
fortunate enough to find this speedy end of their miseries,
and with scarce an hour's delay of our march the bodies
were tumbled in.   This the captain called "Christian
burial."   And I have since learned that when writing of
this removal he used the following words, which surely
must have been meant for unholy sarcasm : " These burials
occasioned considerable expense to the government, but
it is my opinion that the civilizing effects upon the minds
of the Indians more than compensated for the outlay."

One evening, after a long journey through the rain, I
was sitting under one of the wagons bathing my torn and
blistered feet, and listening to the mournful patter of the
rain upon the darkening prairie.   My father came to me,
and without a word beckoned me to follow him.   He led
me to another wagon, and pointing with his finger to a
person lying wrapped in blankets under it, indicated that
I should uncover the face.   I did so, and found it was my
mother.   She was evidently very sick ; a raging fever had
seized her ; her pulse pounded and throbbed like the
swollen Missouri.

" Ná-ha ! * Ná-ha !" I cried.

Her eyes were wild, and she turned them out upon the
drenched prairie as if the Spirit of the Storm beckoned
her away.   But she uttered not a word.

* My mother.

" Oh speak to me, Nâ-ha !" I moaned. " Thou didst brave death for me: conquer it now, and speak."

My father had tried to build a fire in the shelter of the wagon. It had all died out save one little flame, which flickered feebler and feebler for a moment and then suddenly vanished, affording light enough as it expired simply to reveal to us a little spiral of dun smoke curling up to the dark sky. Thus also died the spark of life in my mother's rent, tear-soaked heart; but just before the utter darkness came upon us we caught a glimpse of the soul floating up to the weeping Wakanda. We did not give her " Christian burial." My father and I, accompanied by a guard of two soldiers, took her dear form out to the highest sand-hill we could find, laid it reverently there, and covered it with a strong wicker-work of such boughs as we discovered strewn by the storm around. We breathed a prayer to Wakanda to guard the dear remains. And as I stood there listening to the dripping of the rain and the sighing of the wind through the tall grass, I missed the strong nature and soft kiss of Wâgh-ta as I had never done before.

The next day as we started upon our march I knew that I must sustain my father's footsteps and try to cheer his heart. I therefore walked by his side and gave him my shoulder to lean upon. His weight upon me became greater and greater as we advanced. The next day he seemed scarcely able to drag one weary foot after the other. When we rested at noon I begged the captain that my father might be allowed to ride in one of the wagons.

" Go away, you dog !" was his reply. " Your lazy father must take his chances with the soldiers. Is he not as able to march as we ?"

" Give him the food and coats that the soldiers have," I

replied, "and he would be able. But he is sick and starving."

For answer he caught up his sword and struck me in the face with it.

During the afternoon my father grew rapidly worse. His cough was distressing. He often stumbled, and would have fallen had I not been near.

"My son," he said, as evening came, "the wing of Death cast its shadow over me when thy mother died. According to the belief of our people I should have remained quiet under the spell while a day and night passed over me. But I was hurried on by the soldiers. My son, I must suffer the consequences of having broken the spell. I must die."

All night I sat by his side. In his sleep he moaned and tossed, and I feared every moment would be his last. When the morning came he opened his eyes and said to me:

"Last night I dreamed of the old home. I heard the whisper of the cottonwood leaves, and the murmur of the river, and the voice of the young men in the fields. Thy mother was with me; we were glad. My son, I shall soon be in a better home, and thy mother will be beside me. Watch where they bury thy father, and if ever Wakanda brings you back to the old home, take my bones and lay them beside those of my fathers. See! the sun rises. Thy mother beckons me! I come! The sunshine is bright! Khé-tha-á-hi comes!"

The old chief started up with these words and succeeded in reaching a sitting posture. He raised his hand and pointed toward the light. His long hair streamed in the sunrise breeze. His hand slowly dropped upon the grass We laid him down and closed his eyes.

The soldiers hurried him out to a "Christian burial."

I noted well the spot where he was laid, and when the Wá-gha permits I shall take his bones, as he wished, and lay them in the old grave-yard.

Of what followed I have the most indistinct recollection. Robbed of bride, mother and father, I walked in a maze of woe that rendered me alike oblivious to the sweet sounds and the bitter things around me. We crossed great rivers; we walked many weary miles; we starved, and shivered, and wept; we buried person after person on the way: hardly a child reached the Land of Fire. There the remnant of us at length arrived. A marshy spot of ground was given us for a home. We were huddled into a few tents, while our agent had a substantial house. The reign of death continued. Whole families became extinct; the sad cry of the mourner was constantly in our ears. Our young men had no heart to work, and had they toiled with the greatest energy the scanty soil would have yielded but little return. We could kick our foot into the ground and strike the hard underlying rock. We heard the most distressing reports from all the northern tribes that had been taken to the Land of Fire. In nearly every case one third of the tribe would die the first year, and before the second year closed, one half of those who in joy and gladness had skimmed the old hills would be in their graves.

I roamed the swamps and looked toward the north. I prayed that the fever might attack me next, and that I might die under its hot kisses. I forgot the face of friends, and often would puzzle my brain to know why I was so sad. My people shook their heads as I passed along. Although now the " chief," I could not rouse myself; I was as one in a haunting sleep that cannot be shaken off.

When along the sand bars of the Niobrara the fish-hawk catches the spotted pickerel and flies with it in its claws toward its nest in the high tree-top, how it screams with triumph; how it enjoys the struggles of the victim as they grow feebler and feebler in death. And when that scream is heard, how the young hawks clamber to the sides of the nest, thrust out their sharp bills and sharper eyes, and scream in answering chorus till the woods ring! I have been told that the inspector who removed our tribe wrote an elegant report of exultation over us, and that the noble senators, and officers, and legislators, and commissioners took up the chorus from their nest, and screamed joyously that the blood-thirsty Indian had for once been treated with proper severity.

CHAPTER XXI.

THE TWO VOICES.

ALL this time I had heard no tidings of my bride. I knew not whether she were dead or living, and sometimes I wished it might be the former. At better moments, however, I knew that if she lived she loved me still, and in that thought there was sympathy and solace.

The winter passed at length away, and the warm spring returned. One day word was brought to us that the members of a neighboring tribe would give us some horses, if some one would go to receive them. At the earnest request of my people I consented to go, and, having secured the permission of the agent, started upon my journey the following day. It was a bright morning, and I could fancy how the grass was springing and the early flowers blooming upon the hills of my northern home. I pressed vigorously forward, and by evening had reached the borders of the reservation of the tribe by whose courtesy we were to profit. I was kindly received at the house where I was to spend the night, and, from the people residing there, learned the history of their tribe's removal, while in return I imparted our own sad story. So strict had been the watch kept upon us, and so thoroughly has the agent the control of all communication between the tribes, that we knew scarce anything of what was going on within fifty miles of us. They had come from a region a little north-west of our old home, and had been removed about the time we had been.

The next morning, bidding adieu to my friends of a

night, I started toward the place where the horses designed
for us were kept. I passed many wretched tents and huts
in which the people had spent the winter, and I found
that the same story of sickness, misery, and death was to
be told here as among our own tribe.

About noon I came to a picturesque spot in the side of
a hill, whence a little spring of pure water bubbled forth.
The water that we had been able to procure had been so
filthy and brackish, that I hailed this pure fountain as the
direct gift of Wakanda. I cast myself down upon the
grassy margin of the spring, and drank and drank until
the thirst of a half-year was appeased.

I do not know how long I sat there. At length I heard
the sound of footsteps coming down the pathway beyond
the bushes. I had nothing to lose, so I did not fear, and
I took it for granted that none but Indians would be near.
Oh! I did not think how much I had to gain.

The footsteps came nearer, the bushes parted, an Indian
girl stepped into the open space. Her head hung down
upon her breast, her long hair vailed her face, but I knew
her in an instant. Only one neck could be so shapely
as that—only one footfall could be so soft. Springing up,
I cried :

"Wágh-ta !"

She dropped the pail which she was carrying in her
hand, flung back the hair by a toss of her head, clasped
her hands in passionate surprise and joy, and said :

"Shá-ta-ga-dtá-tha !"

Yes, it was—it was my bride. She hid her face in my
arms and burst into tears.

"My darling bride," I cried, "how came you here? By
what strange working of Wakanda do I find thee in this
lonely place, so far from our old home?"

She could not answer for weeping.

" Tell me at least this, my darling," I said : " do you love me as when we had the bright prairie for a play-ground ?"

She lifted up her eyes to my face a moment, and in them I saw her heart's truth. So sure was I of her love that all shadow of doubt instantly fled from my mind.

We sat down upon the grassy bank. The whole scene seemed transformed, as if by some spirit of magic, into the most enchanting beauty. The weeds became flowers, the marsh a garden. We talked of the old home and the old love. I told her how unjustly we had been removed, how my father and mother were dead. At this her tears flowed afresh. I told her how I longed for a kiss from her sweet lips as I stood in the dripping rain and gloom beside my mother's grave, and she lifted up her lips to my cheek and gave me one as I spoke.

Then she told me all that had happened to her since I had seen her—how she had been given into the hands of the cruel woman Mollie, how the evil man had failed in his purposes, and how he had struck his poor mother to the earth. She said that the day following her escape from him, as she was making her way homeward, she had been taken by a band of soldiers and conducted, in spite of her most earnest appeals, to the tribe in which I had found her. They were then on their way to the Land of Fire, and hither she had been taken with them. One of the families of the tribe had kindly received her, and with them she had remained until that time. In all this tale she did not mention little Swallow's name, simply remark-ing that she had been saved by one of our people.

" Who was it," I cried, " that did thee this great service ? I will bless him with my latest breath. and, were the world mine, would endow him with it."

" It is one," she said, " to whom I will instantly conduct thee. And oh, dear Wolf Killer," she added, springing up, "we should have gone to her long ago. I have been so happy that I have too long forgotten my duty."

She took up her pail, which lay where it had fallen, and I filled it for her at the spring. How strange, how exhilarating it was to walk again by Wágh-ta's side! Again the flowers nodded in joyous sympathy as we passed by; again the grass-spears jostled their fellows in knowing enjoyment of our joy. She conducted me to a wretched hut where lived the family whose kindness and hospitality she had enjoyed. She pushed aside the tattered carpet which formed the door, and told me to enter.

There was but one room. A woman sat beside a basin of coals cooking a little food. In one corner of a room there was a wretched bed, and upon it I saw that some sufferer lay. Wágh-ta motioned to me to go and look at the sick person. I did so.

"Swallow!" I cried in amazement, for it was she.

The hatred I had for her, because of the profession she had made of having aided Scar Face in wronging me and my bride, came bitterly up in my heart, and I was about to turn away, when Wágh-ta, understanding all, came to me, took my hand in both her own, and said:

"Dear Wolf Killer! It was little Swallow that saved thy Wágh-ta. Bless her, then, as thou hast said, for I fear she has not many minutes to live."

Swallow had turned her wan face from the wall toward us, and was now regarding us through wild, staring, sunken eyes. She seemed puzzled, and yet not surprised.

"Has my bright dream become true, then?" she softly murmured. "Have Wolf Killer and Wágh-ta been united? O Wakanda! I thank Thee—I love Thee for it!"

Her tired eyelids slowly drooped. Her breathing grew heavy.

"The old river is roaring loudly to-night, mother," she

said in her feverish stupor. And then, after a pause:
"How the ice crackles, mother! It must be colder. I
am cold. Hear the river surge—it sounds fainter now!"
She seemed to harken intently for a long time, then she
said: "The river grows fainter—and fainter."

After about an hour, just as the twilight was settling
round us, she opened her eyes again and said :

"Where is he? Wágh-ta, where is he? I want to talk
to him before I die! Oh, here he is. Shá-ta-ga-dtá-tha,
can you forgive poor little Swallow, who sinned because
she loved you so dearly?"

"Oh yes," I said, "dear Swallow, I freely forgive you,
and I bless you with all my heart for what you have done
for me and mine."

"I thought it would succeed," she said, looking up to
the ceiling with a far-off look in her eyes, "I thought it
would succeed. Under the sumacs long ago I said:
'Love and hate have failed, unselfishness may succeed,'
to gain his love."

Then in the quiet twilight we talked the whole sad
story over, and she told me all she had said and
done to save my bride. Her mind seemed to retain its
power until she had told all, and then it suddenly failed
her. She fell into a quiet stupor, and her breathing became labored and heavy. We watched beside her while
the long hours passed, and just as the midnight stars had
wheeled into their places a smile played for a moment
upon her sunken cheeks, her lips parted as if before a
scene of ineffable grandeur—the surging of the river
ceased—and with a great sigh of relief her soul burst
forth into the eternal Ma-shán.

When it was over I led Wágh-ta out into the starlight
to stay her weeping.

"What shall we do?" I said.

"I don't know, dear husband," she said.

A great thought of joy came into my heart. For the first time in many months I felt the enthusiasm and strength of a man.

"My Wágh-ta!" I whispered in my earnestness, "will you fly with me from this dreadful land of death? Do you love and trust me enough for that?"

"I would do anything for you," she whispered, "and can brave anything with you."

"We must be all in all to each other, darling," I said, "for all our relatives are with Wakanda. We will fly to our northern home and live together in joy and peace. I can do nothing for my people here; perhaps there some way may open for me to help them."

The little maiden looked up into my face with a sweet, brave smile, and whispered:

"Ge-tha-á-tá-she! Ge-tha-á-tá-she!"*

Our kind friends who had harbored the orphan Wagh-ta were taken into our confidence.

"Go, by all means," they said.

And the father of the household added:

"You must go this very night. Our agent and the police are away in the other part of the Reserve. I will get a brave Shón-ga† for each of you. I will go with you to the borders, and show you the way to safety and joy."

"Oh, we cannot go until poor Swallow is buried," my bride said.

"You must go to-night, or not at all, They would shoot you if they found you stealing away. Poor Swallow is beyond all need of help. We will see that she has proper burial. But you must go to-night."

Wágh-ta wept, went and kissed the blue lips, and then returned to my side and took my hand.

* "Happiness! Happiness!" Literally, "More than glad." † Pony.

The ponies were soon at the door, and in an instant we were mounted. We had no earthly possession but our mutual love, and that was a light burden. Away! away!

" You will send the promised horses to my distressed people ?" I said to our kind leader.

" Yes, yes ! "

" They will wonder much what has become of the son of their last chief. But I could not have had the heart to tell them of our escape. They would have pleaded so piteously to be taken too."

" Think only of your bride—and be off !" our conductor said somewhat harshly ; and we started.

Up dark ravines, over starlit hill-tops, clattering among the rocks, cutting the sod with six pairs of sharp hoofs— away ! away ! away !

The plain is broad, Never mind, love, it will put the more miles between us and death. Start not at the shadows that chase us ; they are but shadows. The night breeze whistles " Hope ;" the coarse shrubs wave " Courage ;" the twinkling lights among the wild flowers cry, " Be brave ! be brave !"

Away ! away ! We pass tottering hovels and rent tents in which our shivering people crouch in sickness and misery. We pass the dying camp-fire of those who have not even such poor protection. Dashing down steep declivities, rattling along the dry, pebbled beds of streams, now in the shadow, now in the starlight, pausing a moment to listen, then galloping faster than before, through tangled brush and over clear spots—away ! away ! Oh ! brave Shón-ga ! strong Shón-ga ! Ha ! ha ! we shall be free ; we shall be free !

Hist ! there is a camp-fire around which we see moving figures. We must make a detour in perfect silence : tread lightly upon the breaking twig, brave Shón-ga ! Now we have passed them—on again! The night grows darker; it would be black to any eyes but those of love, but, dear Wâgh-ta, it is noonday with thee by my side. Our guide is wise, and we shall not miss our way. The deeper darkness now but shows the morn is near. Hark! The surging river is near; beyond it there are liberty and joy! The waters are cold—cling close to me, my Wâgh-ta. On, brave Shón-ga! There, we stand upon the bank.

"Farewell," our guide says: "you are now beyond the border of the Land of Fire. Put many miles between you and this river before the morning comes. Wakanda bless you! Wakanda save all His poor red children as He has saved you. Farewell!"

———

It is two years since the good man spoke these words. I sit in a little cabin on the shore of the same shining river whose smile is my first remembrance. But our cabin stands not on our old home. A hundred miles we coursed along the clear river, beyond the familiar old haunts, and stopped at last where we could find a place which, for the present at least, is not coveted by the white man. There we built us a rude but comfortable cabin. Through the door I see the fields I have with so much joy cultivated. They have given us food and clothing. Our brave Shón-ga, that saved us from the Land of Fire, grazes just there by the doorstep.

By my side dear Wâgh-ta sits gazing up into my face as I write. She thinks it the most wonderful thing that I should dare to write down our simple story for the white men to read in their magnificent homes. There in the center of the room sits another dear object, with her lap full of roses. She laughs and crows, never thinking of what her father and mother have suffered. We call her

" Ma-he-dú-ba," because she is a constant " Sunshine" in our simple home, and she was given by Wakanda.

But I dare not tell you where our cabin stands. I fear some one would covet my poor possessions, and come to drive us away; and I could not claim protection by the white man's law. We are happy in our simple ways; we live in constant love, and for recreation we put our arms about each other, take our little "Sunshine" and walk forth into the world our Wakanda has made, and study all its beautiful things. May we not thus live, and may we not be free?

But my people—O my people! I long to do something for them in their desolation. Yet what can I do? Poor, powerless, I cannot help them where they are, nor effect their return to their homes out of that sad land of death.

As I gaze out upon the shining river, its roar becomes two voices in my ear. One voice swells loudly from the eastward, and cries: "The Indian is an evil thing in the path of civilization; he must be burned off or ploughed under as the trees of the forest are cleared and the weeds of the prairie go down bfore our driving ploughshares. Get him off the earth, as fast as musket balls and bad whisky can do it!"

The other voice comes wailing from the southward, and says: "Are we not human beings? Did not the one Wakanda make us and you? We pray that we may not longer be murdered and plundered in order to enrich a few base men. We pray that we may have our homes in peace and safety, and be allowed, under just laws, to support ourselves and our children. Let us have our lands undisturbed as the white men do; give us teachers to aid and instruct us in your arts of industry; send us good missionaries to teach us from The Book of morality and religion. Be as just to the first owners of the land as you are generous to all other people of the earth, and the Indian too shall enrich the free soil of America without being ploughed under."

It is for the Christian public to say which voice in the river shall swallow up the other. Wolf Killer the son of Eagle Wing has spoken.

THE END.

FIGS AND THISTLES:

A Romance of the Western Reserve.

BY ALBION W. TOURGEE,

Author of " A Fool's Errand."

12mo, Cloth, Handsome Side Stamp. . . *Price,* $1.50.

WITH FRONTISPIECE.

THE pen which so vividly portrayed the moral and political status of the South in " *A Fool's Errand"* has not less graphically delineated in " Figs and Thistles" the social and moral atmosphere of the Western Reserve, where GENERAL GARFIELD was born and reared. To appreciate the life and character of him who has become the President of the United States, every one should read this book. He is simply an outgrowth of the life there described. Indeed, if some shrewd critics may be trusted, the barefoot boy, student, lawyer, colonel, general, Congressman, Senator, and possibly President, may be discovered in even more intimate relations with the scheme of this novel. No American can afford to be without this vivid picture of the home of Wade and Giddings and Garfield and the civilization from which they spring.

One of the striking features of Judge Tourgee's works, and one which has done much to give his " *Fool's Errand"* its vast popularity, is his intense realism and strong sense of local coloring. " Figs and Thistles" has been very generally described by the press as an "Ohio book," "a Western Reserve romance," "the Western Reserve in romantic miniature," etc. Many declare that so life-like is the portraiture, that the models of the characters, although, of course (and very properly), not to be identified in all incidents of their careers, can easily be distinguished.

OPINIONS OF THE PRESS.

"It is, we think, evident that the hero of the book is the Republican candidate for President, Gen. JAMES A. GARFIELD. The author has indulged in the novelist's license, and the story is not, of course, a biography. But the author evidently models the career of his hero upon the life of Gen. GARFIELD. The book is worth reading for itself, but the fact we have stated makes it an unusually attractive volume. It is, in many respects, one of the best books of the period."—*Atchison (Kan.) Champion.*

"Tourgee is undoubtedly the chief of American writers."—*Troy Sentinel.*

"Close observers of our political history will not be at a loss to discover the originals from whom the author has drawn his characters."—*Burlington Free Press and Times.*

"It is a representative American novel, and deals with characters entirely new and fresh, but altogether real."—*Hartford Courant.*

FORDS, HOWARD & HULBERT, Publishers,

27 Park Place, New York.